T0375600

THE
Thank You
LETTER

CAMERON FRAZIER

authorHOUSE

AuthorHouse™
1663 Liberty Drive
Bloomington, IN 47403
www.authorhouse.com
Phone: 833-262-8899

Published by AuthorHouse 04/11/2023

ISBN: 979-8-8230-0598-2 (sc)
ISBN: 979-8-8230-0597-5 (e)

Library of Congress Control Number: 2023907080

Print information available on the last page.

This book is printed on acid-free paper.

Contents

I

Why did this kind of day happen to me? One of those days where nothing seems like it could go right. Well, this is one of those days. I woke up optimistic with my head held high, but everything around was trying it's best to make sure that just couldn't happen. Maybe I'm exaggerating, because my friends always tell me "It could get worse", when I go on a rant.

Obviously it could get worse, but what's going on is making me feel worse. Pretty simple I think. I knew it was going to be this way when I woke up, because there was no way I was out of toothpaste. I still ended up having to scavenge what was at the bottom while still looking in the smeared mirror telling myself that today is still gonna be a good day. As I walked through the door my mom said that Ryan couldn't pick me up on time and would be late. Which he usually can, because he's never really been the type of guy to have plans or things come up to prevent him from his normal routine. Luckily he was still able to get me barring that we were both thirty minutes late to our first class. This isn't a problem worth stressing about on a normal day, but today was supposed to be the day we start a project in biology and we could pick our partners.

My partner should've been Paul, who's always been a really close friend of mine. He's really smart and we have always done projects together since I started cheating off of him on sixth grade spelling tests. He never cared though. Mostly because he is a pretty timid person and isn't very outspoken, kinda like an average nerd, but he's a great guy, I'd cheat on any test with his.

Well on this day where nothing good could happen, Paul and someone else already decided to be partners, because of my tardiness. So when I arrived at class I had no idea what to do and had no help until the teacher decided to assign me partners with Brooke Rose. The name sounded familiar, but I've never talked to her. Even though I knew of her because the school I went to was relatively easy to know at least over half the people you go to school with. I've always kept to myself, so this was an experience I was not looking forward to. It's always been hard to meet new people, and I really wanted to work with Paul. So I asked the teacher with subtle hints so I wouldn't hurt my new partner's feelings, if I could bend the rules this once so I can work with Paul. With no hesitation, or tolerance for the attempt of being appealing Mr. Richards denied my request. Mr. Richards wasn't someone who was very strict, but I can tell he wanted me to go outside my comfort zone and work with someone new. Mr. Richards has only been my teacher for only about a month, and I've got to say he's one of the coolest teachers I've ever had. That's not saying too much considering I'm only a Freshman in high school, but I admire his willingness to help students who learn in a variety of ways. He was also really good at keeping a smile on his face everyday, which can be very difficult when you're around angsty teens all day. So basically I look like the bad guy if I tried to argue my way out of this one. Although, I get to meet someone new? Who am I kidding this day has been awful, and Brooke doesn't seem to be making a change.

The only thing I really knew about her is the fact that a couple of years ago we shared an English class where we never talked much outside of saying the basic generalities like "Thank you" or "Excuse me." This didn't help at all, because we are currently learning about microbiology and we're using words that sound like gibberish, so I'm at a complete loss with someone I don't know.

Now looking from the outside in, someone could be thinking, "this day isn't as bad as you're trying to make it seem". Maybe it wasn't, and I would have to say that person is right, but when you've played out scenarios ten thousand different ways and then the world hits you with one you never thought about. That by itself could cause a bad day, and today was a bad, bad day.

After about five minutes of daydreaming Mr. Richards gave instructions on how the project should be done and the time frame we have to work with. I wasn't paying attention so either this could mean everything or it could mean nothing, but I had to figure it out without making it obvious that I was oblivious about everything going on around me.

So I turned to Brooke and softly said, "So…when is this due?" I think she knew what I was trying to do and could tell that I was pretty introverted and wasn't looking for much social interaction.

She replied with a light smirk and a softer voice than what I remember, saying, "We have till the end of the semester."

WHAT? I thought to myself there's no way that I'm stuck doing this big project with someone I don't know and I have to do well, because I have a C in the class, already, and this could help tremendously. Also, why did she chuckle? Does she think I'm an idiot? Could she tell I'm clueless? Does she think I'm funny? I sound a lot more nervous about this whole situation than I ultimately am. It's not like I'm attracted to her even though she's not too bad looking by any means. Whenever I have heard her name come up in conversation it's always been good, like how she looks and acts. I just don't talk to many people so

I tend to overthink everything that happens. From what I know about her she seems like she is genuinely a good person, but I still don't know her all that well. Maybe I should change that, I thought to myself.

As we sat there in silence for the rest of the class we realized that we got nothing done other than putting our names on a piece of paper for ideas. I'm honestly surprised that even happened, because the way things started and not getting to class on time hindered our ability to even start talking to become comfortable with each other.

After that awkward interaction I tried going through the rest of my day as if I wasn't having a bad day, but I was pretty bad at hiding my emotions.

Later on at lunch my friends caught on to the fact that something was up so they all collectively asked if something was wrong and I denied it. I helped their suspicions by not acting like I normally would. Usually with my guys they'll ask if something is wrong one time, and if the answer is no we'll all move on. Today was different, they were adamant to try to figure out what was wrong. So I gave them the spiel about how I was partners with Brooke Rose, and as soon as I mentioned her name everyone at the table had a reaction. At first I couldn't tell if this was a good or bad thing. I can tell that Paul did this on purpose, because he was the one to start the commotion "You really gotta do this whole project with someone you don't know," Paul mocked. He must've been plotting this, he probably wanted this to happen.

"Thanks Captain Obvious, and thanks for waiting for me until I got there." I answered sarcastically. I looked at him as if I was a detective trying to read his facial expression.

"It's not like I knew you were going to be gone for half the class.

Besides I'm pretty sure she's smart so you'll end up getting a good grade regardless." Paul got what he wanted out of me, but then realized it wasn't as funny as he initially thought.

"I'm sorry for being late by the way, Landon." Ryan was such a peacemaker, so it's always nice when he stops the group from escalating farther than what it needs to. I shrugged letting him know that it was fine. I would hate for me to keep going on when I could've prevented a problem. Ryan was very mature for our age, and acted like a parental figure in a way to us.

"Hey...at least she's pretty cute." We all knew this was gonna come from Matt, sooner or later so we all side-eyed and kept talking as if nothing happened.

Tony sat there taking everything we said in. He wasn't really a talkative person, really none of us were, but whenever he had something to say we all listened. I tried convincing myself for the rest of the day that this will work out in the best way it can. Who am I kidding? I don't see this working out in my favor at all.

II

When I stepped into class the next morning I was excited, I had no reason to be as exhilarated as I was, but I wanted to keep my head held high. No reason not to, yet. I had almost forgotten that I had to be partners with Brooke, and as I remembered that I got butterflies in my stomach. Not because I was nervous to see her or anything, just because this is still someone I don't know. Today that was going to change, I was determined, but "only fools run into unknown situations with high optimism" At least that's what my grandfather always told me.

Whenever I do anything outside of my comfort zone I tend to think back to my grandpa's millions of random sayings he has. Most people think what he says is nonsense, which some are, but I've always taken what he said to heart, because it seemed to be helpful for me. That and he was someone I could always admire, because we're so similar in our character.

As we started working on our project again, I could feel the digging of the uncomfortable chair in my butt. I started squirming around trying to get comfortable. Realizing what I was doing, I looked at Brooke with a faint smile. One that stayed when she relayed the same smile back. As soon as I got that simple reassurance I felt more confident to speak, but when I tried to say something at first nothing would come out. It was so weird. When I tried again she beat me to it.

"So what do you think we should do to start? We're already a little behind, but it's fine it can't be that hard." Her voice still seemed softer than I could remember, but it was soothing and made me relax. I thought about a million things, but I try to be as subtle as possible. I worried and was self conscious about how I was acting.

"To be honest with you, I don't know too much about what's going on, I've just been kinda going with the flow." I gave a nervous laugh hoping she wouldn't think I'm a complete idiot.

"What if we did protein synthesis?" She was being nice and suggestive, basically telling me this is what we were going to do. I didn't have a problem with it, so with a slight look of confusion on my face I nodded my head in agreement.

Protein Synthesis. I knew we should have general

knowledge about it, but I was just drawing blanks. I always have a hard time focusing on school, because my mind loves to wonder about a thousand different thoughts and ideas that I can come up with.

It sounds simple, but I know that it's probably like putting a rocketship together. Seeing that I was already beyond confused she took the liberty in asking Mr. Richards to clarify what he would want the assignment on. As I looked his way waiting for his response I saw Paul already looking at me holding in a laugh. I looked at him with a stern face, already knowing what he was thinking. He just thought it was so funny I was paired up with someone I don't know, but from the little interaction I've had with her, Brooke was pretty alright. Mr. Richards reminded us that he wanted us to become creative and there were no criteria outside of planning, creativity, and presenting the information in a way the class could understand. So the idea of the project sounded like it should be an easy A, but it was all about execution. I hate executing, I suck at it. Mostly because I had little clarity for the full definition of the word. As I turned back to my table Brooke already had her head down writing and sketching. You could tell she was a visual person and liked having things drawn out to help herself better understand things. I felt awkward interfering so I picked up a pencil and wrote on the top right of her paper "Is there any way I can help" with a little smiley face to the side of it. She looked up and gave a warm smile that had made me feel shocked, but more accepted. I thought I was going to look dumb, but her smile was reassuring.

"You can look up and write down the characteristics of Mono-and-Polysaccharides." There was visible confusion on my face, but I didn't want to be the weak link of the group so I did as she asked, and copied everything I could find about anything with the word "saccharide" in it on Google. Which wasn't much, but I was hoping that it would be enough to help her draw, or do whatever she needed. I just didn't want it to be so apparent that I was clueless. I didn't want to mess up at all, because I really needed this grade, and I wanted to make a good impression.

For the rest of class we didn't say much to each other, but I was relieved to find out that she was not weird or didn't think that I was weird, at least she doesn't from what I can tell. The rest of the day was pretty normal, I tried treating it that way at least. It was like any other November day in Colorado: cold, dark outside, bad weather, things of that nature.

I preferred to stay inside anyway ever since I moved from Texas. It always seems cold, but to be fair to me I do live in Colorado where the air is thin and the temperature is low. Although I moved when I was about ten, so I've had some time to adjust to the new climate. It's just not as fun to go out anymore. Especially when it's not your childhood friends you spent everyday every summer with for years. Simply, things just aren't the same anymore.

"Life comes with changes though and the ones you can control are the ones you should be careful about." Another one of my grandpa's sayings. He's right, but it's hard to start your life over especially when it feels like you're in the perfect position you could live in for a lifetime. I assume that's how most childhoods are and then something drastic happens that makes you grow up a lot sooner than what you would like. Which is a big reason I've kept to myself, I wasn't always this way, but whenever I moved it seems like I'm not even the same person. It's not bad here either. I'd hate to make it sound that way, because I still have great friends and live in a great environment where everyone gets along, I just miss the feeling of being a child. Wish I had someone who brought out the missing part of me, but what am I going on about, everyone and everything changes. I just hope it all ends up being for the better.

As the rest of the week went along, I actually learned a decent amount about Mono-and-Polysaccharides, and was actually trying, which was a rarity to see from me in that class. Mr. Richards showed subtle complacency. He probably thought that I was going to drag Brooke's grade down, but so far I've done my part and the project has gotten a lot better. Brooke was still doing most of the work, but I wasn't completely in the way of either of us.

We decided to do a model so the only problem is that when the model becomes bigger we can't bring it into class to work on. Luckily we were still a couple months away from that so we wouldn't have to do anything out of what we were already doing. As the project became easier to work on, and as school became more stressful, there seemed like there was no real reason to talk to Brooke so I didn't. It felt weird though, because I really wanted to. Maybe because I actually found her kind of interesting, and kind of attractive, whatever reason it was, I actually wanted to talk to her.

"We've gotten a lot done, haven't we?" I said it with no emotion trying to sell that I didn't want to be awkward.

"We sure have." The response was a lot more simple than what I was expecting. I knew I had to keep the conversation going, so I tried to be slick about it. It was quiet for a few moments before I decided to say something to her again.

"Crazy." I said in a stale voice.

"What do you mean?" She responded with a confused tone.

"Feels like we've done all this work and I still don't really know who you are." I must've said that a little louder than I expected, because the table of girls behind me started giggling. I immediately felt insecure after saying it. My face was blushed, and I felt myself building an emotional wall so I didn't seem bothered to whatever she would shoot me down with, but to my surprise she said:

"Why don't we change that then." I was taken aback by her response, and didn't know what to say.

She could tell I was at a loss of words. So she tore the corner of a piece of paper and wrote something down. After she finished she looked back up to me with a smile and said, "You can let me know how you want to change it once you figure it out." I looked at the little piece of paper and it was her phone number. I instantly became wide eyed as if someone had just given me life changing news.

Before I could say anything in response the bell rang, and she grabbed her bag and left the room swiftly. I sat there for a moment with slight curiosity. Overthinking a lot of things in a short period of time. Paul came over to me and asked what had happened. I was still sitting in my seat slowly getting my things together for the next class. So I told him what had just occurred and even he looked confused. He knows I'm not the type of person to pursue any type of relationship and was surprised that anything happened at all. I figured that he thought that I wouldn't ever try to get to know her, so he could keep the joke running. Now it was looking like he put me in a position I never knew I would need.

Throughout the rest of the day I noticed her a little more in the halls which made me nervous. Even though she knows I'm not outgoing, it seemed as if I was avoiding her. I wasn't trying to be rude or anything I just didn't want to intrude or make a fool of myself so I kept my distance, and spoke minimally. For the rest of the day I kept my head down. When I was in the halls I kept buried in my phone, finding something on it to distract myself from reality. I could've walked right past her and never knew, but that didn't bother me, because that was better than anything I could do that could potentially ruin what we got started. Which may be a little bit of a reach to say, since I can't even look her in the eyes without being nervous.

Was anything even starting?

Once I got home and immediately thought about what I should text Brooke. It was the only thing that was on my mind all day. I realized it was pretty strange, but since I loved to overthink everything, I thought about all of the positive things that could come from this. Then I paced around my room for a couple minutes thinking of how I should text her, and negative things that could happen started flooding my mind. I must've typed out a thousand responses just trying to say hi. It had to be perfect. Maybe I could try being funny, or maybe I should try to play it cool. If I play it cool she might think I'm being lame and not respond. What if she didn't respond at all? Then I'd really feel dumb, all of this stressing over a little text would be for nothing. After what felt like forever I finally came up with what to me sounded like the perfect response.

"Hey, it's Landon. I think I know how I want to change it now." I didn't think that was reaching for anything, and it was pretty nice to follow up with what she said.

Whenever I heard my phone buzz I picked it up so fast just to see that it was my mom letting me know that she would be home a few minutes late. I got a little upset, mainly because I was hungry, and I wasn't able to cook without mom at home. As I was about to set my phone back down I got another notification. It was from Brooke, my stomach dropped. I wasn't actually prepared for a text back. Not because I was scared, but because I didn't think she would respond at all.

Her text said "So what did you come up with?" I honestly had no idea what to do now. It's not like we can go out. Would it be weird to ask her out? What else would she give me her number for? I can't drive yet I'm only fourteen so I had to think, but I didn't want to keep her waiting. Luckily it was basketball season and I'm friends with some of the guys on the team so I had a plan.

I was pretty tall myself, standing at six foot two but I never took any particular interest in basketball, or at least playing, because it seemed so stressful. I couldn't imagine everyone yelling at you to go really fast while maintaining a dribble with a little rubber ball and throwing it precisely in the air at a small hoop, sounds impossible to me.

Anyway, I responded saying "Do you like basketball,

because if you do there's a home game next Friday that we can go to."

Almost simultaneously she responded with, "That would be awesome, sounds like fun to me."

Such a simple sentence made my mood change drastically. I was having a pretty stagnant feeling day, with everything feeling bland, but this put a flavorful blast into my mind. I was so excited, and couldn't wait until next Friday. I usually don't get excited for much, but I was more shocked than anything.

We continued to talk a little, getting to know each other a little more. I found it interesting that Brooke wasn't short for anything, because usually it would be short for something like Brooklyn, but her name was just Brooke. She also had a dog, a cat, and a sister. Her sister was older than both of us, having already moved out. Everything she told me I felt like I could remember forever. I didn't want to push any agendas so I avoided asking her anything really personal and overall just had a nice talk getting to know her better.

My feelings spilt over into the dinner table and my mother made it very apparent.

"I assume you had a really good day today." I started to chew slower realizing that I was being extra.

"Uhh… I got one hundred on a test today in English and you know how I was struggling with that class." I felt like I couldn't tell her the truth yet, because I didn't know what to make out of the situation.

She believed what I said and we went on as if nothing happened. I asked myself who was on the basketball team, and would drive me to the game. Caleb, who was a junior on the team, and a really great person. I asked if he could take me to his game. He said yes willingly, because he has a huge heart as well as school spirit. He loved when everyone came to the games, so it made sense to ask him first.

"What makes you want to go to this one?" He asked politely. I felt as if I was inclined to tell him, because I could trust him, and he was my ride to the game.

"I told someone I was gonna go to the game with them." He nodded and gave a small grin. He could tell what was going on pretty easily.

"So who's the special girl?" My heart fluttered, I didn't think he would jump straight to that question, but I had no real problem with letting him know, because he was two grades ahead of us, so I was sure he wouldn't know.

"Brooke Rose." I said with a little hesitation. He looked a little surprised which worried me.

"No way. I was actually friends with her sister, who graduated last year." Caleb is a popular guy, so I didn't really bat an eye at his comment. "She's really cool. I'm glad you're going out with her," he added. I just thanked him awkwardly, because I didn't know how else to respond. I didn't want him to think that Brooke and I were together, because that wasn't what was happening. I tried to steer away from what was going to happen, but I knew I had to start to get mentally prepared for Friday. If things don't go right, finishing the project with her will be really hard for the both of us.

Why did I do this? What was I thinking? I should've just stayed to myself.

In the middle of the night I thought to myself, am I going out with her? I am going out with her, but this isn't really a date is it? Oh no I'm going on a date, but that shouldn't bother me. I really like Brooke, but not in a way for a relationship to happen. I barely know her, she probably thinks I'm just some kid she has to do a project with. I just don't know if it would be progressing to a relationship with her. It was normal to think this way, I'm still a teen. I've never had a girlfriend, besides little things when I was younger. That doesn't really compare to what could be happening now. I need to stop overthinking, we're just friends for right now.

III

As Friday came, which followed after the slowest week I have ever experienced in my life. I guess it would have to be the anticipation, because I've been living a boring life ever since I moved. It's been hard for me to really plan things, and I don't go and do things often as it is. I act as if I haven't lived here for years now, but it's still not the same as it was when it was easier to make plans with friends in Texas. It could be part of my mom being friends with my friends' mom, or it could be because I don't put in enough effort to make anything happen.

I still found myself having the same social problems throughout the week with being shy and not necessarily nervous, but more timid. I couldn't really talk to her out of class, because at least when we were in class it was expected and not a surprise.

As I opened up more about the whole situation with

my mom, and as I became comfortable with the fact that I was going on a date with someone I hardly knew, she was very supportive, because this was the first time I really tried talking to any girls. Outside of the little crushes I had in elementary school. Mom was starting to get nervous that I would never try to get with anyone, but she didn't say that, she just always inferred and alluded to it. Which is understandable, I just didn't feel like anyone could support a relationship I was looking for. I also didn't think I would be good enough to keep one going. I wasn't pursuing any kind of relationship, unless what I'm doing with Brooke is considered pursuing. I was more so hoping one would just fall into my lap one day, that day doesn't seem like it'll come.

Mom told me that it was normal for me to feel antsy whenever I'm around her, although the way she was making it sound, either she thought we were already dating, which we aren't, or I was planning on making a move Friday. I honestly didn't know if that's what I wanted to do. I have no clue what I want to do. I mean I really like Brooke and she's cool, but *dating* that's a concept I definitely didn't feel comfortable with quite yet. If it were to lead to that in the future I wouldn't stop it or complain about it happening, but I'm so unsure with myself now. I'm really unsure about the whole situation. I've never had to deal with something like this, not that I was trying to be weird about it, but I felt like I was causing more harm than good.

At this point I was hardly concerned about the project we should've been getting done, which we were at a decent pace. I was more trying to figure out who she was as a person. You know, those talks where you find what makes someone them, and what makes them tick. I don't know why I was trying to have these conversations in school, and early in the morning. It's definitely hard to have those conversations when you're a freshman and only have one class together. I didn't know what to think about the whole ordeal, but I was hoping at the very least we were on speaking terms by the time I got a license and car so it would be easier for us to meet up outside of school. Maybe that was too far in the future to worry about, and I was forcing something that didn't need to happen. She probably didn't care and was still trying to be polite, but I was trying to be optimistic on my side of thinking. Who knows what she's thinking about me, because my thoughts about her were leaning to one idea, but there was still a mix of a lot of other things.

As I walked in Thursday morning, still waiting for what felt like forever, Friday, I met Paul at the door. We had a little small talk about a video game we started playing together. I continued a redundant joke that started while we started playing the game. He was easily annoyed and acted as he blew me off, but I kept egging him on.

After a while I gave up my efforts of being funny, and went to sit down at my desk. As I crouched down to sit I looked towards the front door and I saw Brooke walk in as soon as I sat down. We locked our eyes for a second, a second that felt like minutes. She didn't do anything drastic to change her appearance, but to me she looked stunning today. It was weird, people didn't usually catch my eye that way she just did. She looked really good today, not to make it seem like she didn't look good everyday, but seeing her today felt different. Nothing was different though, I didn't think so at least. I guess it was just my mindset toward what was happening, but it didn't make sense. Why is she making me look at her wide-eyed? Why was she wide-eyed? I did my best to act normal, but something seemed so different about her. She glanced at me with a smile for a moment as she made her way to our desk. She scooted her chair in and raised her eyebrows indicating she didn't want to be there. Who does... it's school, but I ignored it and asked the first thing that came to my mind.

"Did you change something?" I asked in a very peculiar tone. When I heard myself I felt like I sounded rude.

"I-I don't think so." She sounded kind of concerned as if she did something wrong, and immediately tried to take back what I said, because I felt bad. I didn't know how to say she looked extremely good without flat out telling her.

"You look really good today. That's why I asked, I wasn't trying to be rude." I ended up just saying, at very fast pace, hoping she wouldn't think I'm strange. Maybe I said too much, but her face became instantly flushed with blushing colors that flooded onto my face when I fully realized what I said. "Uhhh…I-"

"Thank you Landon, that's very sweet of you." She still had the same bright red face with a big smile.

We didn't say anything for a moment, but then she decided to break the awkward silence with small talk about the project. We went on with the class as normal, even though I had that small interaction it replayed through my head at least a thousand times before the class ended.

When the class Paul came up to me and was surprised I said what I had said. Usually Paul was pretty critical of the things I did like most good friends are to each other. This time he was just shocked, just as much as I was. I really didn't think I said it that loud, but he informed me that Mr. Richards had a slight smirk on his face as well. That means what I did was good, I guess. I really didn't know I was nervous that I might've said too much.

Another thing that surprised me is that Paul didn't decide to tell anyone at lunch, he is perfectly fine telling my business any other time, but I guess he was just so thrown off he didn't know how to tell everyone. It would've been the perfect time, because of what I was saying before class to him. I wasn't going to mention it, because I knew someone would tear me down for it. Not in a malicious way, just in a friendly and playful way to get on my nerves. Paul tapped on my shoulder and as I looked at him he moved his head in an upwards direction, which I knew meant to look up, so I did. It took me a moment to see what he meant, because I looked down to check my phone for a second and as I looked up again I saw Brooke staring right back at me. I felt weird that we made such direct eye contact so I immediately looked back down as if I never looked up to begin with. The whole table got a kick out of it, but I wasn't amused. Not that I wasn't happy to see her, I just didn't like how they mocked me in front of her. Her posture gave away her timidness. It seemed as if they were proud of me for a second, but that was gone almost as fast as it came. I didn't realize that Brooke was so close only being a few tables down. I tried to act as if I wasn't caught off guard, but I'm awful at hiding any emotions that hit me so it was obvious that I was shocked.

"H-hey. What are you up to?" I said I was confused.

"Nothing, I just wanted to show you something before tomorrow" she responded, business-like.

I looked at her phone to see writing asking what time the game had started. She could've got the information from anyone really. Basketball was pretty big at our school and most people were informative about the games.

"It starts at seven." The table all stared at me knowing exactly what was going on.

"Ok thank you. I just wanted to make sure." She said with giddy, as she walked off back to her table. I sat there not knowing if I should say something.

"Brooke." I called out to her. I don't know why I did, but my intentions were good, I just didn't know what to say.

"Yeah Landon?" She made her way back to my table.

"You can come sit here if you want. You don't have to though." I was doing my best to sound polite and not demanding.

"Really? Thank you. I had more things to ask, but I didn't want to interrupt you guys." The whole table looked at each other.

They didn't seem as if they had a problem with it. So she gathered her stuff and sat down next to me. In class we sat across from each other, so we were a lot closer than what I was used to. Being this close made me feel as if I was invading her space.

I could feel the eyes of everyone seeping into me. I sat there in silence with a grin on my face. They were surprised I was going on a date.

I'm surprised they all knew without having to do anything about it. Although Matt saw me with Caleb talking about the game earlier that week, and we all have talked about the game. So I guess they just put two and two together.

"Landon Morgan is going on a date. That doesn't even

sound real." Matt said in complete shock. Brooke and I blushed and looked at each other. My smile was met with hers.

"Well for one, I'm happy for him." Ryan responded with a smile on his face. I still sat there quietly, as they went on and on about it for the rest of lunch. It actually didn't bother me, I was happy.

"I still have to find a ride, so I might be a little late tomorrow." Brooke whispered to me, as lunch was ending. I nodded my head to signify that it was ok.

When the night came it was impossible for me to sleep. I tossed and turned, but was overcome by every thought that made me think of every possible scenario. Sounds like another day I had that started all this. I thought well that it ended up working out pretty good so I tried to convince myself that everything was happening for a reason. It was to no avail, I struggled falling asleep all night. Things became more apparent, such as the room being burning hot. Then it became freezing cold. Polar opposite feelings and thoughts were running all throughout me. I still had no clue how I felt about Brooke and the day was here. When I finally went to sleep I slept like a dog.

When I woke up I got ready very slowly not realizing how nervous I would be to put all the plans to action. To reassure myself I texted Caleb to make sure he could still pick me up for the game. I got even more nervous because I didn't get a reply the whole morning. When he finally answered I was relieved to see that he said that he could. Only thing is that I would be there early, which wasn't a problem. It will just be weird watching a sport by myself that I don't know that much about. I went to science unsure how seeing Brooke was going to be, but it was a lot more casual than I expected. We didn't say anything about the game at first. We really stayed focused on our assignment which was the project we had been accustomed to doing every day for the past couple of weeks. Since the game was big, apparently we had a lesson on physics in basketball. It was getting really hard to deny the fact that we were going to the game together.

I was going to keep avoiding the talk about it, but Brooke decided to say, "You ready for the game?" Only if she knew how over prepared I was, most of the preparation was mental, but nevertheless I was still over prepared.

"Oh yeah. It's going to be a good one, I've been waiting for this one all year." I sounded cliche, but I didn't know what else to say, and that was the first thing to run out of my mouth. She silently nodded her head and went back to the assignment. I started overthinking the gesture way too much. I was self aware of what I was doing, I just couldn't stop myself. It made too much sense to think of everything she was thinking. I just hoped that she wasn't going to bail out on going, because I genuinely was looking forward to going with her. I just didn't know how to express it to her without looking like I was trying too hard. The rest of the class was quiet and so were we as the bell rang, we grabbed our stuff and left with just a simple goodbye. That was that I did my best to go on about my day as normal as I could. Just the thought of the game slowly climbing to the forefront of my mind. As the day went on the further it climbed until that was the only thing I could think about. The time was here. At this point I had to have been more nervous than the players who actually had to play the game. When I got home from school I sat on my bed straight up and sat on my phone while I patiently waited for Caleb to let me know when he was on his way to pick me up. I waited and waited for what felt like days, until finally a buzz in my hand electrified my energy seeing that it was Caleb letting me know he was here. I sprung up from my bed and grabbed my bag, because of the usual routine I was used to. I laughed as I set my bag down, told my mother goodbye and headed out the door.

"Hey hey hey." Caleb said, looking as ready as ever. He was such a great guy. I wasn't just saying this because he was giving me a ride, but he was honestly an amazing guy. He was the type of guy to light up any room he was in no matter how dark it was from just a smile. He could logically get his way out of any negative situation and could match it with positivity.

"How are you doing Caleb?" I exaggerated his name to sound like I wasn't nervous even though my legs were trembling in fear.

"I'm ready. It looks like we both have a big night ahead of us, huh?" He gave me a little nudge as he said the last part.

"Yeah, I guess we do. I just hope I don't mess it up." I answered.

He could tell the worry I had by looking at me. "Look, I think that every time I lace up before a game. I go out there and control what I can and if things don't play out the way I want, I adapt. I'm gonna fight my hardest to get the results I worked for, but that's the fun of the game. Like for you, I can obviously tell you put effort into this, but if it ends up not working out it's not the end of the world. That doesn't mean you don't give yourself the best shot that you can. You worked for and deserve it, but can't control everything." It was crazy, because that was exactly what I needed to hear. My mentality changed my words from his simple dialogue and I was totally ready for the night and felt as if I had all the confidence in the world.

"Thank you, Caleb. I really needed to hear that."

"Anytime bro. Just be you, that's the easiest thing you can do." I took his words seriously and was determined to do what he said and just be me for once.

When we arrived at the gym, I almost forgot that I was early and me being early with Caleb meant I was there before everyone, which felt weird. I felt like I was out of place just because I still had no real connection with basketball. I sat there patiently waiting for the game to start, but I actually enjoyed watching the players do their warm up routine. It was intriguing, seeing as they were tall and had enough hand eye coordination to manipulate the ball the way they wanted to. Although I was fascinated by what the players could do, that didn't take my mind off what I was trying to accomplish, which is trying not to make a complete fool out of myself. Now that I was here I thought, wow I'm really here. What am I doing? I really hope this goes well.

Before I knew it the game started and I was surrounded by a bunch of students, some which I knew and some I didn't but knew they were popular within our school. I felt out of place more, because of me being in the heart of the student section, so I snaked my way out to find a more isolated spot. I looked around for a while not spotting Brooke and started to feel insecure thinking I got stood up. This is one of the scenarios that kept me up Thursday night. This scenario had the worst ending. An ending that sees her not showing up, and telling all of her friends how lame I am. She didn't seem like the kind of person to do that, but maybe I was wrong about her.

Although I had enough courage still to text Brooke to make sure she was still coming. She responded very quickly letting me know that she was just running a little behind because of traffic. It was understandable and she assured me she would be there by the end of the first quarter.

Whenever she arrived I could tell instantly she was there. It seemed as if when she stepped foot in the building there was a different aurora. When I saw her coming towards me my emotions fluctuated all over the place, but remembering what Caleb what had said and looking at him on the court I had enough confidence to not cower down and not say anything when she approached me. We exchanged our hellos and she apologized about her being late. I was just glad I didn't get stood up and told her that it was perfectly fine.

"How much do you know about basketball?" I was just trying to start a conversation, so it wasn't awkward.

"Well, I know that when the ball goes in the hoop from inside the line it's two, and if it's outside the line it's three." This basically let me know we both had no idea what was going on. This also told me that she really came for me which made me burst with happiness inside.

"I guess we're on the same page, because I don't know that much either. I know Caleb though he's a really good player."

"Oh yeah my sister was a good friend of his brother, but I've never talked to Caleb myself." I was surprised to hear this, because I was hoping she would say she did know him, so we can touch bases on something, but I guess it was ok that we didn't.

"You should meet him, he really is a great guy.

Everyone loves him." I was hoping I could introduce her to him, but I didn't want to force anything onto her.

"That would be cool, but if I talk to him I want you to be there, because you guys are already friends." I nodded my head to agree with her.

This so far was going a lot better than I expected. While the players were shooting free throws I saw Caleb look up to the stands and wink at me, because he saw both of us smiling together. My smile became more directed whenever I saw him wink, because he gave me the confidence to do this. I really don't think I would've been able to do this without him, sounds kind of weird, because he gave such a simple speech, but it was touching, because when he said things you knew he meant it.

As the game got to the end it got close. The score was fifty-seven to fifty-nine with seven seconds left, but I wasn't even really concerned about the game. I was worried more about getting to know Brooke. I started to really like her, she was fun to be around. I could tell she liked me too, but I couldn't tell to what extent. Maybe she was just friendly like Caleb and thought I would only be a good friend.

The game saw Caleb at the free throw line to help seal the game for the win. He made his both like it was nothing. This made the score sixty-one to fifty-nine, with only three seconds left. The other team threw in the ball and launched it from mid court. It hit the rim and bounced into the crowd. Nowhere near me, but it was funny to watch.

"GO CALEB!" I shouted towards the court hoping he would hear me. TO my surprise he pointed his finger up at the ceiling. Maybe he heard me, but I don't know for sure.

As the game ended we knew that our night was coming to an end, but we really didn't want it to end. I told her I would introduce her to Caleb and he was my ride back home, so we waited and talked on the court until he came out. When Caleb came I made sure to congratulate him. As I introduced them to each other they exchanged names and Caleb mentioned us together.

"So what are you guys supposed to be?" I instantly became blush, but calmed down seeing that she blushed as well. Neither of us said anything, because we were unsure what we were. I didn't want to say we were just friends in case that would've ruined any chance I had to get with her, so it was silent.

"Well I won't ask anymore questions, I guess." He chuckled. We still didn't know how to respond. She signified that her parents were here to pick her up so she gave me an unexpected hug which gave me butterflies in my stomach and my heart fluttered. I met her with the same hug.

Then she left as we both turned back to blush looking at each other. As I looked at Caleb I felt comfortable, because I knew he was proud of me. We chatted about his game on the way to my house, but then for the last five minutes it was silent. It was peaceful silence. I was satisfied with how the night went, and I was surprised it went as well as it did. I did my nightly routine with a big smile on my face. Told my mom goodnight with the same smile on my face.

"So it went well, huh kiddo?" she asked as I left her room.

"Yep it sure did." I said while giggling a little. I felt like a child, but it was something that I embraced, instead of second guessing.

I went straight to my bed without my smile escaping and went to sleep. Didn't think about anything other than what happened tonight. Monday.....How is that going to play out? I hope it's not awkward and she still feels the same way when she comes back. However she feels. I know how I feel for sure now. It was much easier to see her intimately. I was ok with that being the reality of the situation for me. I didn't want to tell anyone, especially if things did not work out, because then I would look like a fool. I still don't know how to express it out loud with words or actions, but it makes so much sense in my head.

I just hope I don't run her off. I don't think there's any way I could blow this. At least at this moment. If I do, at least I did everything like Caleb said, but I need to stop overthinking. Everything is working out the way it should.

I still couldn't help but to think about how Monday was going to go. I tried my best to go to sleep and at first it was difficult, because I was playing back every word she said in my head, becoming best friends with her voice. Having every detail she told me memorized. Like how her birthday was September twenty-seventh, how her favorite color was cyan, how she wanted to be a neurosurgeon when she grew up, or how she moved here when she was four from Fresno, California.

I tried not to replay it as much but it slowly consumed my dreams as I went to sleep. The idea of being with her, talking to her, and just being around her. It was taking all of my thinking, all the room I had of everything I've been worried about, occupied with the idea of her. I was okay with it, because at least it was her.

IV

A few weeks passed and not much has changed since the game. I've been living life as normal with a little more of Brooke. We've gotten along so well, and honestly I'm surprised. I definitely won't complain, with all of life's changes, this one was something I could say I was proud about. I wasn't prideful that I was starting to have a relationship with someone, more so because I found a way to be happy. Sounds a lot more sad than intended, but at times it can be easy to get caught up with saying I'm not enough. Although, I've always been pretty hard on myself. My mom's always said that it's a blessing and a curse, because I'll always hold myself accountable, but sometimes I take it too far and it's a detriment to me. I know that I fall into a hole that gets harder and harder to climb out of, but it just makes sense to me. How do I expect to improve if I'm laxed about everything? In my mind you simply can't, it's just not how it works.

Recently I think it's been changing for the better. I've found more balance and I'm not so hard on myself. I won't say it's because of Brooke completely, but I can for sure say she's helped tremendously. Which is weird. Who would've ever guessed that the introverted kid would become better by choosing to not be introverted. Sometimes life's greatest opportunities come at you in the most unexpected ways and I'm glad this one did. I still think I'm in over my head about her. Why her? What made me think she was so special? Why is she so special? Such simple questions, but I have no idea how I could answer them.

My mom's been able to tell that I'm getting better. I haven't told her why, but I figured she already put two and two together. I'm glad she can tell though, because in a way seeing me happy I think has made her more happy. She's always had a load on her shoulders which stresses her out, but I understand. Being a single mother with a child in highschool couldn't be easy. Especially because I couldn't drive yet.

I'll be able to drive soon. I already passed my writing portion, which I failed two times before I passed. The way I failed really is upsetting. I got all the way to the last question just to miss it and fail. The same thing happened the second time. So when I took it that third time I inspected every question for at least ten minutes, double checked my answer, changed that answer, and then probably changed it back to my original answer. All that worked out though, because I passed it. I passed the test in October which meant I had to wait at least six months before I could take my driving portion and it was just a waiting game at this point. In my mind I was David Pearson, except I actually drove the speed limit to the exact number. I also turned fifteen in March, so I couldn't even drive alone once I was able to take the driving portion of the test. Once I can drive I feel like so many things I've been planning on doing can actually happen. Mom's pretty strict on what I do so that would be the only thing stopping me from just driving around all the time, or driving to a friend's. I don't go out much so it'll probably be a thing that I would do for a couple weeks but wouldn't carry out too long.

Not having that barrier of driving in my way would be so ideal. All the things my friends and I could do, or even what Brooke and I could do. I might be pushing it saying that, but I don't know. I still have no clue where she's at us. I don't even know if there is an us to be honest. Seeing her at school has gotten easier and easier as the weeks go on, but I think we're just friends. We started texting more so I've gotten to learn more about her, and she's very interesting. Sounds cliche, but she's actually really cool, there's no real other way to put it. She keeps her circle small so I'm more surprised she even talks to me to begin with.

Realizing it was the end of November, meaning Brooke and I project was due in only a few weeks we needed to put the overall model together.

This also meant that we would start having to meet after school to finish it. We already did about a quarter of it in class, but Mr. Richards has us working on the project in our own time now so we can focus on different topics. I don't know why he made it this way because it's kind of awkward having to go to each other's house especially with how parents are when you're the opposite sex. Realizing that we would actually have to plan how to finish the project outside of school, I started overthinking every scenario like I often did.

"How are we going to finish the rest of the project?" I asked bluntly.

"I don't know. Maybe you could come over and we can finish it, because I already have the model at home." She sounded like she didn't care what happened. I was shocked she was okay with me coming over at all.

"When could I come over, because we only have a few weeks." I responded quickly.

"It could be whenever, my parents aren't very strict on who comes over. I'd have to ask if you could first though, because you're a boy." Pretty understandable why she would have to ask, but I'm surprised that she even mentioned the idea of me coming over. This didn't seem like a natural conversation, because that was way too easy. It was a spectacle, but I went along with it.

Class ended and at lunch I was mostly quiet. My friends asked what was wrong, but there genuinely wasn't anything wrong. Paul and Ryan, who sat in front of me, looked as if they saw something either disgusting or alarming. Either way I was perplexed and was scared to turn around. I thought maybe a principal was going to come talk to our table to make sure everything was alright and we weren't doing anything. Although that was a regular thing that happened at school so why would they be so alarmed by that? The seat to my right is always vacant, because we only had five people at our table: Ryan, Paul, Tony, Matt, and then me. Tony wasn't here today who usually sits to the left of Ryan. Now if he was as appalled as Paul and Ryan were there would definitely be a problem. I look left and see Matt looking as confused as Paul and Ryan were. I look to my right thinking what is up with these guys. My face instantly matched thier's seeing that Brooke was walking up to the vacant seat. I was speechless when she sat down. Every word I try to say wouldn't form in my breath.

"Landon, guess what!" She sounded excited which made me even more nervous.

"Uhh-I guess-uhh that..." I was struggling really badly.

"My parents said it's okay for you to come over." She had a wide smile on her face. That slowly dissipated when she saw me not smiling at first. I looked over at the guys and they sat there in awe.

"Do you not want to come over anymore?" She sounded hurt and probably thought I didn't care.

"I'm sorry I'm just shocked to say the least, but I'd love to come over."

I try to give a warming smile, but I didn't want to be weird. I had no idea what was going on. It was all so random. She didn't have any of her friends come over with her. Although she told me she just sat with them so she didn't have to sit alone. I could understand that, so with that in mind I added, "Also, would it be okay with everyone if Brooke sits over here. If she's okay with it." I turned to her and she smiled and nodded. "And if you guys are okay with it." Turning back to my friends and they were still in shock.

Luckily for me Ryan spoke up and said, "That's fine she seems really cool. I know that being the only girl at an all boys table may be weird so if you wanted to bring one of your friends too that would be okay." He knew exactly what to say.

Now that everyone was speechless I felt a little more comfortable. Brooke just smiled at us. I smiled back and enjoyed all of my favorite people's company. Ignoring the fact that I would have to meet her parents, ignoring the fact that it was almost Christmas, and ignoring the fact that I wasn't overthinking.

Once I got home I texted Brooke about what day I should come over. She said, "It would have to be either a Thursday or Friday. My parents don't want us home alone, and they're usually busy Monday through Wednesday." Simple enough. Only thing is that It's Tuesday and I don't know if I'm mentally prepared to do it this week so I asked if it was okay if I went over next week. She said it was. Only problem now was transportation. I had time though, so I would just ask mom if it was okay to go to a friend's house. She was more surprised that I wanted to go to a friend's place rather than them coming over, but she said yes. She never asked who the friend was so I didn't tell her. She probably wouldn't be too fond of me going to a girl's house, but oh well she doesn't know, so I guess I won't find out.

The next day at school Brooke and I spent most of our time talking about Christmas instead of doing our work. Mr. Richards didn't care so we didn't care. The work wasn't very hard, so if I did it for homework it would only take about fifteen minutes to get done completely. I was trying to be slick about how to know what to get her for Christmas, but every question I asked didn't give me any hints. I thought about asking her friends what she wants for Christmas, but then I thought I don't know any of her friends. I guess today that was going to change.

When lunch rolled around everyone took their seats as normal. Tony was back today which was nice to see. We didn't question it, because if he wanted to tell us he would.

"Why are those two coming over here?" He asked after a few minutes of small talk. Brooke approached me with a delightful hello and introduced me to her friend Sara. Sara was a somewhat tall blonde girl who wore glasses. She seemed as if she would be quiet, but quickly we found out that that wasn't the case at all. After anyone would say anything she would comment on it in some fashion she could find. Although after a little bit I could tell that Ryan enjoyed her, he was a nice guy so I thought he was just being courteous. This felt different though. Maybe I was being hopeful, because I love seeing my friends happy. Not that Ryan wasn't a happy guy, he just made up a fantasy in my head that everyone in the group gets that special someone. Except Matt, we all knew that was not going to happen. Anyway throughout lunch we had laughs and everyone seemed fond of Brooke which I was glad about, but I could tell that everyone except Ryan was slightly annoyed with Sara and her comments. They were good additions to our table group and it seemed like this could be a long-term thing. If that's what Brooke wanted. I thought she would think my friends are weird, but she was apparently having a good time with everything that was going on at the table. I tried not to overthink it, and just be glad that she was ok with my friends, and I was ok with hers.

V

The next Monday, I was approached by Caleb in the halls on the way to first period. He didn't say hi to begin with rather saying, "Are you still trying to get with Brooke?" I was kind of alarmed, because it sounded like he said it out loud. I didn't really know how to answer. I would like to be with her, but I'm not trying to be with her.

"I-I guess. I mean I don't know, but I wouldn't be opposed to it." I struggled to find an answer, just letting things roll out of my mouth.

"Well I mean are you guys in some sort of relationship where you wouldn't want other people trying to get with one of you guys?" He started sounding more urgent which worried me.

"I guess you could say that, sure." Made sense in my head, but I still wasn't sure how she felt "Just letting you know. I saw her hanging out with Jayden Culvert at the park on Saturday." I know Caleb wouldn't instigate, but this felt out of the blue. Why would he randomly tell me this? Especially if he wasn't sure if Brooke and I were close. Jayden was a star quarterback on the football team. It was pretty impressive, because he was our best football player only being a sophomore. I didn't know how to process what Caleb just told me, mostly because I still have no idea what Brooke and I are yet, but I wouldn't care if she was talking to other people, but I wouldn't want her to get into another relationship with someone who wasn't me. Sounds selfish, but this for me is a rarity, so I'd hate to watch it walk away.

Being aware of time I walked away from Caleb with no words and headed to class to not be late. Brooke was already sat down and ready which didn't usually happen. I was nervous to say anything even though I knew she didn't know that I knew that she was hanging out with Jayden. I sat down slowly unpacking my things not trying to draw any attention to myself.

"Hey Landon. How are you?" She had her hair in a high ponytail which was different from her naturally flowing hair.

At first I was thinking about everything except what she just asked. I stood there blank for a second and then processed what she asked me and said, "I'm fine, how was your weekend?" Oh my...why did I say that?

"It was nice, I got to hang out with friends and family,

and that type of stuff you know?" Her answer was hesitant and slowly said. Maybe it was the Monday fog that most students get, or maybe she thought I knew something. Regardless I wasn't helping my case with fumbling my binder and notebooks out of my bag. I nodded for a response and tried to cool myself down. Not that I was mad, I was just aware that I wasn't being me. Halfway through class I start daydreaming about all the things that are happening this week, mainly that I have to go over to Brooke's and meet her parents. After a while, Brooke leans halfway over the table and asks,

"Are you okay? Something seems off with you."

I was caught off guard, realizing what was going on around me. I looked dazed and confused for a minute. I looked over at Paul and waved him over to come to my table. As soon as I saw him coming over, I turned around to Brooke and reassured her that I was fine, and that I was just tired from the weekend. She acted like she understood, but her body language told me that she was confused. As Paul made his way over, people started packing their bags. I didn't realize how close to the end of class it was. Paul was about to turn around and go pack his things before I stopped him. "Paul! You think you could come over after school?" I was trying to hurry not fully knowing how much time was left in class because I hadn't checked the time since I got to class.

"You could've asked me this at lunch or something."

He was trying to brush me off, but I wouldn't let that happen. I just needed a quick answer.

"Come on. Can you come over yes or no?" I was trying to sound like I was pleading without it sounding like begging.

"Sure, but why?" I couldn't tell him right now, with Brooke right next to me because it pertained to her, but luckily as I was about to answer the bell rung. Now that Brooke and Sara sat at our lunch table I couldn't easily tell Paul. I had to think of a way that I can tell Paul why he's coming over without alarming Brooke or Sara. Sara wasn't the brightest star so that part should be easy. Brooke on the other hand, she's like a detective. She can deduce things pretty quickly which was worrisome for me.

When lunch came and everyone took their spots at the table Paul eyed me for a minute. I texted him, which would've been a lot easier to do in the beginning, saying "I need you to come over for some advice." I didn't realize Brooke was looking over my shoulder, and she asked about the message. I tried to brush it off like it wasn't nothing and then she said, "If it was nothing you could've just said it across the table."

I look shell shocked. I had no comeback, so I decided to say, "He knows stuff about my family I'm comfortable with talking about." Why did I lie about that? I felt like an idiot, because I don't like lying or having that be my first resort. Tony looked at me confused, he knew it wasn't the truth but he wasn't going to call me out. I tried to ask for forgiveness with my eyes, but he must've thought I was being sarcastic because he rolled his eyes back.

I looked back at Brooke with a nervous smile on my face hoping she wouldn't see through my lie, because I've told her some personal family business over text. "Oh…I understand I won't barge in on you anymore, I'm sorry." I instantly felt bad. I know not to lie and I usually don't unless I absolutely have to, like to save someone's peace of mind. Everything was like normal for the rest of the day, other than the lingering thought of my flat-out lie.

Later that day when Paul came over I gave him a rundown of what Caleb told me and why I was acting so weird. He told me that I was probably just overreacting because he was pretty sure their parents were good friends. That would've been an amazing detail for Caleb to add but maybe he didn't know. If parents were there then why would he tell me? Something wasn't adding up. I didn't want to confront Brooke, because I thought I was being typical Landon and overthinking the situation. Paul presented the idea of texting Brooke and just asking her. At first I was unquestionably not going to text, but as he explained how she probably doesn't like him, and we're not dating, "yet" as he liked to add, there was definitely a reasonable explanation of why she was with Jayden.

After a couple hours of hanging out with Paul I came to a decision. I was going to text her, and just ask her.

How do I ask her though? Do I admit I lied? I still feel really bad about lying, if I didn't lie this would've been a lot easier. I had recurring memories of me doing the same thing when I first started texting her. So I convinced myself that the first time it worked so why wouldn't this time work? I still thought it wasn't a good idea, but Paul wasn't going to leave until I finally asked her. I eventually text her, "Brooke". Paul was disappointed I didn't say more with the first text, but I didn't know how to approach the situation.

"Hey Landon, you alright you've been acting a little strange today." I could hear the concern in her voice, even though it was only a text.

"Hey, do you know Jayden Culvert?" I struggled to allow myself to ask such a simple question. I irked every moment until she responded. Minutes passed with no response. I was getting nervous that I screwed up in some way.

After some time Brooke responded with, "Oh yeah Jayden, he's a family friend. We've been real close since when we were little, even dated at one point." I was relieved to find out that Paul was right. I still shielded my phone so he wouldn't be able to see the response, because I was insecure I would mess up. Although my worry came back when she said they used to date at some point. I was surprised, how come she wasn't more popular because of dating Jayden. That means it had to have been years ago.

Paul kept asking to see the messages, but I was quick with turning down his requests. Seeing that I hadn't responded in a couple minutes Brooke followed up with a text saying, "Why? What's up?"

I didn't know what to say. I was frozen in fear of what to say next. I handed the phone to Paul hoping he would know what to do.

"Ha! I told you so." I rolled my eyes at him. I simply asked for help and not a remark, he didn't know what to say either. I decided to be straightforward and let her know what Caleb had told me. She thought it was funny, because she "couldn't see Jayden in that way anymore". I didn't completely buy it, but I went by her word.

"You don't have to worry about anyone, Landon." As soon as I read that text I instantly became laid back. Paul was glad the stress was gone and decided that he was going to leave.

It was already nine at night so I decided to have a little small talk with Brooke before having to go to her house. I asked what her parents were like, and she described her mom as a nice sweet lady who would help anyone. And her dad was a funny, buff, scary, and tall man. The thought of her dad sounded frightening, because I would have to meet him soon, but I was prepared. I mostly had a bloom of confidence, because of her text.

"You don't have to worry about anyone, Landon." For once I didn't.

VI

I remember being a child thinking that I would grow up alone. I had imagined a big house in the middle of a corn field that I lived alone in. It sounds sad, but to me that was tranquility, it was peace. When mom and I lived in Texas we always discussed what I wanted to be when I grew up and it would constantly change. It's still that way even though I'm in highschool now. I'm just so indecisive, especially with big decisions. Mom says, "It's ok you still have a lot of time before you go to college, and start your life." That was something I pondered often. Had my life not already started. What if I never figure it out. Maybe I need to just calm myself and let things work themselves out.

Things still aren't clear in the present day. I still overthink with Brooke, if I'll mess things up or if I'm enough. There's nothing to indicate whether I'm losing her or not, but I don't want it to even get close to that point. I need to calm down. It's December and Christmas is almost here. Snow glazes everything giving a warm feeling despite how cold it is. I've always loved Christmas. Mostly due to the fact that my mom does everything in her power to make it a "magical" day. We make gingerbread houses, set the tree up, decorate the house, and most importantly open presents. I love that she goes out of her way to make me as happy as possible, she knows how much I stress about little things and the holidays really help me get my mind off of those things. Although if there's nothing to stress about I'll make something to stress about. For example, I'm thinking about what I should get Brooke for Christmas, and I'd love to spend time with her on Christmas.

I don't want to seem like I'm intruding on her or trying to take her away from my family, but she's become a big part of my life and it'd be fun to have her over. Last year I had Paul over for a little bit to celebrate with my mother and I. He didn't stay long, maybe an hour or two, but it was still fun to have him over. I would have more of my friends come to spend time with me and mom, but the people I usually hang around and are in my circle are big on family and usually make Christmas an all-day event with family. Which isn't a problem at all, just kind of lonely when you're the only child and mom is done with festivities.

I'm overthinking, Christmas isn't for another twenty days. Right now I need to focus on school and not ruining anything between Brooke and I.

Meanwhile at school, things have been routine. Just making it through the day everyday. It's been pretty boring, but I have to go to Brooke's house to finish our project. It's hard to believe that it's the end of the project. It's crazy to think that this project is the whole reason I even started talking to Brooke. To see how far we've come from that is mind-boggling.

Today at lunch, a receiver on the football team, named Michael Reed came up to our table. He didn't introduce himself, but immediately started talking to Brooke about school. He said with a very strong voice, "Do you think we have time to finish our homework?"

I could tell she didn't like him and wasn't trying to hear anything Michael had to say. She replied, "No. I have to finish my project with Landon."

"Who cares about this loser." He was pointing at me. "All I need is fifteen minutes with you and I'll get all my work done." I didn't like his tone at all.

First of all, he didn't have to disrespect me, I'm not a super awesome guy, but man that one hit a little bit. Second of all, why is he talking to Brooke that way, it's very awkward. I have to intervene. "Hey! Why are you causing problems man, she said no."

"Who do you think you're talking to, bum?" Michael

was trying to be menacing and intimidate me, but I was having none of it.

Standing up was usually out of my character but I wasn't going to let him heckle her. So I stood up from my seat and approached him. We were right above Brooke. "I'm asking politely, please leave."

"Or what?" He shoved me back two steps. I knew what I was getting myself into, but I did not care.

I couldn't say I would tell a teacher, I felt myself stumbling on my words. I wasn't a very confrontational person so I didn't know what to say in this instance. "I-I... uh-I'll show you, just leave." I walked up and gave him a shove, not as hard as he shoved me. He stepped back maybe one foot, not fazing him at all.

"You got a pair on you dweeb." He balled up his fist. "You don't want this." He was right. I definitely didn't want to fight. I also didn't want him to mess with Brooke.

"Last chance...Leav-" before I could finish I saw a first hurling towards me and I didn't have enough time to react. I got a boost of adrenaline whenever I felt the contact of his fist. I clenched my fist ready to retaliate, but I saw the concern look on Brooke's face, so I eased up.

"What's the matter? Already had enough?" He started hackling, "I was just getting started I thought you would-" I couldn't take anymore of his blabbering. So I used all of the weight of my body and threw the hardest punch I could muster.

BAM! the cafeteria fell silent. I looked over at Brooke and her eyes were wide as if she just witnessed a murder. I looked around and realized what I did. I stare at the floor to see a puddle of blood next time Michael's face is on the ground. He looked up towards me with an angry snarl. We both had no clue how to react, because we felt the hundreds of eyes of our peers glued to us.

Fights were not very common at our school so I knew this would be talked about for a while. That doesn't bother me, but I would hate to be the guy known for punching star receiver Michael Reed. An administrator walked over to see what the commotion was about, to see a blood-leaking Micheal holding his nose trying to contain the bleeding. He was appalled at the situation, and so was I. To be honest I didn't know I was capable of causing harm to others, I've always been very passive, so for me to do this it was crazy. The administrator said no words, he just pointed to the front office, and I headed that way.

I waited in the office for around thirty minutes waiting for the principal to call for me. Michael was in the Nurse's room and he wasn't too badly injured. When I walked into the principal's office after being called in, there was a very ominous looking black chair to match the principal's blank and ominous face. I sat down and sat silent for about fifteen seconds before opening my mouth.

As soon as I did he said, "I already know what happened, your punishment won't be so severe, because it was an act of self defense." I breathed a breath of relief. His voice was very deep and he continued saying, "Now to keep it simple. Your mother will be informed on the matter, but I will make sure to include the whole story and it's details. On the school side of the matter you will have a week's worth of detention. You may choose whether this is at lunch or after school, because it is Friday I will let you ponder the decision. Once the decision is made inform your administrator of your choice and your week will be served."

I said very quickly and with swiftness, "Thank you sir, I'm sorry and you do not have to worry about this happening EVER again."

He could tell I was being honest and replied saying, "I understand why you did what you did, he tried to harass your friend and you prevented it, so I commend you for that. Honestly if it were up to me I would let you walk away without punishment, but unfortunately as head of the school I must follow the hand book, but I assure you this was the lightest punishment you would have received. Now head back to class and try to keep this matter quiet." I nodded my head, said my thanks, and headed to class.

It was sixth period, which is my economics class, and when I knocked I prepared myself for the eyes that would be staring, and probably the millions of questions my peers would ask. A shorter brunette girl came and opened the door, and looked at me wide-eyed, as if she just saw something she wasn't supposed to see. I awkwardly smiled and walked to my desk not knowing how to maneuver myself. The teacher approached my desk and lightly slid our work onto my table. I swiftly grabbed the paper and immediately started getting to work. I could feel everyone's pupils burning into the back of my skull.

This feeling would last the rest of the day. I kept to myself as usual.

When I saw Brooke after school before going home. I apologized to her, "I'm sorry. I saw the look you gave me, but I wasn't going to let him harass you like that."

"I understand Landon." I knew it was a problem when she said my name with a flat voice. "Don't feel like you have to protect me all the time. I can defend myself and I had the situation under control."

I was very confused how she was turning this on me. "What do you mean you had it under control, you didn't do anything to help defend yourself. You just sat there and took what he was saying, and I was not going to let that happen." My tone started to change, but I couldn't keep a hold of it.

"I'm not a little kid! I don't need a Prince Charming to come and save me every time an inconvenience happens." She started to raise her voice.

I knew I shouldn't have kept responding and left it there but I couldn't, "I'm not trying to be that way...I just want you to be ok, and I-I want you to know that I really care for you." I started to talk softer, scared of her response.

"Landon…" I was ready to hear about how she doesn't care about our 'relationship', "thank you. I care about you too" she came up and hugged me. "But you know you don't have to do that."

"I know, I'm sorry." I tightened myself around her. We stood there for what felt like forever, whenever she pulled away I could see that she was teary. "What's wrong?" I asked.

She wiped the tears from her eyes, "Nothing." She was lying.

"You sure it's nothing, I'm here for you." I put my hand on her shoulder to reassure her.

"I'm ok Landon." Then she walked away. I was speechless. Is she ok? Did I mess up? Should I follow her? Following her would be weird. Before I knew it she was gone, and I stood there alone, cold, feeling the brisk air push against my cheeks.

Later that evening, I ended up texting Brooke to clear everything up. She didn't open up much and I made sure I was still ok to come over tomorrow. She let me know I could, but it didn't sound as if she wanted me there. Despite our feelings we needed to finish the project, so I subtly agreed and we kept our text to a minimal. I hope she was ok, I don't know how severe the argument was, if you could even call it that. I usually would ask my mom what I should do in this situation, but I couldn't even start the conversation. I just sat at the dinner table for about an hour thinking about everything. I went to my room and laid there and still pondered what happened. I slowly fell asleep thinking about what I did wrong.

VII

I woke up the next morning frantically, I looked at my clock on the left side of my bed to realize that it was six-thirty. School didn't start until eight-thirty, and it was Saturday. I guess my nerves had woken me up, I felt disoriented when I sat up. I opened my curtain to see a blanket of snow outside and it was still dark. I got up and moved around for a few minutes trying to wake myself, before I headed back to bed to lay down. I stared at my phone with an empty expression. There were no notifications, nothing to look at but I continued to just stare. I turned on a video to watch anything, but as soon as the video started I turned it off and went back to my Lock Screen, to continue to stare at nothing. I don't know what I am waiting for, or if I was waiting for anything at all. It was six-thirty in the morning with nothing to do. I got up and strolled to the bathroom, and gently splashed warm water in my face attempting to wake my brain. I could still feel the empty expression on my face. I ended up walking to the kitchen to open up the fridge. The door handle was cold and the sensation of cold flooded my hand. The light from the fridge blinded me for a second, but as my eyes adjusted to the light I reached for eggs that were at the back. When I reached for them I knocked over a gallon of milk. It ended up not spilling everywhere as I anticipated it would, as I stared at it blankly on the ground I softly chuckled. As I held the eggs and set them on the counter. I picked the milk up to realize it was three days expired. Three days isn't that bad so I just set it back in the fridge, and returned to the eggs. I decided to make scrambled eggs for mom and I so I made four eggs, two for her and two for me. After making them the time was seven, meaning mom wouldn't get up for another hour. I ate my eggs very slowly, taking in every bite and letting every taste dissolve in my mouth. I continued to sit there with my phone staring blankly. Not watching anything just continued to wait, but not for anything in particular.

"You're up early." Mom came in bundled up in a robe. She gave me a hug. "I see you made eggs."

"Yep." I felt as if I was just going through the motions. No reason to be empty, I just was.

Mom didn't say much after eating her eggs; she just let me be with my empty expressions.

I was going over to Brooke's house at one and I was

a little anxious about going. Mom told me I'm allowed to drive to her house, because nobody had time to take me over, including my mom. Which is crazy, because she won't even let me drive to school, but she's ok with me driving to a girls house. I didn't question it, I just played along.

I loafed around my house trying to occupy myself with something. Before I knew it, it was twelve-thirty, so I told my mom I was getting ready to go.

The last time I drove by myself was this summer, and I hung out with Paul. The plan was to go to Walmart to get stuff to build a treehouse in the forest. I convinced my mom for what felt like hours, but she ended up agreeing. That was not a good decision on her side. We spent around two hours looking for the "perfect" tree. That perfect tree had us parking in the middle of nowhere in Colorado, which is never good. Paul grabbed as many supplies as he could, he was pretty scrawny so he didn't carry much. I just carried a tool box, because I had planned on doing most of the building. Whenever we started getting to work, it simultaneously was the beginning of dusk. We didn't mind because we brought two flashlights and eight batteries if we weren't lucky. I became very fidgety with my movements letting my nerves get to me, my palms began to sweat and my hands were trembling because of how cold and dark it was getting.

"Maybe we should go back to the car, I bet our parents

are worried about us." I was doing my best to suggest to Paul we should leave, but he was so intrigued by building our tree house. I became more alert of my surroundings waiting for anything to attack. As I became more fearful I heard a branch snap. I had no idea if it was an animal or person, but I took off in a sprint. I sprinted for around five minutes in the opposite way of the car. I had no clue if Paul was behind me or not, but I was concerned about myself first. I took a minute to catch my breath, putting my hands on my knees, trying not to collapse. Paul showed up whenever I got off of my knees. He stared at me wondering why I ran so hard.

"What were you doing? Why did you run so fast?" He sounded very annoyed, but I honestly did not care.

"Did you not hear that? They were coming to get us." I responded with crackling fear in my voice.

"You're an idiot. It was just a rabbit." He put his face in his hand with disappointment. I stared blankly feeling insecure and dumb. "Let's just go home. It's dark anyway." He continued.

"Like I've been saying for the last forever." I remarked sarcastically.

"Shut up! I don't want to hear anything from you." He was very mad and it was apparent. I wanted to start an argument, but he stormed off in the direction of the car before I could retaliate. We ended up not getting home until around midnight and my mother was worried sick about me. Ever since I haven't been able to drive anywhere, but today that changes.

Brooke sent me her address, and her house was ten minutes away. Which was walking distance from the highschool. I opened the garage to see a light mist, so I ran back inside to grab a hoodie. It was an old gray University of Denver hoodie that was a gift, because I had aspired to go there for college. As I opened the car door I got flashbacks of the argument Paul and I had back in the woods. I was hoping that the same thing didn't happen between Brooke and I. I still haven't spoken to her in person since I got in that fight with Michael. My brain was still on autopilot and I was just going through the motions it felt. I started the car and immediately fixed my mirrors, adjusted the seat, and changed the air conditioning. I moved the car very slowly out of the garage, and with much hesitance. I took in a deep breath and started accelerating. I was overthinking every movement I was making.

After thinking too much, I finally arrived at Brooke's house and I was overwhelmed with nerves. I could barely make it out of the car without falling straight to the ground. I crept up to their door very slowly and very fearfully. When I arrived at her door I pulled out my phone and texted Brooke that I was at her house, before I knocked. I knocked softly hoping they wouldn't hear me, but surely enough they heard it clearly.

As I saw the door open I saw her mother smiling, she

greeted me very kindly. "Oh my, you must be the sweet sweet Landon. How are you?" I've asked about Brooke's family before but she didn't talk about them entirely too much. She was a nice woman that looked to be in her late forties, and was a brunette that's hair was fading to gray, but still looked very nice and welcoming.

"Yes ma'am, I'm good. It's very nice to meet you." I said as politely as possible. I had a forced smile on my face hoping she wouldn't see how nervous I am. I could still feel the tenseness in my hands as they were glued into my pockets.

"You're here to finish up your project with Brooke, right? Well you can head up to her room, and if you need anything just holler. My name's Nancy." She was very welcoming, it was a lot nicer than I had initially expected. My nerves were slowly fading away. She reached her hand out to shake my hand, and I instantly started fumbling. I was struggling to get my hand out of my pocket and I was nervously laughing. I shook her hand softly, but with intent.

After that Brooke was at the bottom of the stairs waiting for me. I looked at her with a faint smile, hoping she wasn't dwelling on Saturday still. She didn't say a word, she just walked me to her room in an awkward silence.

When we got to her room it was a white-painted room that was slightly messy, but not too terrible. She had words above the head of her bed that read, "To be loved, you must

65

show love." Seemed like it fit her pretty alright, but after spectating her room, she got the model for the project we were working on. It was almost complete and it should've taken maybe thirty minutes to finish.

She still hasn't said a word since I've been in her room, and it was starting to concern me. Was she still mad? "I'm sorry." I said flat.

"What are you sorry for?" she said snarkily. I still didn't know why she was being so vile towards me, it was pretty hurtful.

"I was- I just- I just wanted to help." I was stumbling hoping she wouldn't take what I said the wrong way, because I felt as if I didn't do anything terribly wrong.

"What do you think you're helping me with? I don't need you, I have no idea why you think you are." She started tearing up while trying her best to not yell at me and alarm her mom.

"Why are- what- what did I do?" My voice was starting to crackle and fade away.

"Let's just get this over with." She grabbed her sleeve and wiped away the tear that began to fall. I was so confused, I didn't see why she was so upset.

After a few moments of silence I finally broke the still air, "I don't know why you're so upset with me. You know that my intentions were good, and I saw how you felt so I apologized, and I let you know that it won't happen again. So if it's me just tell me, because there's no reason for you to be so mad if I'm trying. I know I'm not the best and I'm probably not good enough, but I promise I'm doing everything I can to keep you as happy as you make me. I'm so thankful for you, but I don't know how to reciprocate my feelings the right way, and I'M SORRY!"

The silence became deafening, and then she started to cry. I knew I was the cause so I immediately tried to comfort her, but I didn't want to invade her personal space.

"I-I'm sorry Landon." she fell into my arms, burying her tears into my hoodie. "I don't want to lose you, I just don't know how to control myself. Everyone in my life has just used me as an excuse to do what they want, and I didn't want you to fall into that trend. I want you to be here all the time. I want you to be with me."

I lifted her head and wiped her tears to stop her from crying and said,

"I'm not leaving, just don't push me away."

"I'm sorry." she clinched on to me harder. I'm glad she actually expressed how she felt, it made some of my doubt go away. Didn't mean it would remain gone, but it helped in the moment, and this was one of the few times I wanted to live in the moment.

"So...are we gonna get back to the pro-" before I could finish my sentence, she locked her lips with mine, shocking me, and giving me butterflies. I was so surprised I had no clue how to react. I barely knew how to process what all just happened in the last five minutes, but I went along with it for the first time in what seemed like forever. I stopped worrying and just started appreciating the moment.

After she pulled away I sat there for a moment in a distraught expression. I was blushing too hard to formulate words, and I could feel the wideness of my eyes.

"Project." she said with a giggle.

"Yeah…that." I still didn't know how to react.

We smiled towards each other as we finished the project. Finishing the model wasn't as hard as I had thought it would be, but we still finished within an hour.

It was starting to get dark outside, so I was about to say my goodbyes before Mrs. Rose came in and invited me for dinner. "How would you like to eat with us, Landon? It would be wonderful for you to meet Mr. Rose." I got a little nervous thinking about meeting Brooke's dad, but I was already on cloud nine so it didn't seem as if it could go too bad.

"Let me ask my mom first, but I would love to accompany you guys." I said with the same smile I greeted her with, just with more confidence.

"I'm sure Brooke would love to have you, because I know I would. You are just the sweetest thing." she pinched my cheeks, as if she were my mother.

"MOM!" Brooke said annoyed while rolling her eyes. I gave a slight smirk watching them interact.

"Oh hush, but we would love to have you have you for dinner." Mrs.

Rose said, looking back in my direction.

I texted my mom to see if she would let me stay to eat with them, even though it was dark outside. She ended up being ok with me staying, which surprised me. A part of me was hoping she would make me come home so I didn't have to meet Brooke's dad, but if he's anything like his wife it shouldn't be too bad.

After the table was set, I looked outside to realize the mist I remember when leaving my house had turned into a downpour. Hearing a loud thud outside matching the opening of the front door. There he was, standing about six foot four. He looked menacing, but it may be because of him running into the rain on the way home. Mrs. Rose was delighted to see him welcoming him with a kiss on the cheek. After that he had lightened up looking more jolly. I still remained with a tense feeling that had me portraying my shyness. After setting his brown suitcase down, he ventured his eyes across the home until he fixed his glance onto me. I nervously gave a smile hoping he wouldn't be mad to see me.

"Oh, this is Landon, he had come over to finish the science project that Brooke had told you about." Said Mrs. Rose, before Mr. Rose could say anything.

He gave a calm chuckle and said, "Is that so?" His voice had a certain flatness that was alarming. "Welcome to our home Landon. Hope you're having a good day." he was staring into my soul it seemed like.

"H-Hi, Mr. Rose. Thank you for having me." I still tried my best to sound as polite as I initially did to Mrs. Rose whenever I first arrived.

After an awkward five to ten seconds of silence Mrs. Rose continued, "Landon was going to eat with us, if that was ok sweetie?" she nodded her head while looking up to him.

Mr. Rose cleared his voice, "Of course it is. Come on, let's eat." After clearing his voice he sounded a lot more welcoming. He also gave a lovely smile with his pearly white teeth. I gave a nervous laugh and eased up a bit. Although it was a brief interaction I could tell that Brooke had an awesome set of parents.

As we sat down to eat Brooke and I sat closely. There wasn't much said as we began to talk, because of how swiftly we ate. Halfway through the meal Mr. Rose broke the silence saying, "So…are you two dating or whatever kids do these days."

I could feel myself blush and she matched my expression, being wide-eyed not knowing how to respond. I was going to give a response, but before I could say anything Brooke chimed in saying, "Yes, we just started dating." This was news to me, because I was under the impression that she didn't want to be in a relationship, but I'm not complaining.

Mr. Rose gave an intrigued look saying, "Well, I really thought it would be the ol' Culvert boy."

"Dad!" She responded quickly, but there was a sign of defeat on my face. I thought I didn't have to worry about him.

"Oh hush, you know I'm just kidding." He said while looking at me trying to get me to laugh along with me. I wasn't, this was not amusing. I played along though, trying not to seem like his comment had bothered me as bad as it did.

The rest of the meal I was radio silent, feeling like there was something Brooke wasn't telling me. The rest of the meal consisted of small talk that I did not engage much in. Whenever we finished I cleaned up my eating area. Mrs. Rose offered to get my plate. Not really knowing what to do with myself I started towards the front door. I tried saying my goodbyes, but before I was even halfway through the door Brooke grabbed my hand.

"Thank you for coming, Landon. It really meant a lot." She seemed as if she was caught.

I rested in a displeased look. I was visibly upset, but didn't want to start an argument so I simply said, "Clearly. Thanks for having me." Then I walked back to the car. As I started the car, I sat there a minute in silence not knowing how to process everything I was feeling. I was glad to feel as if we were together, she even said we were dating. Then her dad had to mention Jayden. I didn't know what she was telling me was real, I didn't know if her parents wanted her to be with Jayden. At the moment I didn't care, I just wanted to be home, I was so upset and just wanted my mom, as if I was a little kid.

When I got home I looked at my phone to see the time was around ten at night. I walked into my mom's room to hand her back her keys. Whenever I lifted my arm to give her the keys back I started balling my eyes out. It was uncontrollable, but felt good.

"I don't know if she wants me mom. Why am I not good enough! I try and try, but I just never seem to be enough for anyone." I said in anguish, just letting my emotions take full control.

As I fell into her arms which gave comfort she said, "You're always enough for me. You're enough for everyone, and if she can't see that she's a fool." I eased up on my crying once she said this, I started to open my mouth when she continued asking, "What happened?"

I instantly started telling her everything that occurred, hoping she would have the perfect answer for me. As I finished telling her the story, she just said "It'll be ok, nothing's wrong." After hearing those last few words I stopped crying and started thinking more clearly again. I looked her in her eye before heading out of the room with a goodnight, as if we had a normal conversation. She knows I hate to show people how vulnerable I am, but I always could with her. Which made talking and crying to her so easy, but I couldn't keep thinking about it so I had to walk off as if nothing happened.

I laid down in my bed and stared at the ceiling like I had done at the beginning of the day. My day, ending parallel to how it started. It's crazy how all the things that have happened, and I still have the same question.

Am I good enough for Brooke?

VIII.

It was the day to present the project. The whole reason Brooke and I started talking. It was all coming full circle, but things between us seemed uncertain. At least for me. I act as if things weren't bothering me, but I kept myself at a distance from her. Whenever we walked into class she beat me to class and already brought the model from her house. I sluggishly walked to my desk and took out my computer from my bag to get myself ready to present.

"Are you ready?" Brooke said with excitement and anxiousness. She looked at me with a smile.

I didn't reciprocate the expression. "Yep." I responded with a very stale voice.

"What's wrong?" She seemed concerned, but I couldn't care less.

"Just tired." I didn't want to tell her, because she herself has been more distant as well. It was probably my fault, but I assumed that we wouldn't talk anymore after the project was over.

"No...it's been like this- nevermind, let's just be ready

to present." I wanted to know what she was going to say, so I became slightly anxious wondering what she was going to say.

"I'm ready...but-" before I could finish what I was saying, Mr. Richards interrupted.

"Today is the day class. You guys have worked very hard for a whole semester now. So I'll give you five minutes to get ready to show the class what you have learned." As the five minutes started I sat in silence already knowing what to do like the back of my hand.

Before our turn, there was a group before us. They did pretty well, but stumbled on their words whenever Mr. Richards started asking questions. Usually this would get me concerned, but today I did not care. I was in my own world in my head. Whenever we got up there, there was an eerie silence. When we started I started daydreaming about what Brooke could have been talking about. I thought out of everything that sentence could have finished with. Was she going to tell me that she wasn't going to talk to me anymore? I wanted to act like I didn't care, but I did way too much.

"Landon." Brooke said softly while nudging me. I snapped out of the trance I was in to realize what was going on. It was my turn to speak. I looked at the audience and Paul looked concerned, because he saw the dead expression on my face. I thought he would've been holding in a laugh like he usually would be. I just did my part and finished the project. The oh so hard project we have been working on for months, done. Hours of learning, hard work, and teamwork; done in ten minutes. Crazy how things we put so much time into can be over so quick. As we got applause from our peers, we went to sit down. I sat with a blank expression as the rest of class went on.

During lunch that day I sat with the same empty expressions, just thinking about the school year so far. Brooke looked at me not knowing what to say, but what could she say. I knew it would just make me upset.

"What were you going to say in first period today?" I said looking straightforward, but meaning the words for Brooke.

"What do you mean?" Paul replied. I get why he responded, because he sits in front of me. It irritated me though, I was hoping I would just hear Brooke's voice.

"What's been going on Landon? You're scaring me, I don't know why you're upset, but I feel like it's my fault." It was exactly what I wanted her to say.

"Maybe it is." I muffled under my voice. "I'm fine-"
"No, what did you say?" I didn't think she had heard me.

"I said I'm fine." I raised my voice slightly.

"No, I heard what you said. What did I do?" The guys at the table were just staring.

Sara chimed in saying, "Guys, please don't fight."

"Shut up!" I said furiously to her. I clenched my teeth in anger.

"Landon…" I could see the fear in Brooke's eyes after calling my name. I didn't know what to do so I just resorted to silence.

As we left lunch, Ryan came up to me with words of reassurance.

"Hey man, it'll be ok. I know you're upset right now, but it won't last forever. Although you owe Brooke an apology. She's the best thing that's happened to you for as long as I've known you, and you're just throwing her to the side as if you both don't care for each other."

"Yeah. I'm sorry man, I just think too much man and I don't know if I'm doing a lot for nothing." I was glad he came and talked to me. Ryan was always good to hear from. He dapped me up and we went on about our day. Ryan had always known how to talk to anyone in our group if there was a problem, and he never seemed to have his own problems. He always kept a good mind and heart, which was admirable about him.

After school I texted Brooke and asked if she could meet me somewhere, so we could talk. We ended up agreeing to meet up at a park that was equal distance from both of our houses. Matt was going to take me, and Sara was going to take Brooke. I told mom my plan, and she had just advised me that I "value every moment with her." I'm surprised she's so fond of Brooke, she's never even met her.

As Matt came to my house, my mom invited him in

before I had a chance to leave. I sat there anxious and worried about time, because I didn't want to be late to something that was actually important. I started tapping my foot on the ground as I was in the living room overhearing the conversation Matt and my mom was having. I was hoping I wouldn't have to go in there so we could hurry up and leave.

As I steadily increased in anxiety levels I got up and walked to my mom's door. "Hey, look at the time. It's crazy how it flies, right?" I said, trying to hint to Matt that we should hurry up and go.

"Oh well, nobody comes and sees old Miss Morgan anymore." My mom said pitying herself.

"You know that's not true Miss Morgan, but Landon's right. We should get going." Matt was very polite with his exit which wasn't like him in front of my mom. Although we've gotten to the point where it doesn't have to be so formal.

"Well you two have fun, and don't stay out too late." She acted as if it wasn't dark outside already, but we both nodded our heads in agreement, and headed out the door.

When we got in the car Matt was pretty quiet. Which usually means he's thinking how he should say something he's mad about. As I waited to hear what he had to say I started focusing on the music to relax myself.

"Why did you yell at Sara today?" He said passive-aggressively.

"I don't know, I didn't mean it, I've just been so mad lately. I'm sorry I let it out, I didn't mean to hurt anyone's feelings." I tried my best to sound regretful.

"Yeah well, that's not good enough. We all have problems, and we're all here for each other." After he said that there was a pause for about five seconds before I decided to respond.

"I know. I know! You just don't get-"

"Don't say I don't get it! You have been so self-centered you haven't even realized what anybody has been going through!" At this point he was screaming.

"NO! Don't act like you're not the same way you-"

"I act nothing like-"

"Stop interrupting me! And stop acting like you care, when I know YOU DON'T!" it became a screaming match.

"The only reason I'm even bringing you is because of Ryan. I didn't even want to look at you." He was just saying anything to be hurtful.

"See…you don't care." I didn't know whether to be sad or mad, but I was definitely hurt.

"No…I do care, it's just- I was mad." He seemed to be sorry, but I wasn't buying it.

"Let's just go." I said softly. The rest of the drive was done in silence, other than the radio. Nothing was helping, so I had no clue how this talk was about to be.

As we arrived, I got out of the car quickly doing my best to convince myself not to slam the door. Whenever I walked towards the entrance of the park, Matt came over and hugged me. I was weirded out because this wasn't like him. He kept apologizing for not being a good friend, but I still didn't say a word. I just reassured him with a reciprocated hug. Afterwards we looked around to see if Brooke and Sara were there yet, but to no avail.

I was about to text Brooke to ask where they were before Matt spotted them out sitting on a bench talking to each other. "Look. there they are over at that bench." He pointed in their direction and we set off. I had no idea what I planned on saying, I was just going to go with whatever came to mind. They were both in a beanie and hoodie. The wind was blowing their hair all over the place while they sat under a light post that was glistening an orange color giving the area light in the dark.

As we approached I immediately said, "I'm sorry Sara, I shouldn't have yelled at you like that today." I was hoping I wouldn't have to say much other than that.

"It's ok. I forgive you." She replied with a smile on her face. Sara and Brooke were both shivering. I often dressed pretty warm so the coldness wasn't bothering me so bad.

I asked if Brooke would want to walk and talk. The park's trail was about a mile long and I knew that she liked to walk so it wouldn't bother her too bad. She agreed and left Sara and Matt to be alone. As we began walking there was silence for a moment as we started on the trail.

I could feel the tension between us. I couldn't allow it to stand much longer.

"Brooke." I said with poise.

"Yeah?"

"I'm sorry for the way I've been acting. I honestly thought when the project was over you wouldn't talk to me. I thought that I was just someone you kept around until you could get with Jayden. I keep thinking you don't want me." I started spilling all of my thoughts into three simple sentences.

"Landon, why would you ever think that?" She seemed to be more concerned than mad. I honestly thought she would be angry that I was still worried about Jayden.

"I." I didn't know how to say what I was thinking.

"You...you what. Landon just talked to me." Brooke was hugged up to my arm.

"I love you...I've never been this way so I don't know how to act." I can't believe what I said. My legs started to shake scared to hear what she would say.

"I-I love you too." I felt a sense of nirvana from hearing her say those words. I could tell she was waiting to say that but was too nervous to let it out.

After we professed our love, I stopped to face her, and what was meant to be a gentle kiss, turned into one of pure passion. Neither of us held back. Suddenly we both became aware of our surroundings and pulled back. The both of us smiled towards each for a long moment.

Whenever we started walking, we admired the start of the snowfall. Although the wind was blowing it was still nice to see the snow, the park, and all its entirety. Everything about the moment was beautiful, how the light reflected off the snow. Time seemed to be stagnant and I wanted the moment to last forever. The wind eased up with its blowing. We made it full circle to where we started going back to the bench she was sitting on when we first got here. Sara and Matt weren't there, looking around we saw them swinging softly on the park's playground. We sat back down, but I realized Brooke was shivering "Do you want my hoodie? You look really cold." I said as a nice gesture.

"Landon, you don't have to." She said as she was still shivering. Without another word I took off my hoodie, revealing my long sleeve that was tight on me.

I handed her the hoodie saying, "But I will." She took it willingly and gladly. From a distance I saw Matt gain some altitude, and then jumped off.

Whenever he crashed to the ground, we all had a laugh.

The night didn't last much longer after that. We hung out for about twenty more minutes then parted ways. On the way home there was a much more uplifting feeling than before. Still not much was said but there was no tension. When we got to my house I thanked Matt and left his car with a smile wrapped around my face.

When I walked in I was greeted by mom who was

giddy to see me in a better mood. "Things went well I guess?" She said with the same warm expression that I had.

"Thank you." I said hugging her. I didn't explain what happened at all, but I thought saying thank you would explain everything.

After mom went to bed, I got ready for bed as well. After laying down I couldn't help but drown myself in thought of her. Brooke was all I could think about. It wasn't anything negative, I wasn't overthinking, I just felt loved.

...

Waking up on Christmas morning was more difficult than it should've been. I struggled gaining consciousness, I tried convincing myself of all the presents I would receive. Although my joy of being a child felt absent. I wasn't sad, I didn't feel any particular way other than empty.

As I strolled my way into the kitchen I saw my mom waiting for me on our couch. She looked very ready and excited, but that look started slowly fading away once she saw that I lost the ambition for Christmas. She didn't question why I had an empty expression, maybe she just knew that I lost the feeling a kid gets for Christmas. Which was really weird, Christmas was so big for us. It was "the" holiday where we don't worry about anything and just enjoy each other's company. I still did, it just seemed like something was missing.

The main thing I was worried about was if Brooke was still going to come over. I invited her over, and she planned on coming for about a week now. I told her that she didn't have to get mom and I a present, but knowing her giving nature I figured she would. So I prepared her a present, it wasn't anything too much, but I was hoping she would really like it. I got her a box of chocolates with a bag she's been wanting for a while. I hoped and prayed that her parents wouldn't get the bag too, I was hoping she would show up first off. It was only ten in the morning so I was getting ahead of myself. She never told me what time she would be here for sure, so I just had to sit and wait I guess.

After a while I just was doing anything to occupy myself. I got a text from Brooke saying that she would come in about thirty minutes. My eyes lit up whenever I saw that. I got everything ready for her: I made my room spotless, got her present ready to give, and made sure everything was perfect. Thirty minutes felt like an eternity. I felt as if I did everything I could do and it was only ten minutes, so I just layed down on the couch hoping that I could take a quick nap.

When I layed down I dreamt of getting a call that she had crashed and wouldn't be able to come. Then I went to her house to see what was wrong just to find that Jayden Culvert was there with her. Seemed pretty vivid even though I was only asleep for about half an hour. After seeing that I woke up to a missed call from Brooke. I immediately called her back, she said she was at the door. Whenever I opened the door I expected her to be here with her mom, but it was just her. She came with two boxes. One was a decent size box that needed to be carried with two arms, while the other one was about the size of a hand.

"Hi Landon, how are you!?" I could tell she was excited. Seeing her caused me to have a smile on my face.

"Better now that you're here. Come in." She wiped her feet on our doormat before coming in. This would be the first time she would meet my mother, but my mom already knew all about her.

She set the boxes by our tree and settled down. My mom was glad to see her. I could tell mom thought she was pretty. There was an awkward tension in the room at first, but my mom was great at meeting new people so she opened the conversation.

"So this is the Brooke I've heard so many good things about? It's so nice to meet you sweetheart." She sounded similar to how Brooke's mom was when I first met her. My mom had a lighthearted tone that was very welcoming.

"Yes, it's nice to meet you as well Miss Morgan." Brooke responded politely.

"Oh please, you can call me Rachel." She never let any

of my friends call her by her first name so I was slightly confused.

"Ok Rachel I-" Before Brooke could finish her sentence she was interrupted.

"Nevermind, just call me Miss Morgan. I'm not used to you younger kids calling me by my first name yet." Mom said while giggling.

"Sorry…" Brooke was laughing with mom. "…but I got you guys presents." pointing at the boxes she placed by the tree.

"Oh, you didn't have to, you are just so sweet. I'm sorry I would've got you a present as well if I knew." I could tell mom was touched by Brooke's gesture.

"No worry, I got her something." I said butting in. I got up to grab the present that I got for Brooke. She seemed surprised when I showed her the box.

"Uh…thank you Landon." She acted as if she's never received a present before.

"Don't say that yet, what if you hate it?" I said jokingly. Mom looked annoyed when I said that. Brooke started opening her gift and her jaw dropped. I was guessing I did good with the present. I could tell she was starting to tear up, so before a tear could fall I asked, "Do you like it?"

"Landon…" during the pause mom and I locked eyes in confusement. "I love it so much, thank you." She grabbed and hugged me tightly. I could still see mom and she just had a face of awe. Mom was glad to see me happy, rather than with the emotionless face I had this morning. When she let go she wiped the tear that nearly fell and said, "Oh I almost forgot." She went to go get the two boxes that she had brought. She told my mom to keep her box up right as she got the bigger one and gave me the smaller one. I watched mom open her up first, curious to what was in there. She opened and gasped happily to see a cornucopia of flowers of all varieties. I don't remember if I mentioned to Brooke that my mom loves flowers, but if I did she remembered well getting her some of her favorite flowers.

"Thank you thank you thank you." My mom said hugging Brooke the way she had hugged me. "Your turn Landon." she continued.

I looked back to the box that fit nicely in my palm. I unwrapped the nice red bow that surrounded the box. I looked in to see a snow globe, with a small construction of Denver's skyline. There were also people holding hands in the globe, and the harder I looked I realized there was a small portrait of Brooke and I on the people holding hands. My heart melted seeing this.

I stumbled trying to find the right words to describe my appreciation. "Th-Thank you." I didn't know what to say. I just sat there not knowing how to express myself. It wasn't anything glamorous, but it was so cool to me.

Something I vowed I would never lose or forget.

The rest of the time Brooke was at my house was filled

with laughter and a good time, but she let us know that she had to go home. We said our goodbyes and she left through the front door.

Before I could head to bed mom called me into her room to talk about Brooke I assumed.

"Landon…" I was prepared to hear the worst. Even though I knew my mom liked Brooke. "I really liked Brooke. You better not do anything to mess this up kid. She's a good one."

"Yeah I know." I closed her door and went to bed. This was one of the most memorable Christmases and I'm glad that Brooke really liked her present, it took a lot of my allowance to afford it, but it was worth it.

IX

Before I knew it, it was almost spring break, and that meant that my birthday was coming up. I didn't celebrate my birthday too much, most people don't even know when it is. Which I wouldn't expect a bunch of people to know I wasn't too popular. The only people that really knew were my close friends. Even with Brooke, I never told her what day it was, I just told her it was in March. It was in three days, so the fourteenth of March.

We've been getting along well, Brooke and I, nothing special has been happening. I think we just really enjoy each other's company. Although we haven't been able to see each other out of school, that's soon to change now that I'm going to be able to get my license. Mom has been open to the idea of me driving whenever I turn sixteen and get my drivers license. I've gained a lot of trust from her with being open about the time I had hoped to spend with Brooke. Mom seems to be very happy that I'm in a "relationship". I'm still scared to call it what it is, but I overthink everything as usual. Although with me not fully on the idea of publicly saying to people that we're together it seems to work out better. To be fair people aren't asking too often if we are together, I think they just kid of assume that we are.

At lunch I sat down to realize most people were sick from our table. Paul, Sara, Ryan, Brooke, and I were the only ones at the table. Sara was pretty quiet without Matt there, which seemed strange. She usually talked until she was out of breath so I was wondering if something had happened between Matt and her.

"Wow. I can't believe everyone's sick." Paul said what everyone was thinking.

"They'll be back, don't worry." Brooke said in a calm manner.

"Nobody was Mrs. worrier." Sara said out of nowhere. I mean, she was right, but her tone was really derogative.

"Excuse me?" Brooke seemed to be offended as this argument was in the woodworks.

"You're excused." Sara rolled her eyes. Everyone at the table knew things were about to go down.

"Hey…" Ryan nodded his head negatively to diminish the altercation from happening.

Sara and Brooke gave each other a hard stare for a couple seconds. Being in the middle of it was a strange feeling that I no longer wanted to be a part of. I wanted to say something to ease the tension, but I didn't know what to say. We just sat there in silence for what seemed like hours.

"So anyway, are you guys ready for Spring Break?" Before anyone could answer he continued, "Better yet. Landon, are you ready for your birthday?"

Brooke's eyes lit up. I shied away from trying to draw attention to myself. I looked down at my phone hoping something would get me to look at anything else.

"So..." Brooke scooted closer to me "...What are you doing for your birthday?"

"Uh...I don't know." I was visibly uncomfortable. Usually I didn't do anything for my birthday, that's why she didn't even know it was in three days.

The whole ordeal was strange, and it remained that way until the end of lunch. After that school stayed the same way other than Brooke trying to find something to do for my birthday. I remained pretty timid about doing anything, which it's not like I didn't want to spend time with her, I just didn't want it to seem forced. I knew her intentions were good, but being alone on my birthday was something I grew accustomed to.

Whenever I came home my mom was already sitting in the living room waiting for me. I immediately thought I was in trouble by the look on her face. I ran the whole day through my head thinking if I had done anything wrong. The only thing that came to mind was in history I inadvertently made a peer feel dumb because they didn't know something the teacher just said. That wasn't that bad though, not enough to warrant a punishment I wouldn't think, I mean we're in highschool that would amount to anything compared to what some people did. I calmly and nervously walked over to the couch to sit down. I felt myself sink into the couch as soon as I sat, because I had been exhausted from school. No words were said at first, so I had just assumed she was trying to come up with a long speech of why I did something wrong and why I was grounded.

She started to give a smile and finally said words. "You know I'm so proud of you. You've done so well in school and stayed out of trouble..." When she said stay out of trouble I instantly thought back to the incident that Michael and I were in, but I didn't decide to mention it. "...and you're growing up. So for your birthday, how about we get you your own car?"

"Really?!" My eyes lit up in excitement, was I really going to be able to get my own car? This would mean I wouldn't have to get rides from anyone.

She nodded her head as a sign of conformation. I was in complete disbelief. I was actually excited for my birthday, which never happens. My jaw dropped and it seemed as if I couldn't close it. I was really going to get my own car. I thought about the millions of things I was actually going to be able to do.

After the conversation, I texted Brooke that I was finally going to be able to get my own car. She was just as excited as I was: she then asked if that meant I was going to do something for my birthday. I still didn't have an answer so I gave a bland response. Despite my uncertainty she told me that on my birthday I should come to her house. I reluctantly agreed. This was still two days away. My birthday turned from doing nothing to doing a lot.

The next day when I came into first period, I walked into class to see Mr. Richards, Paul, and Brooke conversing. Once they saw me walk in they dispersed. We had started a group presentation together, so we were all sitting together. I sat down cautiously expecting something to happen.

"Come meet me outside for a second." Mr. Richards said, tapping my shoulder. I was startled and was hesitant to get up, but once I did, I walked out the class feeling the eyes of my peers stain my shirt. I was very confused of to why I had to talk to Mr. Richards, I just got to class. I didn't think I did anything wrong, but who knows.

Once he met me in the halls I sat there with a disgruntled look on my face.

"Landon, how do you feel about the rest of this year?" He had a calm manner like usual so I was getting more confused.

"Good?" I was questioning myself, wondering if there was a right or wrong answer.

"Well you've been doing well so far and I just wanted to take time to congratulate you." He said while patting my back from being positioned on my side.

"So you brought me out here to just congratulate?" I said blatantly.

"Yes?" I could tell he was trying to distract me from something in the class. I peeped into the class to see what was going on, but nothing was happening. I looked back at Mr. Richard confused, he looked at me with a nervous smile.

I walked back into the classroom, but nobody paid my presence attention. I sat back down, glanced at Paul, then glanced back at Brooke. They were looking down on our presentation. I was starting to get weirded out.

"Did anything happen when I stepped out?" I leaned in asking Brooke with a whisper.

"In here? Uh no." She was hasty with her words, which added to my confusion.

I continued on as if nothing had happened, and went on with the class. Paul and Brooke had still given me little to no eye contact for the rest of class, like I did something wrong. I didn't want to keep asking what the problem was, so I just ignored it the best I could. The rest of the day was pretty routine with the addition of no eye contact from anyone in my friend group. Were they mad at me? Do they know something I don't? What is going on?

I woke up the next day not even realizing it was my birthday, but my mother gave me a big reminder. I was woken up by the delicious smell of pancakes. I walked in the kitchen to see three big ones my mom had made for my birthday. After I started diving into the food, mom walked in and gave me a kiss on my forehead saying happy birthday. I thanked her for the food she had made and went back to eating. I was hoping that things wouldn't have been thrown in my face like breakfast was. Not that I wasn't appreciative of the food, but I don't like things to seem forced. I was alive yesterday, hopefully I'll be alive tomorrow, so what makes today more important than those other days. Although whenever my mother made food that was specially for me, it was special. She can really cook well, but she never likes to and usually doesn't give cooking much effort. Mom got all of her recipes from my grandma. Grandma used to cook for us all the time, because everyone loved her food, but she still lives in Texas so we rarely get her food anymore.

School started off really nice, mostly because I could finally drive to school. I was one of few freshmen that could actually drive. Most people got their cars midway through their sophomore year. Matt fits in that category being a sophomore who is recently new to driving. Whenever I walked into the building, I was met by Ryan.

"Happy Birthday Landon." I almost didn't see him at first. I wasn't a very observant person, but once he said that my full attention was on him.

"Thank you Ryan, means a lot." I said politely.

We had small conversations until we both arrived at our classes, then split ways. When I got in the class, I got ready to sit down and get to work as normal. Before I could Brooke came up from behind and squeezed me with a hug.

"Happy Birthday, Landon." I was tensed up at first from the shock of being snuck up on, but after realizing who it was I eased up.

"Happy Birthday Bro." Paul walked in and joined the hug to make himself feel included in praising my birthday. I embraced them whole-heartedly. Then the bell rang a couple seconds later, and we let go of each other. We all made eye contact noticing how awkward it must've seemed to everyone and went to our table with a blush stuck on our faces. Mr. Richards walked in moments after the bell rang, and was perplexed when he saw our faces. The blush remained on Brooke and I faces.

"Did I miss something?" He questioned. We shook our heads no, hoping he wouldn't call us out in front of the class. He eyed us down until he was finished calling roll. He continuously surveyed the room until he could find a problem. We awkwardly smiled and got to work when he was done with calling roll.

"Hey. You should come to my house after school." Brooke said with a whisper.

"I-I'm allowed?" I was caught off guard with the invitation causing a little shock. I couldn't tell if she was being honest.

"Yeah, and then after can I come over to say 'hi' to your mom?" She was pretty insistent.

"Sure." I just went along with what she said, so I wouldn't cause any problems.

I wasn't trying to make a big deal out of my birthday. It was pretty evident through my actions, and even though Brooke got that notion she still tried to do her best to make me feel special. Along with Paul, and this was just the beginning of the day. I was concerned what all would happen if I've only been awake for under two hours and I'm already dealing with everyone giving me attention. I really do appreciate it, I'd hate to make it seem as if I don't.

Work was pretty standard, we just added finishing touches to our presentation. It wasn't the best, because we just took the opportunity to sit together and converse rather than focus on the work. It was finished, and I was confident enough to get an A on it. I barely knew what we were talking about, for the most part I just copied and pasted what I could find on the internet next to sentences I made up, that I thought sounded good. We also didn't have to present the information to the class; it was just a project that we have worked on, on-and-off for about two weeks. I was hoping that he would just let us keep the seats we had for the rest of the year, seeing as there were under three months left. What harm could we do with that little time left? Everyone in the class had become less engaged with the work after February, as most students are looking forward to spring break.

I also stopped caring after February, but because of Valentine's Day. It was the first real time I was talking to someone I was interested in during that holiday. It was on a Monday this year so I had spent almost all of my weekend trying to make something special for Brooke. I had made a basket of all of her favorite candies and I wrote a love letter. It kind of seemed like a poem looking back on it, but the letter went:

The ways people are put in your life will always be a wonder. I wonder why I was blessed with you being invited into my life. I am thankful for you being here everyday, and I hope I show you that through my actions. If not, I hope these gifts can show a fraction of what you mean to me.

I wasn't the best writer but I tried my best to make it special. We exchanged gifts after school. I wasn't expecting anything from her, because she was pretty quiet about the upcoming holiday, but when we met after school she had a gift for me as well. When I gave her the basket she didn't realize the letter at first as it was tucked to the side, but when she read it later that night, she called me to let me know how much she appreciated I was in her life in the positive change I have brought to her. That was a good conversation, although it was brief and more of a thank you, I will never forget it. She gave me a hat I had talked about periodically. In it was a small slip of paper that read:

Hats off to the boy who always makes my day better. Happy Valentine's Day.

I thought it was a clever play on words, and even cooler that she remembered exactly the hat I have wanted secretly for almost a year now. I never wanted to ask Mom for the hat, because it seemed like something small and stupid that didn't seem like it was worth spending money on it.

When the bell rang I went about to my regular routine, before being called to the office. I wasn't in trouble, it was just a thing our school did whenever it was someone's birthday. I already knew what I was going for, because of Matt telling us that he got scared about it when he was a freshman.

When I arrived at the office the lady at the front said, "Happy Birthday, I hope you have a good day." The lady handed me a sucker. It was a nice gesture, but I hated it. This was definitely forced, no question about it.

"Thanks." I snatched the sucker in a way that wouldn't seem too rude, and walked out to go back to my next class. I sat in class with the sucker in my mouth swishing it around. It did taste good, but it tasted forced and ingenuine. By the time I came up with a negative thought that I could tell the front office, the sucker was gone. There was no point in going to express my mind about how I hate the forced feeling they gave me with a sucker. At least it was a kind gesture. They didn't do this type of thing in middle school, so I tried to have a better attitude about it.

Later at lunch everyone was staring at me walking in the lunchroom with smiles on their faces. I couldn't help but to smile myself, as much as I didn't celebrate myself, they made up for it. These were my best friends, people I could actually trust. We didn't act like this on Tony's birthday, and his birthday was just in January. He didn't seem the tiniest bit jealous, if anything he had a bigger smile than everyone else.

Whenever I sat down in unison they all sang me happy birthday. I didn't know what to do, but I just sat there and smiled. After they finished everyone was speaking at once, but I wasn't focusing on what they said. I just looked at them each one by one. I laid my eyes on Brooke and couldn't take my eyes off of her. She was stunning, and she didn't even do anything to make her look special. It was just her. Time felt as if it slowed down for a few moments so I could take in the moment, but once I snapped back to my senses. I realized what I was doing and simply said to everyone,

"Thank you."

After lunch history was pretty boring and I would do anything to get out. So I decided that it would be a good idea to use the restroom, because at least I wouldn't be sitting down.

Before I could even make it to the restroom, I noticed Paul and Matt talking near a water fountain. I was going to say hey, but I saw them snickering and whispering as if they were conspiring. They saw me and wiped their faces clean of expression and dispersed. It kinda weirded me out. There was no reason they had to stop talking or leave the area because I had arrived. I was too tired to let all of the scenarios that could have possibly happened run through my head. I did wonder what they were conversing about. They should have at least acknowledged me, not just because it was my birthday, but we're all good friends. Unless there was something they were hiding from me. I handled my business in the restroom and then proceeded to head back into the halls to then run into Tony.

"Hey Tony!" I was hoping we could make small talk long enough to get to the end of class.

"Hey." He gave a slight smile and then looked away. Before I could even continue the conversation he walked away. He had seen me open my mouth getting ready to say something, but he just walked away. I know that Tony was a quiet person, but usually he would've at least listened to me. My thoughts started to ramp up. Had I done something to the group? Why were they being so weird?

I ended up going to class and finishing out the day quicker than it seemed. Mainly because I was wondering what was going on with Paul, Tony, and Brooke. Was I still supposed to go over to Brooke's house? That question was soon answered when I received a text from her saying to come to her house. The clock already read four-fifteen, so I didn't have that much time to get ready.

When I walked in mom was reading a Forbes magazine on the couch. She smiled when I walked in, but I was very conscious about time. I hurried up and said what I needed, "Can I go to Brooke's-"

"Yes you may, hurry up." She stopped me before I could even finish. I spoke quickly, so I was surprised she could understand me and knew what I was going to say. How did she know what I was going to say? I looked at her perplexed for a slight moment, and then proceeded to my room to tidy myself up. I was concerned about what I looked like, but I ultimately didn't change much.

Within ten minutes I was back out the door saying my goodbyes to mom. I fumbled with my keys trying to start my car, but then after getting the car started, I took a second to relax. It was only four-forty-five. It only takes me about fifteen minutes to get to her house so I was perfectly on time. I looked back down at the clock and it read: four-forty-six. I instantly got worked up again, and zoomed out of my neighborhood swiftly.

After going twelve over throughout the city, I made it to Brooke's house. I was surprised to not see a cop waiting to ruin my timing, but it never happened. I looked down at the clock and it read: four-fifty-eight. So I got here too quickly, and I would've felt strange and intrusive if I were to go up to her door now. So I faked like I was cleaning the car for what felt like two minutes and then got out of the car. As I was approaching her door Mrs. Rose was already there to open the door. Her smile was as welcoming as ever and I gave her a nice smile back. When I was about three steps away from the door I lost my balance and slipped on ice and resinated outside their house. I tried to regain my balance, I fell and landed on my butt and made a fool of myself. I sat with a disappointed look on my face as Mrs. Rose was doing her best to hold in a laugh. I looked up with an embarrassed smile on my face, which led to her bursting out in laughter.

Once I got to the door she gave me a small hug and let me inside.

"Make sure to wipe your feet so you don't fall again." Mrs. Rose said as I stepped inside.

"Ha, yes ma'am." I wiped off my feet a couple times before heading into their dining room.

Brooke was sitting with her legs crossed over one another finishing a glass of water. I allowed myself to sit down thinking there was something she needed to tell me.

"What are you doing?" She questioned.

"Uh… just sitting here with you." I was confused. Was I not supposed to be here.

"Well, let's go up to my room." She got up and grabbed my hand and started dragging me upstairs.

"You two be careful. Also happy birthday Landon." Mrs. Rose said before we went to Brooke's room.

When we were in Brooke's room there sat a box on her bed. I looked at the box for a minute before guiding my attention back to Brooke.

"What's in the box?" I questioned.

"Slow down. We're opening this at your house." She was quick with her rebuttal.

"My house? What do you mean my house?" Why would we go to my house when I was already here?

"Oh yeah…Can I come over?" she looked at me with a cringed face of apology.

"I mean I gue-" Before I could finish my sentence she interrupted me.

"Your mom already said I could come over, so I'm coming over." She smiled and I just went along. There wasn't much I could do, I was expected to go with everything at this point. There was no need in fighting or starting a problem. It was just her tone that had bothered me. She made it seem as if my voice didn't matter.

"When are we going to my house?" I said with a monotone voice.

"Aww, don't sound sad, but we're going to your house in an hour." She was giddy and full of life. A lot more than me, today was pretty emotionally draining. I hadn't even done too much, but the whole friend group has been kind of secretive and it has me concerned. At least being with Brooke was taking my mind off of all that.

There was an awkward silence at first with just letting time pass, not knowing how to fill the moment. Knowing that we were just waiting to go to my house didn't help the situation at all.

We ended up reminiscing about the year in whole seeing as we only had a couple months until summer. We talked about our plans for the summer and what we should do together. It was hard to come up with too much, because of where we lived and how old we were. Denver was only thirty minutes away from where we lived, and there's a lot to do there. So we thought about things we could do in Denver, but we did not come up with much.

After talking about the year, and what we planned on doing, the hour we were waiting for finally passed. It went by faster the more we talked about our plans, but now we were behind. I was still confused on why we had to open the present at my house, but I was done asking questions, they got me nowhere. Realizing what time it was, Brooke tidied herself up a little, then grabbed my hand like she did once before, and we scurried downstairs.

"Alright, we're leaving mom!" She announced.

"You two have fun." She was calmly reading on the couch, just like my mother would.

"Bye Mrs. Rose." I called out before being led out the door.

We rushed into the car. I was more cautious making sure that I wouldn't fall and embarrass myself in front of Brooke. As I said that she started to slip, but as she fell I caught her. I looked down at her for a moment and gave a slight smirk. She became wide-eyed while looking back up to me. I helped prop her back up, and we carried on with going to the car. Once we got in the car she told me to go without saying anything else. I stepped on the gas a little too hard initially, feeling the car's wheels spin. I got a lump in my throat thinking that the car was stuck. As I was getting ready to panic the car zoomed off. I was going the same speed back to the house as I originally did going to Brooke's house. I took the exact same route as it was the easiest for me to navigate.

"Shit!" Brooke exclaimed. I didn't even notice what happened and thought she just used foul language, because she was upset. Then I looked into the rearview mirror to see flashing blue lights. My heart stopped. I was terrified. I instantly thought that I was going to jail.

Pulling over to the side of the road was performed by me in jagged movements. My heart was racing, my palms were sweating, and my breathing became quickened. I wasn't prepared for this by any means. I looked over at Brooke, trying to see if she was as nervous as me. She had a calm demeanor, as if she has dealt with this numerous times. I felt like an idiot, because of how scared I looked. While she was unfazed.

"It's alright, don't worry Landon. Everything will be alright." she patted my thigh as an indication of comforting me.

As I was taking deep breaths to calm myself, there was a knock on the window. I looked up to see a tall figure that had glasses with dark lenses. The terror on my face was visible. I slowly rolled down the window while my hands continued to shake.

"Do you have any idea how fast you were going son?" He took off his shades to look me directly in the eyes.

"Yessir. I'm sorry, we were just trying to hurry up to my house." He looked at me for a moment.

"License and registration." The officer was very blunt. I opened the glove department, and fumbled grabbing the registration for the car over Brooke. She put her hand on mine and just gave me a look to calm down. I couldn't. I eventually gathered myself and handed the officer the things he asked for. He gave my license a quick glance.

"Happy birthday. How about for a present I let you off the hook, but you got to promise me you won't speed anymore." He said with a more inviting look on his face.

"Yessir. Thank you thank you thank you. You won't ever have to worry about me again." He handed my license and registration back to me. I sat everything in my lap and gave him a thankful smile.

"Alright well you have a good one." He tapped the top of my car, and headed back to his car. I was still in disbelief in what happened. I listened to the crunch of snow from the officer until he got back into his car. As everything went silent, I rolled the window back up. I looked over to Brooke to see her reaction. She burst into laughter. I was confused, was this a prank?

"Oh my. You should've seen your face." I sat there in embarrassment not knowing how to proceed to my house.

"Uhhh…that was my first time being pulled over." She looked annoyed.

"I can tell, captain obvious." I changed my expression to match my disgruntled feeling.

"Alright." I didn't know what else to say, but I was very upset.

For the rest of the trip to my house I didn't speak. I can't believe she would laugh at me during that. I felt completely vulnerable and she didn't have my back.

As we arrived at my house, I did everything very sluggishly. My head was down as we got out of the car and walked to the front door. She still had the box with her. We made eye contact with each other for a moment and we both held two different appearances.

"What's wrong Landon?" She confronted me with such a simple question, that I didn't know how to answer.

"Why were you like that?" I retaliated. My teeth started grinding, holding back what I truly wanted to say.

"What? When?" She put on a face of confusion.

"Don't play stu- the cop." I was doing my best to hold on to all of my confusion and anger built up throughout the day.

"What about the cop?" She was actually confused, and I started to feel bad because I was attacking her verbally.

"You laughed at me. You knew I was scared and you just laughed." I was starting to raise my voice.

"Landon, chill out. I'm sorry I didn't know. I was just trying to ease the tension." She placed her hand up on my shoulder.

"Well, it seemed like… like you just stranded me. I know that's what you were trying to do, but today has been so confusing." I lifted my shoulders up a bit, in response to her putting her hand there.

"It'll be alright. Let's just go inside." She came in and wrapped her arms around me to give me the comfort I was needing.

"Ok." I said while embracing her.

As we walked in it was completely dark. The only light that was emitted through the house was mom's room. The light was only coming from a lamp so it was very faint. Mom was in her room finishing the same magazine she was reading when I got home from school. We walked into her room and turned on her big light to expand the light. Brooke placed the box on the cover of mom's bed.

"Hey Brooke, how are you sweetheart?" Her face lit up as if Brooke was her own child.

"I'm doing good, Miss Morgan." I sat there quietly for while they spoke, but I started to space out not hearing their conversation. I thought about the day, recollecting why everyone did what they did, so I started to walk out the room to go to my own.

"Landon." Mom called out to me. I came back to reality and looked back at them as if I got caught.

"Yeah?" I said slowly.

"Do you not want to open this gift that Brooke got you?" Mom picked up the box and handed it to Brooke. Brooke walked up to me and offered me to finally open the box. I walked back to where they were and met Brooke at the edge of the bed. She handed the box to me and I unveiled it. Inside was a blanket. I was confused why she got me a blanket out of all things. Not that I didn't like it or accept it, but I was just slightly confused. I flipped it over and there read a message saying:

No matter where you rest you're on my mind

-Brooke

It was a very cool blanket, I didn't even know that you could make a blanket that way. It had a small rose flower next to her name, for an obvious reason.

"Thank you." I smiled really big and gave her a more gracious hug than the one we had outside.

"Alright you lovebirds. Why don't you put that in your room?" We blushed whenever she decided to call us out. We looked at each other for a second and I grabbed the blanket heading towards my room. I reached my room and weirdly my door was closed. It's never closed when I leave or arrive from school. Mom must've just changed the sheets or something. So I opened the door and flicked on the light getting ready to lay the blanket down over my cover before I was hit with a-

"Surprise!" Everyone was in my room. I was very startled until I realized it was Paul, Matt, Tony, Ryan, Caleb, Sara, and Brooke. Even more surprising, my best friend from when I lived in Texas, Jackson, was here. Whenever I saw him my eyes lit up in excitement. My mouth dropped and I couldn't articulate any words. I was in complete shock that everyone was here. More importantly, how is Jackson here? I was so happy to see everyone all together, everyone I have gotten close with were all in one room. It was unbelievable. Jackson stepped from the back of the room and came up to me.

"How are you man? I haven't seen you in forever." He still looked the same from when we were kids just with a matured face.

"No kidding, it's been so long." I clutched him with a brotherly hug. Thoughts of nostalgia flooded my mind. I felt as if I was neglecting everyone else, but I couldn't help it. Jackson was my best friend since the day I was born.

"One, two, three." Brooke whispered, as I was catching up with Jackson. Everyone in unison sang me happy birthday. Matt of course at the end added his own little twist, which everyone got a laugh from. I took a moment to remember everything I have experienced with each person. My mom came to the door to see all the commotion. There was nothing, but good feelings being felt through seeing everyone.

We spent the rest of the evening talking and sharing a cake that Matt and Sara brought. Eventually whenever we all settled down everyone who came got their stuff and left. Jackon went to our guest room, so I had guessed that he was going to stay a couple nights. Which I was perfectly fine with. It ended up being just Brooke, Jackson, and I. We sat in the living room catching up and talking about stories that happened back in Texas. We cackled until Brooke notified me that she needed to go home. I let Jackson know that I would be coming back, and just as I said that mom walked in. She joined the conversation while I was leaving.

Once Brooke and I walked outside we glanced at each other and started to giggle. The timing of what went on reminded me of a cliche movie. It was a moment I wouldn't expect myself to be in, or enjoy, but everything was working out the way I could only imagine. The snow layed softly across all of the neighborhood's lawn, bringing and amplifying tranquility. It was all so peaceful.

By the time we made it back to Brooke's house, while I drove the speed limit. It was solemn to feel the night come to an end. I had loved every second of what happened, all the stress and the suspense built throughout the day was worth it.

I put the car in park and made heavy eye contact with Brooke. No words were said, but all of the words I wanted to say were running through my head. Like how beautiful she looked, but I didn't know how to tell her.

"Thank you, Landon. I hope you enjo-" Before she finished I had to interrupt.

"You're beautiful." My eyes widened as our eye contact remained the same. Her face was blushed and she began to look away. As she was looking away I leaned in and kissed her. The sensations I felt ran ramped through my head when she began to kiss back with more passion. After we opened our eyes, we had the same giggle that we had outside my front door.

"Goodnight Landon." She opened the car door. I didn't want the night to end, but I knew that it had to.

"Goodnight Brooke." I softly said as she closed the door. I took a moment to watch her go inside. So many positive things about her kept going through my brain.

I drove in silence on the way back home. Once I made it home, the clock read ten-thirty on the dot. I left an hour ago, so I was shocked that mom didn't call and check on me, but when I walked in, the house was silent. Instead of having a feeling of eeriness, it was a feeling of serenity. I poked my head into mom's room to see her asleep so I left her alone. I then poked my head to see if Jackson was asleep as well. He peered his head up from under the covers.

"Sorry, I was just checking on you." I whispered to him.

"You sound like someone from Colorado." He muttered back to me. I had a small snicker.

"Goodnight, it's nice to see you brother." I closed his door and went to my room. As I layed down, I looked at the snowglobe that Brooke had got me for Christmas. It was standing tall on my nightstand, making itself the most apparent object on my stand. I picked it up and looked at it for a while, thinking about Brooke and I. I looked at the skyline of Denver inside the globe and thought about all of the future adventures Brooke and I planned on going. Before I was done daydreaming about the future I gave the globe a good shake before laying back down.

I was nearly asleep, before I remembered that Jackson, my best friend since I was a little kid, was at my house. I haven't seen him in about half a decade, and he was just in my house. The wonder was confusing, but my mind couldn't decide to rest so I got up and went to the kitchen to get some water. The handle of the refrigerator was freezing so I quickly opened, grabbed a bottle of water, and closed it back. I laid horizontally on the couch, while taking sips of my water, before I eventually dozed off into sleep.

X

The next morning I woke up and went to the kitchen to see Jackson and mom conversing. I approached them as I yawned while stretching. I sat at the table with them and slouched over a hefty amount.

"Good morning guys." I said still continuously yawning. I wiped my eyes attempting to wake myself up faster.

They acknowledged me and went back to talking. I sat there quietly until I realized what they were talking about. They were talking about the time that Jackson and I celebrated Jackson's birthday.

It was fourth grade and it was your classic sleepover. Three boys being Jackson and I, as well as a friend of ours that we don't keep up with anymore named Samuel. Samuel ended up moving away and we didn't keep good contact with him. The last we heard from him was that he was in Arkansas, or somewhere around there. Back then we were the perfect trio. I remember that on his birthday we watched movies that we shouldn't have been watching at ten years old. That night was the night I learned what keistering is, and I definitely shouldn't have known what that is. I shouldn't know what that is now, but nevertheless we all had a very memorable night. It's hard to remember all the things we did, because we got into so much stuff. When we talk it is easy to walk back into those memories I forgot I even had.

"Landon." Jackson put his hand on my shoulder and shook me a little bit, as he caught me zoned out.

"Yeah, my bad." I started focusing on what they had to stay.

"Did you hear what I said?" My mom asked with an excited look on her face.

"No." I hesitated before giving my answer.

"Well you should've because we're going back to Texas." My eyes lit up. Immediately when she said that. I was left speechless, I was so excited. I haven't been there in two years. Last time I went I saw my grandpa and heard a million of his quotes he loved using.

"When are we going? How long are we going to be there?" my thoughts turned into words without thinking.

"Today, and we'll be there for three days." Mom said while nodding her head. I couldn't believe what was happening. We were really going back to Texas. The last twenty four hours have been so exciting.

I scurried to my room and threw a bag together as quickly as possible. I just made sure I had underwear, socks, shirts, and shorts. I came back out with my bag not even halfway zipped up.

"Did you get your hygiene bag?" Mom asked with a stern look. I paused for a moment, and ran back into the bathroom to get the bag I forgot. The bag contained a toothbrush, toothpaste, deodorant, and razor. I don't know why I had a razor, because I haven't started growing any facial hair yet. After I grabbed my bag I ran back into where mom and Jackson were.

"I'm ready." I panted seeing as I zoomed around the house getting ready. They stared at me in slight disgust, but I was anxious.

"We're not leaving until four." Jackson said, holding in a chuckle. I looked at the clock and it read eleven o'clock. I felt stupid as they continued to stare at me already packed and ready to go.

"What are we doing until then?" I asked, looking at mom.

"We're going to spend the day in Denver." This must've meant we were going to fly to Texas. Which had been obvious, because it's not like Jackson's mom would let him drive all the way up here.

After about thirty minutes we got our bags, put them

in the car, and got ready to go to Denver. During the trip we caught up on how our school-lives were going. I told him all about how Brooke and I got together, and about my friend group. He told us that he was playing football. Jackson has always been athletic, he's also six foot five so that helps a bunch as well. He dwarfed everyone at the birthday party yesterday. He was a receiver for his football team. He started and had played a lot in high school. Which was really impressive, because he was only a freshman like me, and Texas football has a huge reputation to be good. He explained how he already has a ton of interest from a couple different colleges in Texas. I felt like I was talking to a superstar, hearing all of this new information about his football career. It's crazy to think we were both just kids with aspirations, and he actually is living out those dreams.

After what seemed like a short drive, when usually it takes forever, we were in Denver. It was cold like usual, but it wasn't snowing like it has been for the past few days. Snow still laid on the ground, remnants from the previous week.

We parked in a parking lot and gave our tickets so we could wander around downtown for three hours. The air was brisk, as it usually was. We were a mile high from sea-level so the air was bound to be thin. We walked around for a while before coming to a large structure. People were taking pictures in front of the building, and I was confused what the building was supposed to be at first.

"That's the Denver Art Museum." Mom could read the confusion on my face. It's not like I've never been here before so I don't know why I was so perplexed by seeing the museum. Although, I've never been inside of it.

I was going to ask if we could go in, because I was intrigued by things like that, but I didn't bother asking, because I thought Jackson wouldn't want to and would be bored.

After a little more walking we ended up going to a place to eat. We could all agree on our hunger, and found a restaurant that looked like it would be good. I got a cheeseburger, and Jackson got the exact same thing. When we were little we used to do the same thing when we ate out. If he got a sandwich, I got a sandwich. We had a short held laugh when the food came out.

"There's a park a couple blocks away, if you guys want to go." Jackson suggested.

"That's a great idea, Jackson." Mom responded with a higher pitched voice than normal.

We finished eating and made our way to the park. Jackson walked with haste and began to leave mom and I behind. Mom and I started walking a little faster, so we could catch up.

"Hey, not all of us are superstar athletes, wait up." I called out to Jackson hoping he would slow down.

"Oh…I'm sorry." He looked back and seemed surprised by the distance between us. He stopped and waited for us to catch up.

There wasn't as much traffic downtown as I thought. So the street that usually took forever to cross even with using the crosswalk button.

We got to the entrance to the park and Jackson was stunned by how it all looked. You could see the look on his eyes indicating his amazement. I thought that this would be a great place to bring Brooke at least one time. Despite seeing a friend that I haven't been able to see for the past few years I still couldn't get her out of my head. I couldn't help myself, she was my main priority.

We ventured farther into the park finding all of its fauna and flora. It was still cold outside, so all of the birds were still migrated away and wouldn't be expected to be around for at least another month. The sun reflected off of the snow that was still laying on the ground. There also weren't that many people in the park. All of these factors made the park quiet, but it was peaceful. I enjoyed the time being mom and Jackson, it brought the feeling of a child back into me. I reflected on what overall brought me to Colorado, and the friends I made here and I had in Texas. Then I remembered that time that Matt, Sara, Brooke, and I were at the park. Being here reminded me of when we told each other how we really felt. Although that was a night and it was daytime the feeling was eerily similar. It was a good feeling, it was warm-felt even with the temperature being low. I imagined the park at night and being here with Brooke and what it would be like. I found myself daydreaming, until Jackson patted me on my back.

"Nice isn't it?" Jackson said with a positive expression on his face.

"Yeah…" I looked around for a moment, thinking about Colorado and its differences from Texas. "…I miss being a kid." I continued.

"Yeah, no kidding. Everything was so much easier." I was confused. I thought his life was really good. I didn't question him, but we sat on a nearby bench admiring the view.

Time passed over and soon enough it was time to go to the airport.

We went back to the parking lot to retrieve the car and made our way to the airport. The airport in Denver was the biggest in the country. The only other time I was there I met a man from Korea who had a very American name, Chris. As well as a man from Ukraine named Marat. They were really fun to get to know even if the conversation only lasted under an hour. I liked to explore, so when our flight got delayed I went to the other terminals to see what they had in store. I almost got lost forgetting what terminal I began in, and had to wait for mom to come get me. Not one of my fondest memories, so I try to forget it. Especially since I wasn't even a teenager yet.

When we actually got to the airport, we had to get through the TSA. Since it has been a while since we had been to the airport I was nervous. I thought they would get mad of the jeans I had on, because of the metal that was on them.

I read the sign that had instructions on what to do, and we followed them. I took off my hoodie, and then put the things that were in my pockets into the plastic tubs they had placed out. The lady that was waiting to clear me to let me through gave me a stern look, as if I had done something wrong. I tried my best to avoid straight eye contact. I felt as if I had been violated. She started scanning me with a hand held metal detector. I heard the beeping of it and immediately became shaky. I hoped they didn't think I was carrying a weapon. I stood there in fear.

"Move on." she said bluntly.

I was confused. I heard it beep, does that not mean I'm in trouble. I sat there for a moment before the lady waved her hand at me to go on. I proceeded with caution, and was prepared to stop if called on.

After that strange encounter, we all made it through. Our flight would start boarding in the next thirty minutes. We had to get to Terminal C, that's where the interstate travel was for the United States.

By the time we got to our flight we only had to wait

about ten minutes, before boarding the plane. While sitting there I played a game on my phone to make the time pass a little faster. Eventually they started boarding the plane.

"*Line up in numerical order according to your ticket.*" The public announcement system said.

I thought It was so cool how there were so many flights going at once when entering the tunnel to board the plane. The bag I had brought fit nicely into a compartment that was meant to hold it. I watched as an older man came up behind me, and shoved his bag behind mine. I sat there frustrated, but I didn't want to cause a scene, so I remained quiet. I sat next to Jackson and mom, but I could tell it would be an uncomfortable trip. Since Jackson and I were so big, it was hard to get into a position that would make the trip easier. I ended up trying to put my feet in the aisle, because they didn't fit well under the seat in front of me.

"Please move your feet under the seat in front of you." A flight attendant said to me, as soon as I set my feet out. I gave her a quick glance to see an absolutely gorgeous younger lady. Stunned by her looks I moved my feet back to in front of me, even if it was uncomfortable.

Most of the ride there was me switching my positioning to try to get more comfortable, but my efforts were to no avail. Before I knew it we were alerted that we were going to land in fifteen minutes. I looked out to see the skyline of Dallas, Texas. It was just as good as I could remember.

When we landed it was still evening. There was a vibrant range of colors that painted the sky a beautiful color. Once I was allowed to use my phone again I first texted Brooke to let her know that everything was alright.

She thought I was lying when I first told her that I was taking a surprise trip to Texas. My mom helped verify that we were and I wasn't just trying to avoid her. Especially since we had planned on going on a date in three days. I still felt bad, because I felt as if I opted out on her, but my hands were really tied when it came to making decisions. She didn't seem as if it bothered her too much, but I only could hear her words over text rather than seeing her in person.

When we left the airport, we had an hour and a half trip ready for us. Jackson's mom, Mrs. West. I could tell she aged from the last time I've seen her. Not to sound disrespectful, but that was the only noticeable difference I could tell when seeing her, after all of these years. She came and gave me a hug first.

"I know I'm late, but happy birthday." She said with a tearful smile written on her face. Her hug brought a wave of nostalgia. She stretched her arms to create distance to see me in whole. She noted how tall I've gotten over the years.

I didn't want to comment on what initially came to

my head. So I didn't give much of a response, outside of gratitude for her happy birthday wishes. She then hugged my mom, then hugged Jackson after.

"The car is ready if y'all got your bags." Her southern accent was showing. It was hard not to notice it, I wanted to laugh because I became accustomed to the proper English I learned from my community in Colorado.

We all got our bags and headed to the car, and caught up with Mrs.

West on how Texas has been since we last visited. She retold about how Jackson got his football recognition, which I still found amazing. She also told us how Mr. West has been traveling a lot for his job and that we shouldn't expect to see him until the third day. Hearing this I got a little bummed out.

Jackson and I had a lot of memories together, but the one who supervised us was usually Mr. West. He always had a big heart and loved playing with us. From jumping on the trampoline to playing in the park, we did everything.

Once we eventually made it, I took in a deep breath thinking back to when things were simpler. I don't deal with too much as it is, but dealing with the drama from my peers, and the pressure from school made things harder than it used to be. It seemed like a bit of a wasteland from just looking beyond the population sign.

Driving through the city made me realize how big

the city really was. When I was a kid everything seemed so much more compact. Now that I'm bigger and have a better understanding of the world, I could actually take in everywhere more clearly. There still stood the McDonald's that we would beg to go to when Jackson and I were little. Mostly because there was a kid play area, and we would hide from our parents. We used to do that all the time, until one day our mom pretended to leave us. We cried and begged for them to come back until they eventually did. They told us to not act like we were hiding from them, and we promised we wouldn't. It was crazy to think about all of the things I would promise as a child. Mom probably knew they were an empty promise from a clueless child, but sometimes I was taught really good lessons.

We made it to Jackson's house after a while. Or what I guess was there was their old house, because we drove right past where I remember spending half of my childhood.

"You guys moved out of your last house?" I was taken aback seeing this.

"Yep we did." responded Mrs. West.

"Why?" I said almost simultaneously.

"Well you see, Mr. West ended up getting a really good promotion so we decided to upgrade a bit." I was intrigued by her response. I was also surprised to hear that Mr. West got a promotion. He used to say how he loved the position he worked, but I guess money talks.

Once we finally arrived at their new house I was

shocked to see how big it was. I could only remember being in that two bedroom, two bathroom house. Now, it was triple the size of the last house. It had a nice white picket fence surrounding the front yard. As well as being painted with what looked like a fresh coat of white paint. We got our bags out of the car and headed inside.

"Here we are!" Mrs. West exclaimed with her hands out showing off the interior of the house. Jackson showed Mom and I into the guest rooms.

I've never been in a house with multiple guest rooms. Besides James Crowder's house. We used to be good friends when I first moved to Colorado, but after my first year we ended up not having classes, so we grew apart.

The guest room that I would be staying in had a queen sized bed and was filled with paintings. There was a painting that portrayed a vase with two roses in it. The painting sat right above the bed frame, and I took a moment to admire it. I set my bag in there, then headed to mom's room to see what her room looked like. When entering her room it was similar to mine but inverted. The bed was on the other side of the room with a singular painting. The painting was a large lotus flower that sat across from the bed.

It was already late by the time mom and I got all of our stuff unloaded, and settled down. Mrs. West told us that dinner was ready, and wanted us to come down to eat with her and Jackson. We made our way down there to be met with chicken alfredo. She made it special for us, because she knew that was our favorite meal she made.

Mom learned most of her recipes from Mrs. West. Although when she tried replicating her famous chicken alfredo, she almost burnt the house down. She said that she just forgot that she was cooking and walked off.

Ever since then we let Mrs. West have that be her famous meal.

We continued to catch up over the meal at the dinner table, but something felt off. I couldn't put my finger on what was wrong, but I could definitely tell there was something wrong. Although we were talking, it seemed quiet. It was an uncanny feeling, it was unsettling. Looking at Jackson and his mom's face they had an empty expression. While I wouldn't expect them to be exhilarated, that's not realistic. We have already grown accustomed to each other's company in the time spent together. My mind decided it was just because Mr. West wasn't home.

After dinner I went to Jackson's room for a little bit to hang out with him. He had the tv on already autoplaying a tv show, I assumed he had started before we went to dinner. I stood beside his bed before sitting at the end of it.

"Is everything alright?" I spoke with hesitance. I avoided eye contact at first until he spoke.

"Yeah...why wouldn't it be." He responded without a

care. I must've been over thinking, but I had to explain myself.

"I don't know, it seemed...weird." I started to become more open, with my body language.

"Everything's alright Landon. How's you and Brooke." I instantly was flooded with thoughts about Brooke. Then I realized he was trying to distract me from the problem.

"What are you hiding Jackson?" I was locking my position to show my focus towards him.

"NOTHING! Nothing." He was trying to hold back and I could tell. I didn't want to bother any longer so I felt like it was time to go to bed.

"Alright, I'm going upstairs. Goodnight." I was stale with my voice. He looked down while I walked out not saying a word.

The next day, Jackson approached me with a smile. It seemed genuine so I didn't question it. Our moms were already in the kitchen by the time we went in there. They pretended as if the eeriness from yesterday never occurred, but I was still skeptical of everything. I've known this family too long to not notice if something was wrong.

I didn't know what the plan for today was, but my mom told me to get ready to head out. So I grabbed my travel bag that I almost forgot in Colorado, and maintained my hygiene. While I was finishing brushing my teeth Jackson appeared at the door frame. He had an envelope in his hand.

"Here you go. I know I should've given it to you at your house, but mom wanted to see you open it as well." He handed me the envelope, indicating that it was a belated birthday present.

"Thank you." I said while my mouth still contained toothpaste. He headed back downstairs, to get ready to leave, and I finished getting ready as well.

When I came downstairs I still had the envelope in my hand. Jackson and Mrs. West were standing next to each other waiting for my mother and I. We stood there for a brief moment in silence, I didn't know if I should wait for mom or not so I was at a stalemate for the time being. My eagerness won over my patience and I started opening the envelope. I was assuming that Jackson and Mrs. West were watching me, seeing as there was nothing else to do. Once I opened the gift I realized there was a twenty dollar bill inside, but I didn't want to seem greedy so I ignored it at first. I took out the card and read it aloud:

"No matter how far, no matter the distance, we love you no matter what, because that's the kind of family we are."

Those words meant a lot, especially from them. I walked over to Jackson and wrapped my arms around him. He gave me a tight squeeze before letting go. No words were said, but we had a full conversation through our emotions.

Mom finally was ready and was enthusiastic to go.

She saw the card in my hand, and knew that it was a gift immediately.

"Aww. I missed it, didn't I?" We chuckled and nodded our heads yes. She didn't dwell about missing the moment, and was still ready to go. So we did, and made our way to the car.

"Where are we going?" My curiosity forced the words out of my mouth.

"The ol' Cotton Belt Trail, but you boys better not try to run away this time." Mrs. West responded in a joking manner.

She reminded me of the time when we were eight that Jackson and I went on the same trail with our moms, and wandered off. Our moms were deep into a conversation and Jackson and I wanted to race to see who was faster. Back when I could keep up with him. We ended up getting lost on the trail and made it to a veterinarian clinic. We begged them to call our moms while we were crying, but we didn't know their phone numbers. They helped us by calling the cops, and luckily for us our moms had already called the police to report us missing. We were "lost" for about seven hours that day, but our parents were still visibly mortified when they saw us. They must have thought that we had died. After that incident they never let us back on that trail no matter how much we begged to go back.

Eight years later, I finally got my wishes fulfilled. Better late than never I guess, but it didn't feel like it was going to be as special as it should've been. The feeling of being a kid was almost depleted, or at least it was getting that way. The trip has been fun so far, but things just weren't the same. Maybe it was because I was worried about what Brooke was doing, instead of living in the moment. Maybe it was because I was overthinking. I wasn't going to be looking sorrowful, this was a time to enjoy myself, and that's what I'm going to do.

After a small drive we had arrived. The weather was nice, but also very humid. A lot more than what I was used to in Colorado at the very least. The sun was kissing my skin and it felt really good at first, but after a couple minutes it was getting too hot. We had only begun the trail and I was already starting to crisp. My mom was the same way, which made sense, because we weren't adjusted to the climate. The trail started off as paved ground, but once we got farther in it was only a dirt path. The shoes I was wearing were an older pair of Nikes anyway. I usually wore running shoes no matter the occasion, so I was prepared without knowing what we were going to do.

There wasn't too much talking along the trail. Mostly because mom and I were focusing on how hot it was and how exhausted we were becoming. We chose not to say anything, not even asking for a break. You think since we live in a place where the elevation is a mile high that breathing wouldn't be an issue, but the humidity was killing me. My breathing felt as if it was wet. Despite this it was very visually pleasing being on the trail. I thought this could be another thing that Brooke and I did. I couldn't help but to get distracted by thinking about her. My focus was once regained after I tripped over a log. Everyone stepped over except me. Once I fell I became face to face with a snake. We had a staring contest for a moment until I got a grasp on what was actually happening. I looked up at Mom, Jackson and Mrs. West and terror was written on their face. Looking back at the snake I saw it hiss, got up, and sprinted at least two hundred meters away. I stopped to catch my breath. This trail must be haunted. I put my hands on my knees, and waited for everyone to catch up.

Luckily there was an exit very close to where we were. We left as soon as we could. Once we got back to the car, everyone started dying laughing. I couldn't help but to join them. I admit that I overreacted, but I'm glad that everyone could at least get a laugh out of it.

By the time we made it back to the house it was getting dark outside. We grabbed a little snack after leaving the trail initially, but it was only for a few moments. Once we got back to the West's house, we went to the living room to watch a movie together. At first Jackson and I decided we didn't want to, and started heading to his room to play video games, but our moms wouldn't let that happen. They didn't let us have input on the movie we were going to watch. Our moms decided on a romantic-comedy, but whenever the movie started, Jackson got on his phone. I look over to see what the illumination was, and I saw that he was starting to call someone named mackenzie.

"Who's that?" I asked. I didn't mean to tell that he was on his phone, but the words slipped out of my mouth.

Mrs. West peered over to see what Jackson was doing. She saw that he was calling whoever Mackenzie was, and seemed appalled. Not knowing much I just assumed that it was a girl that Jackson was with or something close to that.

"What do you think you're doing young man?" She grabbed the remote to pause the movie.

"C'mon mom. Dad never lets me bring her over, please." He said in a childish tone.

"Absolutely not. You have a guest over." She responded with no hesitance. I felt weird that I was being put in the middle of the situation, but I decided to remain silent.

"She could meet Landon. That's the only reason I even called her." Not realizing it at first, I noticed that he was actually on the phone with her.

She could hear what was happening.

"Hmm...but you're not going to leave out Landon are you?" Mrs. West looked back and forth to Jackson and I.

"Of course not, this is my guy." He hit me on the shoulder in a playful way.

Jackson got up and walked away from the living room to continue his call. He came back to the room and put up all of his fingers. I guess that meant she would be here in ten minutes. I was intrigued, it was going to be a little more exciting than watching this movie I had no interest in.

After those ten minutes passed, there was a knock at the door. Jackson got up and sprinted to open it. Once he opened to answer who it was at the door, there she was. She was a blonde curly-headed girl, who stood about five foot five inches. They hugged each other and she leaned up to give him a kiss on the cheek. I looked away to see what Mrs. West thought. She seemed as if she was used to seeing that, but I knew if I ever did that with Brooke, mom would kill me. Jackson waved me over to come follow them to his room. I felt out of place, not having Brooke with me.

"This is Landon, he's been my best friend for forever, and he lives in Colorado now." Jackson said to Mackenzie as soon as we walked into his room. I put my hand out to shake and she left me hanging for a second, which gave off a wave of awkwardness.

"Hi, Landon." Mackenzie said after finally shaking my hand. Her voice was soft.

"Hi." I didn't display much emotion on my face, which probably made me unapproachable.

For the time being Jackson did most of the talking. I wasn't good at meeting new people, and Jackson knew that. He tried easing the tense feeling I had by cracking jokes. Which I was a little more of myself than I would normally be if I met someone new. Mackenzie didn't speak much as well, maybe that was her personality. It could be because she thought I was weird, but she was on her phone for the most part.

"You should call Brooke." Jackson suggested.

"I don't know about that." I said while shaking my head no. He must've been thinking that if Brooke was on the phone it wouldn't be so quiet. I did plan on calling her to fill her in on what was going on, but I wanted to be alone when I did.

Jackson kept on asking me to call her but I continuously declined his propositions. After a room that wasn't as talkative or exciting as I thought it would be, Mackenzie told Jackson that it was time for her to go. She gave him another kiss on the cheek, and Jackson went to walk her out the door. I sat on Jackson's bed waiting for him to return. When he came back he said:

"I don't know what her deal was." He said as if he had a problem with her.

"Maybe she just didn't feel comfortable around me." I said, trying to lighten his mood.

"No. That's not like her, she loves talking to everyone. Something's up." I didn't want to challenge what he was saying, but it seemed like he was overreacting. Who was I to comment on his relationship, I didn't know what was going on.

I sat there confused with my silence, until there was a

knock at the front door again. Did she come back? I peered to where I could view the front door. To my surprise, Mrs. West answered the door and it was Mr. West. He wasn't supposed to be here until noon tomorrow. It was good to see him, but he held a grim expression on his face. He's probably just tired, I thought to myself. I bet that Jackson was glad that Mackenzie left when she did. Whenever Jackson saw who had come home, he went back to his room. I ventured away to talk to Mr. West.

"Hey Mr. West." I said when I approached him.

"Is that Landon Morgan?" He smiled while still holding a grim look.

"Yessir. How are you?" I responded, trying to keep the conversation going.

"Not as good as you, you look like a million bucks dude." He still sounded like the Mr. West from my childhood.

"Thank you sir." I said with a small giggle.

"Happy belated birthday. It's nice seeing you, but I got to go to bed.

I'm exhausted." He said while walking away.

"Alright well goodnight." I went back to Jackson's room to see him sitting on the edge of his bed texting someone.

He looked up at me, and then went back to his phone. I didn't say anything for a moment. I decided to sit next to him and glance at his phone. He moved the angle he was holding his phone, so I couldn't view it.

I didn't want to intrude his space.

"Why didn't you say anything to your dad?" I asked.

"Because he probably doesn't want to be bothered." He said it in a way that seemed like there was some underlining to why he really didn't. He knows I've grown up without my dad, so I always tell him to appreciate him. This built on my suspicions that started yesterday. Was Mr. West causing problems within the family? I must've been missing something or maybe I was missing nothing.

The next morning I woke up slowly. I slept well, but I was starting to miss home. It had only been two nights since I've been home, but this was the longest I've been away from home in years.

I wondered what last night was all about. So much had happened last night, and I didn't really know what to make of it. I didn't want to bother Jackson, because maybe there was a lot more than what I was being told.

I looked at the clock that sat on the nightstand to see that it read eight forty-three. I was up very early, everyone usually wakes up after an hour I just did. I didn't want to just sit there for an hour so I went downstairs to see if anyone else was up. I heard whispers when I reached the bottom few steps, so I decided to stop, before proceeding.

"What are you doing?" I made out that it was Mr. West talking to his wife.

"I'm sorry, I didn't mean to." She was answering submissively as if she was scared. Why would she be scared?

"You never mean to." Mr. West was screaming in a whisper.

"Why do you have to be like this? I just wanted to ask what you did while you were-" Before she could finish I could hear that Mr. West had slapped Mrs. West, not letting her finish her sentence.

I was stunned, I felt powerless, and didn't know how I could aid Mrs. West. Why would Mr. West ever do that? I didn't want to be caught so I scurried back upstairs as quickly, and as quietly as I could. I don't want to believe that Mr. West did what I think I heard. Is that why Jackson didn't want to say hello to him yesterday? Was this why they seem so different? I was full of fear. I didn't know how to tell mom, there wasn't anything she could even do.

Mr. West was a bulky guy, he was also very tall so he was already intimidating. Added on to the fact that he was bald, I don't know what it is, but that was an additive to the intimidation he brought.

I went back to my room and waited for everyone to wake up. When everyone did wake, I was scared to even go back downstairs. My mom greeted me in the living room with a smile.

"Why do you look mortified?" My mom said jokingly.

Was it that apparent that I was? If so I need to wipe my face to put up a mask, to ask as if I don't know what happened.

"I'm just tired." I had nothing else to come up with to give her a non-concerning reason.

When Jackson, mom, and I met at the dinner table there was complete silence. I didn't want to say anything to raise any alarm. Mom ate happily and without a care in the world. Jackson and I shared the same expression. Jackson and I made subtle eye contact, having a whole conversation without saying a word. He must've caught on that I knew something.

Whenever we finished, Jackson signaled me to come to his room. I excused myself from the table, and followed Jackson to his room. Once we were in his room, there was a moment of silence. I opened my mouth, but words wouldn't come out.

"Did you see something Landon?" Jackson was blunt and flat with his question.

"Uh-y-yes." I didn't want to tell him, but I knew he would ask.

"What happened?" The words hit like a bullet that shockwaved my body.

I sat there paralyzed thinking about everything he would do if I told him what I truly saw. Would he be mad at me for not doing anything? Would he try to do something himself? I didn't know if he was at his breaking point. I would hate to push him past that point.

"I'm-I'm sorry Jackon I didn't know what to do." I was on the verge of tears. How do I tell my best friend that his household was broken? I was stuck.

"Landon, it's ok just tell me." He was becoming tearful as well.

I tried to tell him, but I couldn't. My body wouldn't allow me to break my best friend. I couldn't let him suffer knowing that his mother was being hurt and there wasn't anything either of us could do. I wanted to tell my mom, because she knew how to fix everything. Could she fix this? Was there any way to fix this? We didn't know.

We carried on the rest of the day as if nothing had happened, although you could tell Jackson and I were carrying a burden. Mom tried asking us if we were in a disagreement, but whenever she would ask we would shake our heads no. The rest of the day was uneventful. Jackson and I were too scared to want to do anything. A trip that was intended for fun, turned out to be one full of despair.

Later that evening we all decided to eat together. I was very uncomfortable, and I didn't care that it was visible.

"Are you ok?" My mother became more concerned with my posture.

"I'm fine." My head was down and I stopped raising my fork whenever she asked her question.

Jackson, Mrs. West, and I all had our heads down

avoiding eye-contact. It was a room full of trepidation. Mom could tell there was something wrong.

"What's going on with everyone?" Her question was directed towards Mr. West.

"They're just not grateful, that's what it is." His southern drawl was more apparent with his attitude.

"Grateful?" I muttered under my breath. It must've been louder than I thought, because Mr. West was seeping his sight into my skull.

"Got something to say boy." His voice was subtly raising. I became fearful.

"Landon, is there a problem?" My mom seemed as if she wasn't in my defense.

"There is a problem. Your son doesn't have any damn manners." Mr. West said to my mother while looking at me still. I drew my eyes towards him, which commenced a stare-off.

"Excuse me?" My mom pushed her chair out and stood up after her comment.

"Don't excuse me, excuse your little brat." Mr. West stood up, revealing his height. I stood up as well.

"What in this whole-wide world makes you think you can talk to my son that way." She was giving Mr. West a stern look.

"Please honey sit down." Mrs. West said while grabbing the arm of the disgruntled Mr. West.

"Get your hand off me woman. Don't make me teach

you a lesson too." He jerked his arm away and reared back his hand.

He looked as if he was getting ready to hit her. Before he got the opportunity to, Jackson got up and rushed at his father. He pushed him hard, and Mr. West's back hit the wall.

"Look who thinks he's grown up." He chuckled as he stepped away from the wall.

Jackson stood his ground not showing any fear in him. He looked strong and his courage was the source of his strength. Mom and I sat there in disbelief.

"Don't you ever touch mom again." Jackson balled up his fist mean mugging his father.

"Or what?" Mr. West said menacingly.

"I'll show you what the fu-" Before he could finish his curse. Mr. West punched his own son. Hitting him in the stomach.

Mom and I couldn't believe what was happening. This family used to be so happy, so peaceful, but all of that tranquility had vanquished. We were watching them fall apart not knowing what to do. Mom and I stood next to each other holding hands. My legs were physically shaking from the amount of fear I was experiencing. This was too traumatic for a kid who just turned fifteen. This was traumatizing for anyone at any age.

"NO! My boy." Mrs. West went to the aid of Jackson.

Mr. West made his way to us, but Jackson was stronger

than anyone I've ever met. He stood back up and attacked his father to protect us. He threw a punch that looked like it took everything out of him. When he made contact with his father's jaw there was an audible pop. Mr. West freefalled to the floor.

XI

Mr. West layed on the floor. His jaw was dislocated, and he was knocked out on the floor. He looked as if he was deceased, with blood leaking from his temporal area. My eyes were like a deer in headlights. He was supposed to be so powerful, and we were supposed to be scared of him. Now he lies on the floor, and we look like the witnesses to a murder.

Did I cause this?

Mom, Mrs. West, and I sat there with our mouths on the ground. We were dazed and confused on what to do next. We continued to look at his body that remained on the floor. After looking at him for the extended period of time we were, you could tell he was breathing. I was slightly relieved to see that he wasn't dead, but that means we have to go before he wakes up. Although where do we go?

I instantly thought that we should invite them to Colorado to stay with us until things could be figured out. That outcome seemed very improbable in action. I was no help to the situation, I felt so small. I hate that my suspicions of something being wrong were true. Why did I have to think so much? This wouldn't have happened if I just kept my mouth shut. Why did I do this? I was about two meters away from Mr. West's body staring in terror.

After my mom assessed the situation, and came to the conclusion that Mrs. West should call the police. What sense would that make, he was the one who was on the floor looking lifeless. Mrs. West and my mother bickered about what the right thing to do is. I looked over at Jackson to see a look that should never be in a kid's eyes. He was staring at his father, his hands were shaking. I wanted to approach him, but how could I? No words I could say would be of comfort, I just had to watch from a distance someone I would consider family destroyed.

Mom devised a plan that saw us going to my grandparents house that lived just out of town, to see if they would be willing to help. My grandparents also had a big house, not quite as big as the West's house, but enough to support Mrs. West and Jackson if they were brought in. They gathered bags that would be enough for a week's worth of clothes, and got into the car. This was all done in silence, it hurt me to not be able to help in any way. I just followed suit and gathered my things to put in the car.

After a short drive to make it to my grandparents house. I was somewhat excited to see them, but I was still gripping on to the fear that Jackson had. Once we arrived at my grandparents' front door my mom knocked and we waited for them to answer. I stood by my mothers side as if I were a small child, scared of being lost. They were in their late sixties so I assumed they either may not hear it, or it would take them a while to answer the door. After a minute of waiting they finally came to the door.

"Rachel?" My grandmother still held on to her youth, looking to be in her late forties even though she was sixty-seven.

"We need help, please." Mom's voice was trembling.

"Come in." She opened the door fully to allow everyone to come in.

As we sat on their couch we were quiet. My grandfather came in from the kitchen to see who was here. He looked confused to see Mrs. West and Jackson. They knew Jackson, because we used to play at their house for its size. Mom gave them a rundown of what happened, and politely asked if They would be willing to take in Mrs. West and Jackson until they get their situation resolved. My grandparents loved taking care of people so of course they obliged.

Jackson went back out to the car to grab him and his mom's bags. They decided to not bring them in at first, so it wouldn't seem as if we were forcing them onto our grandparents. Jackson already knew where the guest rooms were so he brought the bags to those designated rooms.

"They can stay as long as they need. Although I have to tell you guys something." My grandfather said in a saddened voice. It was so nice to see him after all of these years, so I hate to hear the sadness in his voice.

He was a very good spirited man that couldn't harm a fly. He was also very positive and fun to be around, so hearing his tone the way it was, was concerning.

"What's wrong?" I was focused on him, wanting to know what could possibly be wrong.

"I have Alzheimer's." He said softly.

I wasn't aware of what it was, but it sounded like a disease. It couldn't have been good at all, because my mom put her hand over her mouth, and became teary eyed.

"When were you diagnosed?" My mother asked abruptly.

"About half a year ago." My grandmother noted. She looked very sad as well.

Mother got up and excused herself. I stayed put, and layed with my confusion. It couldn't have been good at all, because my mom bursted into tears before she could fully leave the room. I became more worrisome, not knowing what was going on.

"What's that grandpa?" I just wanted to know what was happening to him.

"I'm going to forget a bunch of things." He made it sound like it was simple memory loss. My face showed my confusion.

"Is that bad enough to warrant tears?" I was trying to get a better understanding of what was happening.

"Well, how much do you love me?" He lightly chuckled. Did this mean he would pass away soon?

"Grandpa, what's wrong with you?" I was becoming teary eyed myself, waiting for the inevitable answer I was waiting for.

"Little Landon, I don't even know who you brought here son. Soon I'll even forget you." I was shocked by his response. I had so many questions.

"Then, why would you let strangers stay with you if you don't remember him?" I thought to myself this was a prank, because I didn't want to face the reality of the situation.

"I may forget who everyone is, but I'll never forget my character, and the value of helping those in need." The word hit my chest like a bullet.

Another one of his famous quotes, at the worst time possible.

"Thank you." I didn't know what to say but that.

I hugged him crying profusely. This day was too much to handle, I lost so much in such little time. I still didn't fully understand his illness, but I didn't want the man that meant the most to me, just forget who I was. I didn't have it in me to be able to lose him.

I went to bed crying, not knowing how to deal with losing so much. I wanted to be comforted, I wish Brooke was here. She would be so helpful, but I didn't want to call her crying. So I just went to sleep hoping that it was just a bad dream, or at least that I wouldn't have to remember anything tomorrow.

The next morning I woke up with my head pounding. I went to the kitchen to see who all was in there to see complete terror. It was only Jackson and my grandfather.

"And what is your name, young man?" My grandpa reached out to greet Jackson, as if he's never even seen him.

"It's Jackson." Jackson was laughing, thinking that my grandfather was joking.

"Well it's nice to meet you sir." He had such a simple response, but it was so powerful. He truly didn't remember him.

"Do you not remember?" Jackson was starting to look concerned.

"I'm sorry, have I met you before?" My grandfather was doing his best to be polite.

"It's me, Jackson." He stood up from his seat, and spread his arm, hoping that maybe a full view would help him remember.

I watched from a distance, holding back the tears, letting them only be for last night. I couldn't believe what

I was watching. We were here so often together, that it was breaking me to see how clueless my grandfather was to who Jackson is.

I entered the room fully hoping to break tension. I greeted both of them with a goodmorning. The sun was shining into the kitchen revealing particles that were swarming the air.

"He doesn't remember me." Jackson whispered into my ear. I could tell he was confused.

"Yeah…don't worry." I didn't know how to tell him, because I didn't fully understand myself.

Today mom and I had to leave to go back to Colorado, and I wasn't prepared to leave yet. This trip has been awful, but I still love being in Texas. I wish I could bring all of my friends from Colorado and bring them to Texas.

I didn't want to speak to anyone for the remainder of the time here. So I didn't, I gathered my stuff and got ready for the ride home. I didn't speak to anyone for hours.

Whenever we got ready to leave I hugged my grandparents without a word. I was the last one out the door to go home. Before I could go, my grandfather stopped me.

"If this is the last time I speak to you, I want you to know you're a great person, you are greater than your worries, and overthinking is a gift. Most importantly I want you to know that I love you." He gave me another hug and I broke down.

I could barely stand. This may be the last time I ever talk to my grandpa, the man who's taught me the most in my life. My best role model, gone.

"I don't want you to go." I could hardly form the words through my tears.

Although I was the one not wanting him to leave, I was the one to walk out the door. I was paranoid if this would be our last interaction. The ride to the airport was grim. So much agony bottled up inside, not knowing how or what to do to express the feelings I had. I wasn't even sure about the feelings I had. I was glad that we would be back home soon, it would help me get my mind off of the trip. Maybe telling Brooke would help, but how could I?

When we made it to the airport, not many words were said. As we got our things to leave, we gave each other goodbye wishes, and hugs for comfort.

"I'm so sorry." the only words I could mutter to Jackson after ruining his life.

"Landon, it's not your fault." He was like my big brother telling me I was okay. I wasn't okay, there was nothing that would make me feel better at this moment.

I stayed a moment waving as we drove off. Staring, knowing that it truly was my fault. The events that occurred wouldn't have happened if I was just quiet, but I didn't know any better. I was ignorant and naive to what had happened. I know I shouldn't blame myself, but I was at the center of everything. It sounds sorrowsome and narcissistic to make it sound like it was only my fault. I do understand that it was partly Mr. West's fault, but I fueled the already lit flame. I engulfed the entire family in the flames, because of my ignorance.

On the ride home, I stayed on the side closest to the window, hoping the views would take my mind away from things. Seeing the skyline of downtown Dallas was majestic. It eased me for a moment, but that moment didn't last long. When the plane ascended past the clouds, not seeing anything brought the memories back. They came flooding in, and I had no escape. I was trapped inside my head, and trapped inside a confined area without a way to leave. The stress made my face heavy, and the uncomfortability of the seat I was in made me squeamish.

Later after all the trouble from the ride, we made it back to Denver. Finally we were home, I was still uneasy about the images that were left imprinted in my mind, but at least we were home. Now that we were here I realized how little being back to a familiar environment was. I was still tearing myself apart with the ideas that scared my brain. It was my fault, and now Jackson was alone. I did that to him, after everything he did for me, I repaid him in the worst way possible.

I told Brooke that we made it back to Colorado home safe, and an hour later, we were home. Walking through the front door, it felt empty. It was strange, and the silence was killing me. The wave of emptiness was hollowing me out. I looked around to see things that were so familiar, it now felt uncharted.

I went to my room, and layed in my bed after setting my bags down. I guess I was expecting all of my friends to be back in my room. I was hoping that they would be there to comfort me, let me know that everything would be alright. No friends, no family, and no Jackson. I was alone, stuck with my thoughts. I laid my head down just wishing for any serenity. I ended up going to sleep, I was exhausted.

I was woken up by someone tugging on my foot. While I was gaining consciousness, I rubbed my eyes to see who was bothering me. To my surprise it was Brooke, she was at the foot of my bed.

"Hey Landon, are you okay?" The concern in her voice was very obvious.

"Yeah." I was yawning, trying to figure out what was going on. Why was she here? What time was it?

She crawled into the bed on the right side of me and hugged me. I was confused about what was going on, but I was glad she was here with me. The emptiness was filled in at that instance.

"I'm here." She said softly. Did she know what happened?

I didn't know how to respond, but she was here when I needed her the most. There wasn't too much said between us, while we were laying down. There was no need for a heartache conversation, because if she did know, there was no reason to waste my tears when she's here.

I could feel her breathing, as she slowly drifted away to sleep. I thought about her, while my arms were wrapped around her, clutching her the same way a child does a stuffed animal. I longed for her while I was away, thinking about how much I was waiting for this moment. It came unexpectedly, but nevertheless I'm glad that it did. It was so peaceful to watch her lay on me, trusting me enough to fall asleep in my arms.

At first I could feel myself drifting away to sleep, but I tried to stay awake, wanting to protect her if any problem was to occur. Although I ended up falling asleep as well, happier than I have been the past three days. I thought to myself, what would I do if I didn't have her? She was everything I needed, the comfort I was wanting, and she was here with me at last.

XII

Before I knew it, the school year was at its end. Seemed strange to think that everything that happened this year finally had come to its conclusion. This was the same school year I met Brooke. Everything working out the way it did seemed so unlikely. My year would've been so drastically different if I was just on time that one day. I'm so thankful things happen the way they did. The smallest mistake, convenience, happened to be one of my greatest blessings this year. What are the odds that any of this would take place, especially for someone like me.

It was the second to last day of school and the feeling of summer was upon me. I was anxious for what the summer had in store. I had imagined that everything would be perfect: being with Brooke everyday, being with the friend group, and getting to go and drive places. It felt as if I had no limit to what I could do this summer.

I used to be the type of student that didn't really like breaks, because I wouldn't do much at home to begin with. I also didn't like my routine messed with, so when summer comes it tends to throw everything out of whack. It was a rarity that I would see too much out of the state during the summer, which was boring, but not terrible. I was a homebody, I loved being in my bed with all of my things.

Now that I can drive, the opportunity to actually go do fun things with my friends sounded so good. I sat in my fifth period very patiently watching the clock tick. Just waiting for the next class to start, so I would be closer to summer. It also wasn't like the teacher's were teaching anything this late in the school-year. Being in the building felt pointless, which added to the long feeling of sitting in class.

There was ten minutes left of fifth period, meaning that there was only three hours left of school. Three hours doesn't seem like a long time, until you sit around counting down the hours, minutes, and seconds. I fidgeted with my utensils, waiting patiently. I could sit in hours of quietness with no problem, but the longer I sat, the longer I thought of all of the things I would do this summer.

After the gruesomely long three hours left of school, I was finally out. When I was leaving the vicinity to go to my car, I saw Paul. I walked up to him, because I wanted to talk to someone about the summer. All the ideas that were stuck in my head were bursting, waiting to be put in action.

"Are you ready for summer?" I asked Paul enthusiastically. I held a very bright smile on my face.

"Of course I am! Are you?" He was matching the enthusiasm in my voice.

"Oh yeah, I wanted to see what you planned on doing." In asking I had hope that plans would be similar.

"Oh I thought I had already told you, I'm going to Europe next week." After he said that, there was a shockwave throughout my body I felt.

Europe? How in the world have I not heard about this? I was a little disappointed, but equally happy for him, that he got to do something cool and interesting. While he's in Europe, I'll be stuck in Colorado. How fun.

"Dude, that's awesome! How long are you going to be in Europe" I wanted all of the details for the trip, because I was thinking at the very worst he might be there for maybe two weeks.

"I'll be there for about two and a half months." Once he said that there was slight frustration in my body language.

You gotta be kidding me, two whole months with no Paul. I know it's not that big of a deal, especially because he'll have fun, but what am I going to do now? I do still have Brooke, so it wasn't all bad. What about the group? Paul was the life of the group, and he's not going to be here, for basically all summer.

After the exchange I went to my car frustrated, and perplexed. It was strange how this wasn't brought up at all until he's about to leave. I went around the fact that Paul wouldn't be here, and came up with a barrage of more things I could do with different people.

When I came home I rushed my routine, hoping that the clock would read around night, so I could get ready for the last day of my freshman year. It's crazy that this was the end of the beginning. This year was great, so I wonder what the next three have in store. I was ready and prepared. I didn't want to wish my life away, but I was ambitious.

I managed to go to sleep early, and woke up with a full set of energy. This was it, the last day. I knew it would be like any other day, but I was so ready for what would follow. Everything I had planned I just knew it would work out. Obviously it didn't start good with Paul going to Europe, but other than that everything was going to go according to plan.

When I walked into the first period I didn't even set my bag down. Instead I walked straight up to Mr. Richard's desk, and gave him a warm-felt hug. It seemed necessary, he helped me beyond my imagination. Without him, I would've never started talking to Brooke. I wouldn't have gotten more comfortable out of my shell. He really helped me grow as a person. I knew a hug wasn't much, but I was hoping it would be enough to show my gratitude towards him.

"You're welcome, Landon." He whispered trying to make it seem less strange to my peers.

I didn't care. The girls who always bickered and laughed wouldn't understand. The two basketball players that sat in the back wouldn't understand. The only person who could possibly understand was Brooke, and when I let go of Mr. Richards, she was looking at me with a lovely grin.

I sat at my desk, which was just Paul,. Brooke, and I, and talked about the details of Paul's trip. Apparently Paul didn't tell many people, because Brooke was as surprised as I was when she heard that he was going to Europe.

During his trip Paul stated that he would be visiting: Italy, Greece, France, and Spain. His family was spending two weeks in each country. The sights he would see intrigued me, so I asked if he would take pictures for me. He nodded his head agreeing he would. I was still bummed out that he wouldn't be able to hang out with me this summer, but I did my best to act as if it didn't bother me.

The rest of the day seemed oddly standard. Nobody seemed as excited for the break as I was. Seeing the dull expression of the school kind of hollowed me out. It was strange to see everyone not as happy for the end of school as I once anticipated.

When I was getting ready to go to my car Tony approached me. He looked very tired and filled with anxiety.

"Are you okay Tony?" I knew I had to say the first words, or we wouldn't talk.

"Yeah I was just gonna see if I could come home with you today." he gave a fake smile, trying to mask his real emotions.

He had a sense of fear in his eyes, and that he was hiding something. I was slightly concerned for him, and he knew that he was welcome to my house.

"Yeah of course. Is everything alright?" I wanted to make sure he was safe when asking my question, because he was starting to look around like someone was coming for him.

"Yeah I'm fine, I just don't want to go home yet." He continued to look around, while he got closer to my car.

Seeing how anxious he was I unlocked the car, and we both got inside swiftly. I looked at him to see if anything was indicating he was in danger. He wasn't breathing hard, wasn't sweating, and wasn't bleeding. I felt weird continuing to ask what was wrong, so I decided to comfort him instead.

I turned on his favorite musician on the way to my house, and turned the volume up loud enough, so if he wanted to talk we could. We didn't talk the entire car ride, which made sense for Tony, but was slightly concerning me.

I didn't want to make a big deal of it, but I had to. So when we made it to my house, invited him into my room, and told him I had to talk to mom really quickly. Mom was home early, because she got off early every other friday.

"I think there might be something wrong with Tony, but I don't know what it would be." Mom could hence the concern within my voice. I kept a low tone, so there wouldn't be a chance that Tony would hear me talking about him.

"What do you mean?" Mom began to share my worries. The look of concern I had traveled to hers.

"I don't know, he just seems scared." I held a stale voice while talking.

"Scared?" She was becoming confused, the same way I was.

"Yeah. Like something's out to get him." I responded. We wondered what to make of the situation.

Even mom didn't have the answer I was looking for, so I left the room to go back to where Tony was. He sat on the side of my bed with an empty expression. He was playing with the snowglobe tha Brooke had gotten me.

He acknowledged that I entered the room, but didn't pay me any attention. Just sat there and played with the snowglobe. I sat there next to him, and turned on the television.

"What do you want to watch Tony?" I tried to portray an inviting voice, but it was to no avail.

"It doesn't matter to me." He said with his head down. His voice made it seem as if he was sad.

He was admiring the look of the gift I received from Brooke. I know that he was a shy guy, but this seemed so strange. There must've been something wrong. Maybe he was just tired, I don't know, but I hope if something was wrong, that it isn't too bad. Last time I had suspicions like this, I ruined Jackson's family, and I'd hate to repeat that.

I still blame myself for what happened in Texas. I was ashamed of what I had caused, and decided to not tell anyone here, besides Brooke. I asked her that she wouldn't share that with anyone, and I only assumed she did.

Tony looked up to the television once the flashing illumination from a show had started. Once the show started his demeanor slightly changed. It was for the better. He held a better posture to watch the show, and seemed more engaged.

This is not how I imagined the start of summer would be like. It wasn't even the start of summer yet. We just got out of school only two hours ago, but the uneasy feeling I had with Tony was not a great way to begin this break. Not that I have a problem with Tony, because I don't whatsoever, but his grim mood was bringing my mood down with him. I just felt bad for him, but I didn't know what for. I also didn't want to keep asking him, because he kept to himself. I also knew that his life at home wasn't the best, and school was a get away from that.

The rest of the time we spent, he slowly increased his mood positively. It was nice to watch how he was becoming happy, if only for a short period of time.

"It's getting late, man." I didn't want to sound as if I was kicking him out, but I knew his parents would want him home by now.

"Yeah I guess so. It's time to go home." He sounded as if the thought of going home made him depressed.

I was doubting if I should even take him home. He seemed so uncomfortable with leaving, and I hated seeing the despair in his eyes. How could I help him? It's not like I could just kidnap him. I had to take him home.

When we got in the car and started driving, he stared out the window looking at the stars. He wasn't as dull as he was when he was looking at the stars. I wanted to talk, but I didn't want to interrupt whatever was going through his mind. So I kept driving, while occasionally peering over to him.

We made it to his house after a short period of time. He let out a big sigh after seeing that he was home. It was sad, I knew his home life wasn't the best, but I didn't know to what extent.

"Stay safe, I need you dude." I lightly said while he stepped out of the car.

"Thank you, Landon." He closed the door and slowly trudged to his front door.

I couldn't imagine what he was going through. Although what if it's not bad at all? What if it has nothing to do with his home life? He wouldn't leave school looking around if he worried about his house. I absorbed my thinking of what he could possibly be going on with him. Tony didn't deserve any pain in his life. He always follows suit and never causes any problems.

Once I got back home I called Brooke to see what she wanted to do tomorrow to help me get my mind off of Tony. Which sounds selfish, but I didn't want to assume, or even worse, I didn't want to be right. Once Brooke and I started talking my mind focused more onto summer. I wanted to see what would be fun to do, but we couldn't come up with anything at all. We lived in a decently populated town, but nobody ever did anything. There weren't any venues to visit or activities to do. Both of our minds drew blanks.

We decided on meeting up together and just figuring out what to do. That worked with me. I just wanted any reason to be with her, even if nothing happened. At least I would be getting to waste my time with her if we ended up doing nothing.

I slept that night tossing and turning and was not

able to sleep. I was still thinking about Tony. Who would know what to do? After thinking, the obvious answer was Paul. I texted Paul asking what was wrong with Tony, if there was anything we could do to help him, if there was a potential problem. As I sent the text I realized it was one in the morning, so I probably wouldn't get a text back until the morning. So after hoping that Paul would have the answer I went to sleep.

The next morning I woke up thinking of things that Brooke and I could do, so she wouldn't be completely bored. Recalling my main concern from last night, I checked my phone. Paul answered very bland, it may be because he was still waking up and wasn't answering fully consciously. I decided not to answer him right away, and went to the living room. The sun looked colorful and vivid, as it touched the sky. Something was telling me that today would be a good day.

A couple hours went by while I was waiting. I didn't want to bother Brooke, but I also couldn't wait any longer. With slight hesitation I started typing to text her. As I was she had already sent a message saying that she would be ready by four o'clock. That was another two full hours of waiting. I was getting more bored with each minute passing. I could have easily texted Paul back to see what the solution to the problem could possibly be, but I didn't know how to initiate that conversation. It could all be just a figure of my imagination, making problems where there doesn't have to be one. Sometimes I overthink for the better, but I would rather just not think about anything at all.

While I was waiting I decided to go lay back down to take a nap. I was hoping that I would sleep for about an hour and a half, so I would still have time to make it to where we planned on meeting up that afternoon. When I initially laid down, it didn't seem likely for me to fall asleep. I wasn't tired at all, I was just hoping I would convince my body it would be a nice way to pass the time. After about fifteen minutes of just laying down, I started to drift to sleep. As I was drifting to sleep I felt a vibration from my phone. I picked it up momentarily to see what it was from. It was a message from Paul, asking why I was concerned. Many ideas for answers came rushing to my head, but I became fatigued with making my way to sleep, so I decided to not answer. As I was falling asleep I was thinking of the reasons I was concerned about Tony.

A part of me couldn't let go of what happened to Jackson, no matter how hard I tried to suppress the feeling. I couldn't go a day without thinking of that failure, and now he has to live with a childhood friend who can't even remember him. It hurt, because I knew that I ignited the flame when the box was full of matches. I haven't even talked to him since I left Texas. I wanted to really bad, but I was too embarrassed. What can a person do to the victim of their own malicious actions? It wasn't done because I wanted to ruin his life. The malice of everything that happened wasn't intentional. It felt as if there was a domino effect and I had a chance to stop the piece from falling, but I continued to let everything fall into disaster.

So much negative self-talk I had for myself, because I didn't know what to do about the mistakes I made. I could still see Mr. West's body on the floor when I closed my eyes. I imagine being in Jackson's position with the blood of my father stained to my hands. Now I've never had a father, but I know that's never how the relationship should be. The bond between a son and his father should be unbreakable, but of course I broke it.

When I woke up for my nap I checked the time to see that it was already four. Immediately panicked when I saw that Brooke had already tried to call me. I hopped out of bed as fast as possible, and ran to tell mom that I was leaving. She let me go seeing that I was in a rush, just saying to "be careful." I didn't care if I was careful or not, I didn't want to be late.

I zoomed across the city to meet her at the burger place I promised to meet her. While I was driving fast, but careful enough to not get pulled over again, I thought about the text from Paul earlier. I went to my messages to see Paul's text again. I started to text and drive, looking up at the road every other second to make sure that I wouldn't crash. I continued to text while I was driving, and as I finished the text I saw a car incoming. I became shocked and my reflexes took over, making me veer over to avoid the car.

After that near-crash experience I paid full attention to the road until I eventually got there. As I pulled into the parking lot, I saw that she was still in her car. I could tell she was waiting for me, and I felt really bad seeing that I was ten minutes late.

I parked the car and jumped out to greet her by knocking on her window. She invited me into her car with a wave of her hand. I walked over and opened the door hoping she wouldn't be upset in my tardiness.

"Why were you so late?" She put her hand on top of mine, with some concern layered in her voice.

"I woke up really late, I thought I wouldn't sleep as long as I did. I'm sorry." I was hoping that I would have good enough reasoning so she wouldn't be concerned or think I was lazy.

"It's ok." she said after giving out a sigh.

She smiled at me knowing I felt bad that I was late, but I didn't want to seem as if it was okay that I was late. I didn't want to make a big deal of it, but I also didn't want to make a habit out of being tardy to Brooke and I's dates.

Instead of going inside to eat, we continued to sit inside of the car and talk about what we planned on doing. Our conversation turned to what we wanted to do during the summer. I didn't want to tell her that I really wanted to spend most of the break with her, because I was afraid I'd sound too clingy. Which I didn't mean to sound weird, but I really wanted to spend a lot of time with her. She made me not have a care in the world, as if nothing could make me worried as long as she was in my presence.

There was a brief moment of silence. We locked our eyes and I just couldn't help but to smile. I was just admiring the way she looked. Everything about her was perfect. It didn't matter to me what we planned on doing, at least we would get to be together. If I could hear my thoughts I probably would laugh at myself. I didn't care, I was content with what I had.

"Do you just wanna drive around?" She sounded enthusiastic, which made me want to nod my head yes. So I did.

She put the car in reverse and drove out of the lot. I had a small rush of adrenaline, seeing that we got out of the parking lot so swiftly. I had no idea where we were going, but wherever we went wouldn't bother me.

Then I realized we left my car.

"What about my car?" I was a little paranoid, thinking about the possibility of someone breaking in.

"Don't worry about it, we'll be back." She responded while taking a hard left that led to the interstate.

I didn't know what we were about to do, but I was concerned, because she didn't even have her license yet. Mom knew I was going to be with Brooke, but I anticipated she wouldn't want me going on the interstate. The nerves started rushing my thinking. Were we safe? That was the one question that continuously came to mind. Before I knew it we were on the interstate going over seventy miles per hour, with someone who isn't legally allowed to drive. My breathing became quickened, and panic started to come in.

"Relax, we're going to be alright." She said while trying to catch my gaze with her, but that only put more worry into me.

"Look at the road! What are we doing?" The fear in my voice was audible.

We were passing cars regularly, so I thought that we must've been speeding. It was only a matter of time until we would get pulled over, and she gets arrested.

We drove a little more until she got off at an exit. I recognized where we were going. It was a national park. Why would she want to come here of all places? I didn't want to question her thinking, so I just agreed to follow her. Other than her driving, I knew she wouldn't put us in harm's way.

"Alright let's go." Brooke said as she parked the car and unbuckled her seatbelt.

I didn't say a word, and just got out of the car. The air was a little brisk, but it was definitely bearable. Was she wanting to go on the trail? If so I wasn't well equipped for what could happen. I had on a plain hoodie that wasn't fit for the weather over a long stretch of time. How long did she even intend on being here? I wanted to stop her, but before I could she looked back at me with a smile.

"C'mon Landon, I want to show you this view." She kept her smile after saying her comment.

I couldn't stop her. I've already been on this trail numerous times, but never with her. She also wasn't the type of person to go on any trails, so this might have been an experience she wanted to share.

As I caught up to her, I couldn't help, but admire her beauty. She was beautiful, and the most eye catching person I could ever lay eyes on. I gave a smile of my own, that wasn't visible to her. I still couldn't wipe the grin from my face, just thinking about her.

I continued to follow her, and listen to her talk about her reflection of the school-year. She said a lot of things pertaining to me. Maybe because I was in her presence, but it genuinely seemed as if I was a huge factor in her school-year. I didn't want to chirp in, and sound self-centered, but I was just so surprised how much I affected her. It really put some of my overthinking into perspective. Should I have really worried as much as I did walking into Mr. Richard's class every morning? If this is how she felt about me, why was I scared to mess up? It was crazy to see how oblivious I was to how reciprocated my feelings towards her were. Hearing her speak about some things that occurred throughout the year made me think that she may be a really bad overthinker as well. Maybe it was my fault because I wasn't very clear-cut with my communication at times, but when she mentioned the time she spilt her water over herself one day it made me realize.

She said that she was on the verge of tears when she did that, because it was in front of me. I didn't make a big deal of it and got up to get her napkins to help dry off her accident. While I was gone she explained how she felt like a complete fool, and that I would think less of her, because of something that insignificant.

It really amazed me to listen to her and hear her perspective fully when I've been so narrow-minded with my own thinking. She was telling me all of this in an enthusiastic tone, as if she was waiting till she had the courage to tell me some of the stories she did. I wondered how she thought about what I thought of her. Should I even ask? I assume that it couldn't be negative or we wouldn't be all the way out in a national park hiking together, but a part of me wanted to know for sure.

"Brooke…" I called out to her from a few steps away, while I grabbed her hand.

"Landon." She responded in a mocking voice, teasing me.

"I think you're perfect the way you are." I wanted to drain any doubt of how I felt about her.

She seemed speechless. She looked down at my hand holding hers, then looked back up at me. She had to have something on her mind, but I didn't want to intrude her thinking, so I just looked into her eyes with the same smile I had from before.

"Thank you…the end isn't that far now." She responded as if she snapped out of a trance.

The rest of the walk was awkward silence, and I was confused. Did she think negatively about the comment? I convinced myself to stop the needless worry and enjoy the time being spent with her.

We finally arrived at our destination. The view was astonishing, the sight of the fauna and how it clashed with the sunsetting-sky was picturesque. There was a nearby bench we went over to, to finally relax after that hefty walking we did. When sitting I got to enjoy the moment a little more, not worrying about the throbbing pain in my feet.

"Isn't it beautiful?" Brooke said to me, as we looked over everything.

She was admiring the view, but I couldn't help but to admire her.

"Not as much as you." A response that would take everything in me to muster up, flowed out of my mouth. It was how I truly felt, so it seemed natural to say.

We watched the sunset in its entirety. It was very calming, getting to experience this moment with someone I had deep intimate feelings for. I looked over to her, and she was already looking at me. Her gaze was more of a side eye, but I could tell she was wanting to say something, so I turned my attention fully towards her. I felt as if I knew what she was planning to say. She directed her attention to match my demeanor. I wrapped my arm around her shoulder to be closer with her.

We both at the same time while having our eyes interlocked, indulging the feeling said, "I love you."

XIII

A month of summer has passed. Paul off doing who knows what in Europe. Brooke and I have been together a good amount through this beginning stage of summer. It's been all I could ask for, but even with things going right something felt off. It may be because I was overthinking every time that Brooke and I hung out. I thought about each possibility and its outcome.

It was near the end of June and the summer wasn't everything I imagined it to be. Something was just making the break feel as if it was just another long weekend, before school starts again. I was having fun, but it didn't feel like summer fun. I wasn't having the late night experiences with friends, and that's not gonna happen with Paul in Europe. That could change soon, we still have a month and a half before the thought of school is even brought up again.

Was I supposed to be doing something? I didn't want to keep bothering Brooke. She doesn't want to see me every single day I imagine, but as always she's been the main source of happiness. I couldn't see her perspective, so it became a little harder to keep asking her to hangout with me. I didn't know if I was starting to become intrusive, and not letting her enjoy her break the way she intended.

For the rest of the week I didn't ask her to do anything, and decided to stay to myself. I had nothing else to do, so I sat around staring at my four walls. What else was I supposed to do? Paul was in Europe, Matt was always with Sara, Tony seemed like he didn't want to be around anyone, and I couldn't keep bothering Brooke. That means the only other person left is Ryan. I've never really been with him, and it's just him and I. I have no idea why we haven't been around each other with just the two of us, but it just never seems to happen.

Ryan's family is definitely the most financially stable, and he acts very classy. Although he doesn't act like your typical rich kid, you could just tell the economic difference between us. His father is a neurosurgeon, and his mother is a pediatrician. Meaning, they make a lot of money. Ryan could probably ask for a brand new lamborghini for his birthday, and it could happen without hurting his family's pockets. The whole friend group knew this about Ryan, and he is a very humble and modest person, so we don't really talk about it. He's more kind than his parents from what I've heard from Matt. Maybe because his parents were stressed from their jobs, which is completely understandable, but he made them sound like arrogant people. Which doesn't resemble Ryan at all.

While I was thinking about Ryan, I got a buzz from my phone. I picked it up to see what the notification had to say. I couldn't believe it when it said that it was a message from Ryan. He was inviting me to dinner and to stay over. The last time I stayed over someone's house was Jackson's house. The memories from that situation came flooding back, when having the initial idea of spending the night away from home. I didn't want to answer right away. I didn't even know what to say, to be honest. I couldn't shake my lingering thoughts of how I ruined Jakcson's life by staying at his house for only three days. What if I do the same thing to Ryan's family? I've already heard things about his parents that put them in a negative light. I also didn't want to have prejudice against people without giving them a chance first.

After a little while more of nulling Ryan's offer, I finally decided that it would be better for me, than continuing to stare at the same four walls I've been looking at. I answered back, asking when I should come over. He let me know that I should be there by seven, because that was the time they intended to eat dinner. That was about four hours from now. I didn't worry about getting ready until about thirty minutes until seven.

Our city was broken into different financial districts, and the middle class people were positioned relatively close to those of higher class. I told myself when I got there that I would be extremely quiet, outside of kind generalities, and thanking his family for the meal.

The time to go over to his house hit me quicker than I expected. I got myself ready to go over, with slight hesitation. I still feared that I would cause the same problems I did for Jackson. I convinced myself that it would be unlikely that those things would occur, but what if they did?

On my way out of the door, I got a text from Brooke asking if she could call me. I answered as soon as I got my things in the car, and was ready to leave. I let her know that she could, and after a couple of seconds of sending the text I was receiving a call from her. I picked up after fumbling my phone in my hand, and put her on speaker so I could drive and talk to her.

"Landon." Her voice was soft. It sounded like she had just woken up from a nap.

"Hey Brooke. Is everything okay?" I was a little concerned, thinking that there might be an issue.

I stopped at the end of my driveway waiting for her response, because her answer would determine the way I needed to turn. I was very willing to make the trip to her house if anything was severely wrong. "Yeah, I was just wondering why we haven't seen each other all week." My heart fluttered a little bit, mostly because I was stunned with confusion.

"I-I thought you didn't want to." I didn't want to make it seem as if I was making an excuse so I said more words cautiously.

"Why would you think that?" She began to start sounding aggravated, and I wasn't meaning to provoke her.

"I didn't think you would want to be with me every single day." I emphasized the last two words to add effect.

"Landon, why would you think that?" Her question put me at a stalemate, and had me staring at my phone, which was displaying her name.

"I really don't know, I just didn't want to intrude on you honestly." I said after moments of silence on my end.

"You're not intruding on me, I want to see you, Landon." She chuckled a little while saying her response.

"Today?" I wasn't considering canceling on Ryan, unless she had something going on.

"Can you see me today?" I didn't like how she answered my question, but now I felt obligated to tell her what my plans were.

"I really would, but I already told Ryan I would eat dinner with his family." I replied with a very basic sounding voice so she probably thought I was lying.

"What about tomorrow?" she asked.

"If I'm not busy, then yes." I said with optimism audible in my sound.

"Fine." Then she hung up the phone.

Was she mad? Did I do something wrong? After hearing the call hang up I looked at my phone to see if there was a problem. Should I call her back? Her hanging up so abruptly caught me off guard. She hung up on purpose so there was no reason to call and bother her.

I drove with curiosity about how I should handle the phone call. The drive to Ryan's was brief. Whenever I arrived at his house, I decided to text Brooke to ask if she was upset. Maybe the answer was obvious, but I wanted to make sure. What was I supposed to say? I was surprised that she even wanted to see me after spending almost every day together. It seemed like since I was the one continuously asking, that I was becoming a nuisance. I didn't want to seem like a chore for her, so I thought that providing space between us would be helpful.

Ryan's driveway was very lengthy. It could've probably fit ten cars. the way it looped around making it easily accessible to enter and leave. It was kind of nice, this is the first time I've been over to see his house. The house was very similar to Jackson's, when comparing the sizes. I was stunned at first, because we had a relatively decent sized city, but I didn't know that we would have houses like the one Ryan has.

As I planned to go in, I got a responding text from Brooke. She asked a question that sounded rethorical. "Do you think I'm mad?" The text read. How was I supposed to respond without making her upset? Was she actually upset? I couldn't read her tone through text, so I was confused on what I should say back. I wasn't wanting to go in before I responded to Brooke.

I decided to call her back, and let my thoughts develop on the spot. As the phone began to rang I was worried she wouldn't even answer. After a couple rings she picked up the phone.

"What?" She sounded annoyed, and not willing to talk.

"Would you be mad if I came to see you tomorrow?" I was hoping to spend time with her and explain why I was hesitant at first.

I didn't want to make it sound like she was ever the second option. I was only worried that I would become redundant in my attempts to see her. Maybe I was her second option, and her first option became limited throughout the week. I think too poorly of how she perceives me. I do know that she loves me, at least I'm pretty sure. It's hard to know for a fact all the time. What if her love from me runs dry? What if she loses her interest all together? Things make me doubt myself. I hate to make it seem as if I need constant reminders of things that should be known, but how can I truly know?

"I wouldn't be mad at all. Come and see me tomorrow, please." Her voice started to sound more inviting, making me feel more comfortable.

"Alright well I'll see you tomorrow, I'm about to go into Ryan's house.

Bye." I said quickly so I can hurry up and go inside.

"Okay, tell Ryan I said 'hi.'" She said as I hung up.

I still had five minutes to spare until seven, but I didn't want to just sit in my car, so I got ready to go to his door. As I walked up the red brick steps that curved upwards, I admired his front porch. The decorative theme was nice, portraying summer colors. I knocked on his door and felt a sense of nervousness blanket my body. There's no reason for me to be nervous, Ryan was one of my closest friends. Why shouldn't I have a nice casual dinner with his family?

Ryan answered shortly after I knocked and welcomed me inside. I looked up to see a crystal chandelier hanging and emitting a beautiful light. Ryan's house was extremely nice. I'm surprised the friend group has never been invited, because there's a good amount of unoccupied space. Ryan did have a sister but she graduated about three years ago. She still had her room ready for her, when she came back from college. They had five bedrooms in the house so it would take a lot of people to fill all of the rooms.

I took a minute to take in everything the house had to offer visually. I can't believe I've never been here. We've been this good of friends, and it seems like he's never even mentioned his house. It was also very random that I was in his house. Why was I invited to his house? Of all people he could have invited he chose me. I didn't want to seem as if

I was being ungrateful, but I was just surprised. Maybe he found himself in the same dilemma, with everyone gone with the summer. He knows I rarely ever leave the state, so I was probably a really reliable person to choose.

I made it to his kitchen to see his parents. They were very short, or at least more than I was expecting. Ryan was an average size guy, so I just assumed his parents were average height as well. His mother was just a hair over five feet tall and his dad was maybe five foot five inches. I towered over them, when they came to greet me.

"Hello, I presume you are Landon?" Ryan's dad said while reaching his hand out to shake mine.

"Yessir, that's me. It's nice to meet you." I said while reaching out to meet his gesture.

"The pleasure is mine." He readjusted his glasses, as he surveyed the way I appeared.

I didn't dress the nicest. I didn't think I had to, I dressed pretty casually, and not like a slob. I didn't think the way I appeared was a problem, until I read the expression on his face. He looked as if I had disgusted him, which I knew that I wasn't the best looking, but he didn't have to make it obvious. I kept my mouth closed unless spoken to, so I wouldn't cause any problems.

His mother simply looked up at me with a forced smile. I was taken aback by the way I was being approached, but I was a lot taller than them, so I might've been intimidating to them. I was doing my best to not say anything, so I wouldn't ruin anything. If I was being judged, I did not care.

Well I did, but I didn't make it look that way.

I sat down at their table, which was very elongated. It was rectangular shaped, with a single chair at each end. I didn't want to cause attention towards myself so I sat along the side, parallel with Ryan. His father sat at the end of the table, which I predicted he would do. It was obvious he would be the type of person to have everyone sit on the sides, besides him. I didn' think too much of it, and just sat properly in the chair I was in, waiting patiently for food.

Ryan's mother brought out a full course meal. It was more food than I was expecting for sure. It all looked so good, and you could see the steam coming out of the food. My mouth watered seeing how good the food was. She made a full turkey, corn on the cob, rolls, gravy, and stuffing. It was a classic Thanksgiving meal, made in midsummer. A part of me wanted to reach out and grab the food with my hands, but I didn't want them to think I was greedy. They definitely had preconceived notions about me I could tell, but I wanted to prove their negative thoughts wrong. I wasn't bothered with having their validation or not, but I wanted to respect their home.

I was still thinking about the phone call with Brooke earlier. I would be spending time with her, instead of eating this amazing food, if I didn't think she wouldn't want to spend time with me. She did seem eager to see me, and I wasn't being forced to be here. It's not like I could just show up at her house this late, and expect to stay over. The Rose family was very fond of me, but I knew they wouldn't let me stay the night. Although it's been a week, and I shouldn't miss her, I did because I feel like she's becoming a part of my routine. So I did miss her. Very short period of time to start missing someone.

The food was looking right at me, ready to be consumed. I was starving, and hadn't eaten all day. I was waiting for my turn to get food, but I didn't want to seem rude.

"You can grab whatever you want, Mr. Morgan." Ryan's mom said to me. I realized I was zoned out and snapped out of my trance when she called out to me.

I acknowledged her words, while keeping my mouth closed. I reached out for the tongs, seeing that I was the last one to grab food. I could feel their eyes seeping into my skull, as they were looking at me grabbing food. I tried my best to have manners and be presenting with my presence. I took each piece of food very cautiously, and carefully. I made sure that nothing had a chance to fall or cause any problems.

By the time my plate was made, I started eating in complete silence.

The table was quiet at first, chewing being the only thing that was audible. The silence was starting to bother me, the closer I got to being finished with my food. Luckily Ryan's father broke the silence.

"So Landon, what are you looking to do after High School?" He folded his hands together, directing his attention to me.

"I'm not one hundred percent sure, but I'm figuring I would want to do something in the medical field." I answered as genuine and truthfully as possible.

"I suppose you are young, but it's good to be prepared." He said with a soothing voice. He was impressed I had an answer ready.

"Yessir, of course." I was trying my best to sound appealing, knowing that they were also in that field.

"Ryan here said he was 'interested in anesthesiology.' Why don't you tell him about that, son?" nodding and focusing his recognition towards Ryan.

"Yeah, I was hoping to go to CSU to get a degree in that, but nothing major." Ryan spoke softly. I could tell he was being timid.

"Good to know what you want." Ryan's father said, as a knock to my response to his question.

I didn't take offense to his comment, and remained silent. I was surprised that he said what he did. I didn't know if he meant he was glad that his son knew what he wanted to do, or if he was encouraging me to have a plan. Although I wasn't even a sophomore yet, so why does it matter yet. There's a lot of seniors that just graduated with no clue on what they want to do.

I really wanted to leave their house, because of the awkward tension I could feel throughout the room. I felt very out of place, and that I didn't need to be there anymore. Would Brooke let me come over this late? It was only half an hour before nine, but being with her would be better than this. Something that seems forced, I hate when things feel forced. I hated that I didn't feel as comfortable as I should around one of my closest friends.

I texted Brooke to ask if I could come see her this late, and almost simultaneously she answered, saying I could. After the meal was finished, I thanked Ryan's family for the meal and was seeing myself out.

"Are you not going to stay the night, Landon?" Ryan asked by the time I was by the front door.

"Uhh-I would, but umm- my mom was wanting me home before ten." I responded by trying to come up with a decent lie on the spot. I felt bad for lying, but I was going to feel worse being in a situation where things felt forced.

"I thought you said it was okay with her." He said. Which is true, mom did say she would be okay with me staying.

"Yeah she just texted me, saying I should come home, because she was worrying about me." The lies were flowing out of my mouth, and it was terrible.

"Oh…well okay. Have a good night." Ryan said while waving goodbye.

"Yeah you too…goodnight, and thank you for having me over." I said while walking out the front door.

When I closed the door to leave, I could hear the crickets outside, and my thoughts talking to me. I felt really bad for lying, I hated to lie, but I did want to see Brooke. I also was not feeling as invited as I should've while being there. The whole ordeal was off, and I wanted to avoid the same mistakes I made when in Texas.

I had some nerves in asking for confirmation, to see if I could go to Brooke's house. It was late, and although I was on friendly terms with her parents, what were the odds of them letting a teenage boy stay the night at the house. I needed a back up plan, so when this doesn't work I'll have somewhere to sleep. I can't just go back home, I'll get grounded, especially if I go and stay at Brooke's for a couple of hours. I had no ideas for a plan, I just texted Brooke to make sure I could come.

She notified me, letting me know that it would be okay. I made sure that she double checked with her parents, and she said I would have to talk to them when I got there. That struck fear into my heart. I wasn't very intimidated by her parents, mostly because they were very hospitable and welcoming, but I didn't want them to have the wrong impression of me. Would I look like a bad person for trying to stay the night? Do they think that I would be trying to do sexual things with their daughter? I mean we've only ever kissed, and I'm pretty sure neither of us are ready for that next step. What are even the odds that they think that fifteen and sixteen year old kids would be wanting to do that in an occupied house. That would be flat out weird.

The drive on the way to her house I was thinking of all the ways I could come off as respectable as possible. I was willing to sleep on their couch, or even on the floor, it didn't matter to me. I was building up with anxiety, just knowing they would say no. I could've easily made up a lie to convince them, but I wasn't even letting that idea materialize. I couldn't fathom using their kindness, to avoid warranted trouble I would get myself into.

By the time I arrived at their house, my nerves started to dissipate. Why should I be worried? Especially when my expectations are for them to say no. What's the worst that could happen then? Well I guess they could make me stop talking to Brooke completely, but that seemed like an extreme. It was a possibility though, was I really risking the relationship that Brooke and I built for one night's sleep. When I parked the car all the bad possibilities came back to storm my mind. I was really about to ask if I could spend the night at Brooke Rose's house. What was I doing? Was this really my best option? It had to be my only, because I found myself walking to her front door. I was built up with the same nerves I had when I came to her house and met her parents for the first time.

I knocked gently, hoping to not raise any alarm, or maybe not even be noticed. Within seconds, Brooke came racing to the door to answer it. She had a big smile when she opened the door. My face matched her expression almost instantly, because of how much I've missed her. Even with it being a short period of time. She looked so good, even with only standing here in pajamas. I was so glad to see her, but super nervous to do what I mainly prioritized.

When entering her house I immediately saw her mom and dad sitting in the living room with their pets watching television. Mr. Rose was in a recliner with their dog in his lap, while Mrs. Rose was at the end of the couch. She was sitting proximal to Mr. Rose, to where they could touch each other. They all looked so happy. They seemed even more delighted when they saw me enter. I was thankful that her family viewed me so positively. They were watching a family movie, and invited me to watch it with them. I quietly walked over and sat on their couch politely. I was trying my best to not disrupt the movie. As I settled in, Brooke came and sat next to me. She got really close, and put her head on my shoulder, and let out a big sigh. I peered over to her parents to see their reaction, but they looked at the two of us together with a warm grin. Seeing how they viewed us so close and didn't have a problem with it, made me relax. I felt content with the moment and joined in with watching the movie without really knowing what was happening. Brooke positioned her blanket she had so we could both share it.

"Here you go, I don't want you to be cold." she whispered, while trying to find the perfect way to lay the blanket over the both of us.

"Thank you." I said while embarrassing her more.

My face relayed a smile that went from ear to ear. It was so peaceful being here. I didn't care about what the movie was really about, I was just glad to be with Brooke.

"Does anybody want snacks?" Mr. Rose said while getting up from his chair.

"No sir." I said after a few moments of silence.

I looked at Brooke to make sure the random raise of my voice to call out to her dad didn't bother her. She looked up at me, and we locked eyes for a few seconds. We both looked back at the television to break the tension. In the movie there was a scene of the two main characters sharing a kiss.

"Aww isn't that just the cutest thing?" Mrs. Rose said, with a tone that made her heart seem like it was melted.

I looked back at Brooke and she looked up at me. After another few seconds of eye contact, we both let out a little chuckle. I couldn't take my eyes off of her. She was so beautiful, and everything was so peaceful and perfect.

By the time the movie came to an end Brooke was

completely asleep resting on my shoulder. I didn't want to move and disturb her at all, so I sat as still as humanly possible.

"She's going to be like that for a while honey. Feel free to stay the night if you guys can keep everything 'PG.'" Mrs. Rose said while preparing to go to her room.

"Are you sure you're okay with me staying?" I was making sure I heard her correctly, while maintaining a whisper so I didn't wake Brooke. "Of course we trust you, you're a good kid." Mrs. Rose responded calmly.

I looked over to Mr. Rose to see what he thought of me staying, and to my surprise he nodded his head in agreement to his wife. Mr. Rose was getting the dog to leave the room. You could hear the jingle of their dog's collar. I looked at Brooke to make sure it didn't bother her, but she didn't budge.

"Goodnight kiddos." Mr. Rose said while him and Mrs. Rose exited the room to go to theirs.

They turned off the light making the living room pitch black. I closed my eyes, making my current position a resting position, so Brooke could sleep in peace. I didn't want her to feel alarmed by any movements so I paced my breathing to slow down, so I could match hers.

"Did they leave?" She whispered with her eyes closed. I was startled at first, when I heard her speak.

"Yeah. Were you awake this entire time?" I was very confused, if she was faking the whole time.

193

"I'm almost asleep, but I didn't want you to be uncomfortable." Her response made my heart shake. She was thinking of my comfort, before even letting herself sleep.

"Well thank you, but I'm okay." I wanted to reassure her with my words, so she could sleep, because I viewed her comfort and safety way more important than my own.

"Well we can lay down if you want. I also really want you to hold me, so we should lay down." She was very suggestive with the way she spoke.

After hearing that I repositioned myself so we could lay together. She moved the blanket with her so we would both be covered. My feet were exposed, but it didn't matter to me, because Brooke was okay. Her back was to me so I could fully grasp on to her.

"Landon." Brooke lightly said to me.

"Brooke?" I was concerned that I was doing something wrong, and making her uncomfortable.

She turned over facing me, so we could be face to face. Her looks were breathtaking. I had so much on my mind, about all of the positive things I could say to her, but I didn't want to interrupt what she could potentially say. We closed our eyes for a few moments in unison.

"Thank you for coming, Landon." she said calmly, as if she needed me to be here.

"I'll always be here if you need me, I promise." I opened my eyes to look directly into hers.

I was stunned to see that she was already looking into mine. She made me feel wanted, and that I belonged with her. Even if we were only on her couch in the living room, while her parents were sleeping about twenty feet away.

She kissed me and held contact for a moment that could last forever. Although the occurrence was very spontaneous, everything felt very intimate. As her lips left mine she put her head against mine.

"I know you will be, thank you." She whispered with a very soothing voice.

I didn't know what to say, so I just held her hoping that my presence would be enough for her, because she was everything I needed. She was in my arms, just like I could ever wish. Finally able to sleep with the girl I loved. A night that I wish I could live in forever, because I just wanted to be with her as my eyes closed. No matter the circumstance, because when we're this close I know nothing could possibly go wrong.

XIV

The next morning I woke up to Brooke petting her dog. He had come into the room licking her. I didn't have any pets, so the thought of that was weird to me, but she seemed to enjoy it. She slowly wiggled off of the couch that we were on and headed for the kitchen.

Her parents were already in the kitchen, sharing a cup of coffee. I was surprised to see that they didn't wake us when they got up. I was even more surprised that they were okay with us sleeping together. Although it's not like we were being inappropriate in any way. We were just young, I couldn't imagine my mom letting Brooke stay the night at our house. I remembered that when we came back from Texas she was there with me when I was sleeping, but then it was only evening.

When I woke up that same night, she was gone. At first I thought it was a dream, but when I woke up I could tell it was real. I still smelled her fragrance, when I went to the bathroom, and came back to my room. I was glad to know that moment was real, even if she didn't get to stay the whole night. Maybe one day she could stay at my house, and without having an excuse of being traumatized. At least with the trauma I developed from going to Texas I would remember how Brooke was there when I was back, but essentially broken.

When I walked to the kitchen to join Brooke's family, they had food prepared. They had a nice plate of eggs and bacon ready for Brooke and I.

I was still waking up with yawns and stretching.

"Did you two sleep well?" Mrs. Rose said while sipping on the rest of her coffee.

I felt weird to answer from my perspective, so I sat down and looked at Brooke hoping she would answer for me. She looked at me, looking as if she was waiting for me to answer. She was visibly holding in a laugh. I was trying to signal to her subliminally, so they wouldn't think we did anything bad. The fact that they had enough trust for me to stay the night spoke levels to me.

"It was…nice." Brooke muttered, continuing to hold in her smile. I looked at her wide-eyed thinking that we were going to get in trouble, because of her tone.

Her parents didn't seem to care too much about what we did. Maybe they checked in on us periodically, to make sure we were being respectful to their unwritten rules. I wasn't sure but I was glad that they didn't appear to have any problems, at least not on the surface.

I was very hungry, so in the most polite way possible, I scarfed the food down. I looked up while I was half way done, to see that everyone was looking at me. I became self-conscious, and slowed down eating. They all collectively laughed, and I started to laugh with them, because I knew they weren't laughing at me. Her family made me feel like I belonged, the best feeling a family could ever give an outsider.

Once we were all finished with our food, I helped Mrs. Rose clean up the mess. I decided to wash the dishes, because she mentioned the dishwasher being broken recently. I grabbed Brooke and I's plate and took it to the sink to clean it. Mrs. Rose attempted to not let me wash it, but I was adamant with my attempt to clean, and she eventually obliged to letting me help.

"Thank you for letting me stay the night." I said while still looking at the first dish, while cleaning it profusely.

"Of course, we trust you, we know you won't do anything to disrespect us." Mrs. Rose was very understanding, not even knowing that I wanted to originally stay, but still allowing me to.

The rest of the talk was small, and I felt like being quiet, knowing that I would be having to go home soon. I prepared myself to get ready to leave just in case I was told to leave bluntly. I figured they wouldn't do that, but

I didn't want to feel like I was extending my visit more than I should.

As it started to seem necessary I started saying my goodbyes and saw myself out. They all wished me safe travels back home, and I was out the door. I didn't have any text from anyone besides Paul. He informed me that he was back in the United States after what seemed like forever. I haven't seen my best friend since the very beginning of summer. Even that time was short lived.

I started my car and made it home without the radio on. I just wanted to reflect on last night, no sound was needed. I have all of the noise saying how much I appreciated the time I spent with Brooke. After what was a short trip, because of my time spent reminiscing I was home. My mom greeted me with a smile and a hug.

"How was it?" She was interested in how my night went, not knowing what I truly did. So I had to be uncommunicative.

"It was really fun." I was being generic but she could tell I was hiding something.

"Oh really? What did you guys do?" She took a moment to look at me after asking the question. I started to get riled up with nerves, but did my best to keep composure.

"We…watched a movie." I wasn't lying so I sounded confident in my answer when I spoke.

"Hmmm sounds fun. I guess." Mom was skeptical, but decided to not question me any further.

I'm glad she didn't, because I definitely would've broken my self-control. When I got to my room I wore a smile that went from ear to ear, not being able to help myself, but to think about Brooke. She really made me feel wanted, even with us not doing anything too special. Just the reciprocated feelings that were displayed physically and emotionally made me feel like everything was worth it. She made me feel a certain way words couldn't describe, but a way I knew that nobody else could make me feel. It was so strange to me all of the different sensations I could feel after just one night, but I'm glad that it was with her. Maybe it's because I'm young and immature in relationships, but I think this is what love is really like.

I responded to Paul, to see when he would get back. He said that his flight was delayed, so he wouldn't be back in the area until tomorrow. I'm sure he wanted to rest at least a couple days, so I wanted to just leave him alone.

...

Before I knew it a month had passed and things were looking very normal. Things became routine again. I was hanging with Brooke, Paul, and the rest of the friend group regularly. School was about to start in a single week, and it felt like summer went by so fast. During the break some days felt so long and now that it's over, I look back and think I should've valued that time more. The time I spent with Brooke was worth every second, and that was only our first summer together. Although I got to spend a lot of time with Brooke, I really missed Paul, and the rest of the group. Usually I spend most of the summer with them, but we all became so distant over the break. I knew it wouldn't be a problem when we got to school, because we've all been so close for as long as we can remember, even after not seeing each other over long periods of time.

I was supposed to get my schedule today at school. I was a little nervous, just because this meant school was really here. That means I'm really a sophomore, and I only have three years left until I'm done with school. Well there's still college, but the fact I have to actually consider college now made me realize how fast time was going by. A weird realization to see how close I am to the end.

I sat around my house waiting for the time to for me to get my schedule. I was praying that I would have similar classes to all of my friends, especially Brooke. I had a certain amount of doubt that made me believe that I wouldn't have classes with anyone I liked.

Even with the redundancy of school, I still was anxious to go back. Even though it irked me, there was comfort in having a routine. I knew I wouldn't be thinking the same thing when the time comes, but being out of the loop of seeing all of my friends on a daily basis was bothersome.

It was finally time for me to get a schedule, and mom said she would be going with me. It seemed strange that she was coming. Not because I was embarrassed, but I felt like I was getting to the point where I'm grown, and I don't need my mom to be by my side at school. There was probably a good reason for this, making sure the kids don't go haywire after not seeing each since last school year.

In the car I was pretty quiet, contemplating the different outcomes, from different schedules. It seemed very unlikely that I would be in a class with most of my friends, but I wanted my delusions to materialize. School was easy for the most part, so I was really going for social interactions. Mom tried to talk to me in the car, but everything she said was going in one ear and out the other. Not to say what she was saying didn't matter, I was just too involved with my worrisome thoughts.

Once we made it to school, I was too nervous to even leave the car, but I knew I had to. I thought about how I wouldn't have these nerves in just a month. With thinking that I was hoping those ideas would translate to now so I wouldn't be as trepidatious to go in. Even though I've only been to the high school building for a single year, coming back felt nostalgic. The school looked old, which it wasn't new by any means, but coming up as a freshman everything appeared brand new. True imagery covered by my own figmentary imagination.

On entering the building I was immediately greeted by Mr. Richards. He was good to see and made all of my nerves release. I was glad he was here, even with a slim chance of me having him again this year, because he primarily taught freshmen. His only other class he taught that wasn't freshmen, consisted of juniors and seniors, so I was ways before that was even a possibility.

"Hey Landon! You're a sight for sore eyes." He smiled as he greeted me, with the smile I've grown accustomed to him having.

"Hey Mr. Richards it's good to see you." There was an act of a small child when I answered him.

"It's great to see you as well. How was your summer?" He sounded genuinely interested in my break.

"Really good." I didn't want to go into too much detail, seeing that he was probably busy.

"Are you still with Miss Rose?" He smiled seeing that I started to blush when he asked about Brooke.

"Yessir." I broke eye contact, trying to hide my blush and embarrassment.

Mr. Richards chuckled, and patted me on the shoulder as he walked away. Mom looked at me with a peculiar face, probably wondering why I blushed. I don't even know why I did it myself, I thought I would be used to this feeling by now, but every time I hear her name it's like a new sensation.

Students and parents were instructed to go to our cafeteria, to receive our new schedule. In the cafeteria they had different tables designated to our names. It was pretty easy to find my table, because they were alphabetically organized. I saw the table that everyone would sit at, and took a moment to reminisce about the memories shared in this confined area. It was funny to think that nobody besides the people that sit there, know the significance of that spot.

Once I got to the table marked "K-M" I asked for my schedule. After about a minute of searching they had my paper ready for me. I practically snatched it out of the lady's hand, and read it over to see what I had. I saw that it was similar to last year's structure, with most of my common classes being towards the end of the day. I also had interesting electives, like Spanish, art, and psychology. I was really interested in psychology so seeing that I had a class to actually learn more about the topic intrigued me. I didn't know what anybody else had, because they just now allowed parents and students to come get schedules.

"Do you want to meet your teachers?" My mom asked suggestively. I could tell she was really invested in me getting better at coming out of my social shell, but I didn't want to have to see my teachers until school started.

I walked off without saying anything thinking that maybe, she'll get the hint. Mom kept egging me on trying to convince me it was a good idea, until I was subtly shell-shocked. I saw Brooke here with her parents. Our parents have never met, so I got nervous that if there was an interaction to be had that it would be bad. I thought a million things at once, as I continued to see her parents come closer I got more concerned that something bad would happen.

Brooke and I made eye contact, and pointed me out to her parents. I thought to myself why would she do that? This is going to be terrible while I watched Brooke and her parents approach mom and I.

"Hello Landon." Mrs. Rose said nice and calmly.

"Hi Mrs. Rose, how are you guys?" I said while shifting my attention from solely Mrs. Rose to all of the Roses. Mom could tell who they were.

"You must be Landon's mother." Mrs. Rose said, reaching out to shake my mom's hand.

"Yes ma'am, and you are Brooke's mother?" Mom started to act shy, which wasn't her character usually.

I was embarrassed, analyzing everyone's facial expressions, trying to decipher how everyone perceived each other. I was more disturbed by this interaction than anyone else. I was waiting for anything to go wrong, and for our parents to hate each other.

"Thank you for letting Landon stay the night a little while ago." When mom said this my heart dropped.

How did she know? Why did she not say anything if she knew? Why would she bring this up now? I was so confused, and overwhelmed with emotions whenever she said that, thinking that something bad would definitely occur after that statement.

"Of course we love Landon. He's always welcomed and

very trusted." Mr. Rose said of all people. I was surprised that he was the one to say anything. I still had it in the back of my mind that he would prefer Brooke to be with Jayden.

"Thank you, that means a lot. Brooke is also welcomed to stay if ever needed." I knew that probably would never happen, but I'm glad there was no animosity whenever she said that.

The whole interaction went better than expected. I laid my eyes on Brooke while our parents got to briefly know each other. Once she realized I was looking at her, she smiled back without having to say any words, for me to fully understand what she was saying.

Once our parents were finished talking they walked off and took Brooke with them. I waved goodbye to them, and got mom to forget about meeting my new teachers. I expected a lot more with our parents meeting, but it was very simple and brief, which was better than most of the scenarios I made in my head. When we made it back to the car it was quiet at first until I broke the silence.

"How did you know?" I asked mom, really confused on how she knew that I was there and not Ryan's house.

She took in a deep sigh, and then gave a subtle smirk indicating that she was trying to cover her anger or frustration. I sat in the passenger seat in confusion wondering what she was going to say. Was I going to be grounded? Why was she being so calm? Her being at bay with her body language made me more scared, than if she was flat out angry.

"Landon...I know everything." She didn't look at me at all, rather kept her same demeanor while looking at the road.

The ride home was made with no exchange of words. The radio was occupying the empty noise. Even with us not talking, mom didn't seem mad like I thought. She was showing no signs of disappointment or anything. I was waiting for her to snap, and go on a rant. I was trying to prepare myself for the tantrum she was bound to have.

Whenever we made it home, mom started laughing. I looked at her, while being jittery, thinking this was a build up to something that was about to be bad. She was about to blow up on me, I could feel it. I just waited for my fate. Waiting for how I was grounded until I graduated high school, or how she never wants me to see Brooke again. I was expecting the worst. We walked in the house and mom continued to chuckle, keeping me and my nerves on high alert.

With all my waiting, the explosion of words never came. I sat on the edge of my bed for probably an hour before easing up. I guess I was expecting her to come into my room screaming, but that never happened.

Was she really okay with what happened? How did she know?

School starts in a week. I intend on making this last

week of summer as calm and relaxing as possible. I didn't want to stay at home the entire week and do nothing, but I'm still worried that mom is waiting to go off on me. I was probably overthinking, but it's good to be cautious, so I won't be grounded at the start of my sophomore year.

It's still crazy to me that I'm already a sophomore. The feeling really hasn't kicked in, but I did realize that I'm nearing the end of high school. So far high school has been pretty good. Only because of my friends and Brooke. The way things are looking, I'll probably continue to be really quiet in school, because I only have one class with Brooke, and one with Paul. Ryan and Tony were in my eighth hour, so at least I get to end the day around them. I had no idea what was in store for me this upcoming year, but I could somewhat say confidently, I'm ready. At least I hope I am.

XV

It was my first day being a sophomore, I wasn't ready for this at all.

I'm a lot more nervous for today, than I was for my first day as a freshman. My nerves felt unwarranted, because I was going to be with my friends regardless. Although now that I'm not a freshman, there's a higher chance I'll be in class with juniors and seniors. I wasn't one to be scared of older kids, but the senior class was a little intimidating this year. That class is notorious for bullying and causing all sorts of problems, and whether I liked it or not, I was an easy target. An underclassman that was quiet.

When I got out of bed I stared at my closet with a blank expression for about ten minutes, without making a decision. I wasn't even overthinking about what I should wear, I just couldn't think at all. School was going to start in twenty minutes so I had to hurry, so I grabbed a basic pair of jeans and a nice t-shirt. I didn't want to look too nice, but I couldn't look completely homeless. I didn't want to be the target of bullying the first day of school.

Before I could make it out the door mom stopped me. She wanted to check me out to see how I was looking on my first day. I was very tired, and I made it obvious. I also made it apparent that I didn't want to go, because even with me not doing anything for the last week of summer, it would be better than waking up this early for school. Which is funny, because I was just saying the other day that I wish I had some more organization in my life. Now that it's here I want to avoid it at all cost.

"You look so good Landon." Mom said motherly. She said it as if I were still a child.

"No I don't." I was very blatant in my response, not entertaining anything that wasn't true.

Mom kept talking to me, but everything was in one ear and out the other. I trudged my way out the door, hesitating each step. No part of me wanted to do this, but at the very least I would get to see Brooke.

I forced myself into my car and took a deep sigh before turning it on. I was really about to go to school with the title "sophomore." My thoughts were clustered around negatives. I wanted to make the best of this, but I didn't know what could go right. I just hope by all costs I can avoid the upperclassmen, besides Matt I didn't like any of them. To be fair I hardly knew any of them, but with the reputation they've built I have no interest in getting to know them.

Once I made it to school, I drove to my parking spot I've grown accustomed to. To my surprise there was already someone parked there. Of course, I just knew this day would be terrible. Luckily the spot next to where Brooke parks was vacant, so I settled to go there instead. Before Brooke could even get to her spot someone took it. I was very annoyed, why? Just why did this have to happen? I don't want to be here.

I just ignored the parking situation, because it ultimately didn't matter that much. On the way in I saw Tony by himself walking with his head down. He was wearing all black, and had earbuds in. His manner was a little off-putting, so I walked up to him to make sure he was okay.

"Hey Tony, how are you?" I try to mask my own frustration and displeasure, so I would sound uplifting for him.

"Oh hey Landon. I'm good…" He gave a small grin as he looked towards me.

"How was the break?" I kept talking to ensure he was okay, and so I didn't have to walk into school alone.

"It was alright, I didn't do much of anything." His answers were very bland.

Something still seemed off. The same feeling I had at the beginning of the summer break as I do now. What was wrong with him? I didn't want to intrude on him, so I just walked by his side until we had to split ways to get to class.

When I got to class I sat near the back trying to avoid being by anyone I didn't know. To my surprise Matt walked in the door right as the bell rang. He put his bag down and sat next to me. He looked exhausted, as did everyone else. Which was expected when coming back from a break, especially with the freedom that kids our age have. Nobody was forcing us to go to sleep before midnight, so we got used to staying up until early in the morning.

"I'm so glad you're here. I was worried, I wouldn't know anyone." I said to Matt just to start a conversation.

"Yeah it's good-" before he could finish a random kid neither of us knew sat down.

He was dressed with style, and had a decent amount of energy. He looked cool, but I didn't want him to sit at our table. I didn't know who he was, but I'm assuming he only sat back here, because the bell rang. He sat with his legs stretched out, and looked as if he didn't have a care in the world. Matt or I didn't say anything when he first sat down.

The teacher came in and introduced herself. She was a shorter woman named Mrs. Cambridge. She started off talking about herself and what the class was about. This talk was expected so most of the students channeled it out. The guy who was sitting at our table was completely ignoring Mrs. Cambridge, and was on his phone. After seeing him on his phone I checked mine to see if I had any missing notifications. I didn't.

After about a ten minute lecture of herself, Mrs. Cambridge instructed us to get to know each other. Matt and I looked at each other and nodded our head in agreement that we weren't going to participate in the activity. We both looked at the guy at our table and acted as if he didn't exist. Not as in he was below us, but just because we didn't want to talk to someone neither of us knew.

"Carmelo!" Mrs. Cambridge called out looking at our table.

The guy at our table sighed, and put his phone down. He fixed his posture slightly to direct his attention more towards the teacher. You could tell he still didn't care what was going on. I didn't know what to think of him, rather he seemed like he was supposed to be cool. He was very nonchalant in all of his movements.

"What's good, my name is Carmelo." He greeted himself, to Matt and I.

"Hi, I'm Matthew." I was weirded out when Matt used his full name to greet himself.

"I'm Landon." I said quietly not trying to make things about me.

Carmelo went back to his phone after doing the bare minimum to do the assignment. I didn't think I was going to like this guy. Something about him made him seem cocky. I wasn't going to judge him too quickly, and decided to give him a chance, because maybe he would end up being a cool guy.

The bell rang, and before I could get my things together Carmelo and Matt were both out of the door. Luckily when I left the classroom I saw Brooke. I smiled when she came up to me looking happy.

"How was your first period?" She said with giddy.

"It was alright, I met this guy named Carmelo." After I said his name she had a concerned look on her face.

"Carmelo May?" She said sternly. She looked as if she knew this guy for the wrong reason.

"I don't know. He was just at my table last period. How was your first-" Before I could finish Brooke interrupted.

"Don't hang around that guy. My sister knew his big brother and he was a bad influence on everyone. Carmelo is the same way." After she said this I thought a little differently about Carmelo.

I still didn't want to judge him too quickly. What if he's just misunderstood? It's not like I'm going to go out of my way to get to know this guy anyway. I tried not to think about it too much, just because he was just a guy who happened to sit at my table during first period.

My next class wasn't very eventful. I sat practically by myself and listened to the teacher talk about the general knowledge things we would need to know. I expected the day to be more like this, isolated from the rest of the class. I knew that my second period would be very boring after one day.

After that, my third period was my class with Paul. When we saw each other we gave each other dap, and sat next to one another. We talked about his trip, because we really never got to. He had a bunch of pictures of famous places like: The leaning tower of Pisa, the Coliseum, and the Eiffel Tower. I was very intrigued by everything he was talking about, because I never thought I was going to be able to leave the country. So I was living my dreams through his experiences.

Our teacher was an older man who seemed like he was going to be strict on us. He wore a plaid shirt with khaki pants. He spoke with the intent of being heard once. He didn't talk about himself as much as my previous teachers have done. I was slightly intimidated by him not knowing if he would get mad at the sight of Paul talking. Which we were going to do regardless of what he said. I was surprised he didn't have assigned seats for us.

I lowered my tone to talk to Paul after Mr. Owens was finished talking. I looked back and forth between Mr. Owens and Paul while we were talking to see if he could hear us. I was also looking to see if he was paying attention.

After a while I stopped looking at Mr. Owens, and gave my full attention to Paulm while he continued to give details about his trip. Everything he was saying was awesome. I could only imagine being on a trip like that and getting to see so many famous places.

Paul randomly stopped talking and looked over my shoulder as if there was a problem. I looked at him with confusion, and then turned my head to see what he was looking at. Mr. Owens was standing behind eavesdropping on our conversation.

"Will this group be a problem for you young men?" He stood with his hands behind his back.

"No sir." Paul and I said in unison. We both looked at each other worried.

"Okay, I assure you, you two will not sit next to one another, if you are a distraction to the classroom, and your peers' ability to learn the material." He spoke very intelligently and calmly, which made him more intimidating.

Paul and I were silent until the end of class. We were freaked out by the calm intensity that Mr. Owens showed. When the bell rang Paul and I walked out of the class and burst in laughter. I mocked Mr. Owens, although I was intimidated by him, I didn't take him seriously. I didn't think that Paul and I would actually get in trouble. We're in high school, why does it matter what two students do in one class for one hour?

My next two classes were unexciting, and not even worth mentioning. At lunch Paul, Ryan, Brooke, and I all gathered together getting ready to meet Sara and Matt at our table. Before we could get there, there was a group of freshmen sitting at our table. We were all perplexed by the sight of a bunch of younger kids taking our spot. I didn't want to say anything, because it's not like they knew. They didn't take our spot on purpose, it was just a coincidence that everywhere there is to sit in the cafeteria, they chose our table. Luckily one table over was available, so I made my way there instead. I didn't want to make a big deal out of nothing, so I put my head down and sat down at the table.

"Are we not going to tell them to move?" Asked Paul. I looked at him for a brief moment making sure he really meant what he was saying.

"Why would we? They got here first." Ryan with the perfect response, to diffuse anything from starting.

I'm glad Ryan decided to say something, and I didn't have to, because I didn't want to be confrontational. They're just freshmen like we were. We possibly could have taken someone else's seats last year, but they didn't make a big deal about it, so why should we?

Everyone took their seats at our new found table, and we started conversing like normal. Matt and Sara came in together a couple minutes after we did. I didn't want to assume anything but Sara's hair was frizzled and she wore a blush face. I didn't make a big deal out of it and started to ask about all of Brooke's classes.

"We have next period together, right?" I was just making sure, so we could just walk to our next class together.

"Yep." Brooke sounded plain, as if she was bothered by something that had happened today.

"Are-are you okay?" I struggled with asking, because I didn't know if my delusions were feeding into a false narrative that I've made for this day.

"Yeah I'm fine. Just a little tired I guess." She closed her eyes and faced my direction with a smile.

Brooke gave out a small sigh, and dropped her shoulders. I wasn't going to intrude on her feelings, because if she wanted to tell me something, she would. At least I hope she will, and I hope nothing's wrong. I don't want to keep asking and bug her, so I'm just here to be a form of comfort.

The rest of lunch was filled with me overthinking about what could possibly be bothering Brooke, if anything even was. As we got up to leave, I read an expression on her face showing that she was stressed. I was getting good at realizing what she thinks by just looking at her. Then again what if I'm making things up.

We were walking our sixth hour together, and she didn't say anything. This was unlike her, because she always loved to talk about the smallest things that were an inconvenience to her throughout the day. I loved listening to her rant about things she would forget in a week, but today she wasn't doing that. What was wrong? She just won't say anything.

Even when we made it to our class, she still didn't say anything, I just followed her to where she wanted to sit. Sara was in the class, but I didn't even see her on the way to this class, so I was really confused. They sat right next to each other, and I opted into sitting across from Brooke. She started to Sara like everything was normal. Did this mean she was mad at me? Why was she acting as if nothing was bothering her now? I'm glad she wasn't bothered anymore, but I wondered if I did something wrong. Was it because I was trying to advocate for Carmelo, because I thought he had a chance of being a good person? I thought my actions were justified. Why would I judge someone who I barely know? What if I didn't give Brooke a chance, and vice versa.

Brooke and I didn't converse much for the rest of class. It was more of me listening to her and Sara talk about things. Even in my seventh hour I wasn't in a talkative mood. I didn't know anyone in that class as it is, so I was bound to not speak. I still sat with my thoughts pondering if she was mad at me or not. She couldn't be, there's nothing to even be mad about.

I stuck with those thoughts all the way until my eighth hour, until I saw Paul and Ryan. I plopped into a seat that was next to Paul. I sat sluggishly still thinking to myself.

"Landon, what's up with you?" Ryan asked me, because he could easily read my expressions.

"Man, I don't know. Am I doing the wrong thing?" I was glad someone asked me.

"What do you mean?" Paul entered the conversation, acting as if he knew what was going on.

"Brooke isn't talking to me, and I can't figure out why." They could hear the subtle concern in my voice as I responded.

"What did you do?" Ryan said right after.

"I don't know, I think it's about this guy in my first period named Carmelo." I was waiting for someone to ask me these questions.

"Carmelo May." They both said simultaneously.

"Yeah...why does everyone find that so bad?" I was so confused by the notoriety his name held.

Paul and Ryan looked at each other, as if they were conspiring to tell me something. Carmelo seemed like a chill guy. I wasn't going to judge someone before I even got a chance to know him. I didn't even talk to him, I didn't even know his last name until Brooke told me.

"He does- things." Paul said after a short moment of silence. He was trying his best to sound comforting.

I blew off what they said, thinking about Brooke. Why would she be upset, about Carmelo of all things. Her silence seemed pointless, but then again I could be stressing about nothing. She's obviously very comfortable with Sara, so maybe she only wanted to talk to her. I don't know, I just don't want her to be mad at me.

The end of the day was very uneventful. This whole day just felt like a continuation of last year. If this is how everyday was going to be, this year is going to be confusing. Obviously I wasn't going to learn anything today, but today seems worthless. I didn't learn anything about my classes. All of my teachers decided to talk about themselves. Everything they said went in one ear and out the other.

When leaving the school Brooke approached me by the time I was about to get to my car. I figured she would talk about how I didn't park next to her. Maybe she would tell me why she's upset. I was honestly just ready for the day to be over. I didn't do that much, but I was mentally exhausted. I was ready to take a much needed nap. I calmed down when she prepared to talk to make sure I wouldn't be snappy with her. Although I was confused, and she was mad I presumed, she didn't deserve for me to be rude.

"Landon." She grabbed my arm to further the attention that I was paying to her.

"What?" She could hear the annoyed tone that layered my voice. I didn't want to be rude, but I thought she was going to start an unnecessary argument.

"Wait. Are you mad at me?" She changed what she was going to say to ask that instead.

"Are you mad at me?" Now I was confused. Was there not a problem? Was I just making things up?

"Why would I be mad at you?" She seemed perplexed that I even had a hint of curiosity.

"I don't know, you tell me." I was trying to figure out if she was actually holding something back, or if I was just being dumb. All of my overthinking for nothing.

"I'm not. I was actually going to ask if you wanted to eat later tonight." She shifted her tone to a more upbeat sounding voice. Seeing how she didn't look as if she held any animosity towards me, I felt dumb.

I really thought there was some kind of problem, and it turns out she wants to go eat. I was still confused as to why she was quiet all day, but I decided to not question it. Maybe we could talk about it over dinner. Maybe I'm thinking too much. Seeing her now, she looks like nothing was bothering her at all.

"Yeah, I'll totally go eat with you. I do want to talk about things." Realizing what I said, I instantly wanted to take it back.

"What do you have to tell me?" She sounded anxious to know what I had to say, and I knew what I said was misleading.

"I promise it's not bad, but I just want to talk over dinner." After my response, Brooke looked annoyed.

"Whatever. I'll see you there." Now I knew she was upset, and a flush of regret washed over my brain. I couldn't let her leave, with a negative way of thinking towards me.

"Brooke, wait..." She started to walk away, but I couldn't watch her go.

"What Landon." Her frustration was audible, and I was beginning to freeze up.

There was a short minute of silence of me trying to think of the right words to say. I walked closer to her to shorten our distance, because I wanted her to know what I was going to say was heartfelt. I didn't know what to say, so I stopped thinking and let words run through my mouth.

"I love you." I gave her a hug, to comfort her frustrations and worries, thinking maybe she won't think about what I said too negatively.

"I love you too, Landon. I'll see you later." Once she left my grasp I could see her face change to a light smiling expression. That indicated that she took what I said seriously.

As I got in my car, I sat there for a moment thinking about Brooke and nothing else. I didn't know what music to listen to. No music that I could listen to would fully help express the feelings I felt for her, so I rode in silence.

I sat around the house waiting for dinner to come. I paced around my room trying to find something to occupy myself. I couldn't get my mind off of her. How do I tell her what I've been thinking? It wasn't anything detrimental, I was just fearful she would take what I say poorly.

Once I finally received a text I picked up my phone immediately. To my surprise it was her saying she couldn't go. I initially acted as if it didn't bother me, but it did. Is she mad at me? Did I do something wrong? I overthink too much. Why don't I just say what's on my mind.

Brooke and I didn't have much of a conversation afterwards. I thought she wanted to be left alone, and that I was bothering her. I was a little insecure about how she felt about me at the moment. I know I shouldn't be, but today has been so strange. It was only the first day of school, and she was already becoming distant. I hoped that this wouldn't be a continuous problem. I really want to spend the rest of my days with her, but does she know that? Does she even want that? Was our relationship only meant for our freshman year? Did things change just because we're sophomores? What if there was another guy in a class of hers that caught her eye. I didn't know how to make a big deal out of it. She never cancels plans on me, ever. Even during the summer, she would be upset if I didn't spend time with her. I even stayed the night at her house. So what happened? Why is she becoming distant? Even though it was subtle I could tell it was happening, and I wanted to know why. I wanted to know if I was the problem, or if I was bothering. Sara would know, but all of these thoughts made four hours go by in a flash. I can't text her this late.

I decided anyway, asking if Brooke had an issue with me. I got no response the whole night. I was slowly falling to sleep waiting for a response from her.

Why did I overthink so much?

XVI

Brooke's birthday was in a week, and I was struggling with what I should do. Things became a lot better since the beginning of school. My overthinking was proved to be unwarranted, and now it's almost her birthday. If I didn't make this perfect for her, things were sure to be bad for our relationship.

I've been stressing myself over what I should get her for about a month now. I've got a couple small things like her favorite candy, and little things like that, but I didn't know what to top off her present with to make it special. Anyone could get her candy, so what is something that would separate me from everyone else.

I've asked everyone I could think of, even to the point where I got Brooke's mother's number to see what her parents got her. They got her new clothes that she's mentioned wanting. I didn't want to flat out ask them what I should get her, but I did ask for hints. They said that Brooke is a very hard person to shop for, but since it would be from me it would be appreciated. That doesn't help. I don't want her to feel forced to like what I get her. I want her to love what I get her. For her to cherish it, and it reminds her how much I care for her every time she sees it. What could that thing be? I couldn't mess up.

Luckily for me, Brooke wasn't in class on Tuesday. So I could ask Sara what she thinks I should do. That is her best friend so she should definitely know what I should do. It had to be perfect, flat out. I was so worried if what I got her wouldn't be everything she wanted, because of how special she made my birthday.

"Sara." I yelled in a whisper, because getting her attention was difficult.

"Yeah?" She said, while looking up deliriously.

"If you were in my position, what would you do for Brooke's birthday?" She looked at me appalled. Her look made me very confused, as if I had done something wrong.

"Landon! Do you not have anything for Brooke?" Her demeanor shifted to show anger in a passive-aggressive way.

"No no no, I have things, I just need something to top it off." I was doing my best to explain to her that I wasn't not thinking of Brooke's birthday.

"Oh. Well, you could take her somewhere nice where it's just you two. A little birdie told me that she would want to do that." She was hinting that Brooke has been talking about what she wants.

Why is it that Brooke can easily tell her friends what she wants for her birthday, but not me? I just thought it was strange, because I expressed to her many times that I want her birthday to be as special as possible. Brooke was a really good and humble person. She says how she doesn't want all the attention on her, but she deserves that attention. It sometimes bothers me that she doesn't see herself as perfect as I see her.

After discussing it with Sara, I had devised a plan of how I was going to propose to Brooke, so we could do something for her. I still had it in my mind that I might be pushy, but the way Sara made it sound, I could really ask her to go anywhere, or do anything and she would agree to go. The plan was that I could give her the first part of her present after school that day, because we tend to meet up as is. Then I'll ask her to go on an evening picnic with me, so I can give the second part of her gift to her.

A picnic wasn't something I would usually do, but I remember when Brooke and I went hiking during the summer, that she wished we could do what we did again in a picnic-type setting. She probably doesn't even remember telling me that, but I always kept that memory in the back of my mind.

Now that I have my plan together, and confidence that it may work, I just need to wait. The rest of the week went by normal, with nothing really happening besides Carmelo talking a little more to me in class.

Carmelo really seemed like a cool guy, but I knew that Brooke wouldn't like the sound of him and I being friendly with each other, so I never brought him up. I really do think she should give him a chance, because he's shown to be a pretty good guy. For example, throughout this week he's been helping one of his friends who was on crutches get to class and made sure he didn't have a problem. Obviously it was his friend, but the fact that he would even do that, gives me hope that he really isn't what everyone paints him out to be.

Today was Brooke's birthday. I ran through my entire plan again to make sure that it was solid, and nothing could go wrong. Of course I thought of a million things that could go wrong, but all of my worries melted away when I saw her that morning. As always she looked flawless.

I met with her in the hallways, and didn't say anything at first. I just stared at her adoring everything she had to offer. Her beautiful luscious hair, her perfectly matched outfit, and her heartwarming smile.

"Happy birthday Brooke!" I said a little louder than intended. I didn't want to keep looking and not say anything.

She said her thanks, and while we were walking to class I listened to her talk. I loved hearing what she had to say. She seemed giddy and said what she had to tell me, so I gladly took in everything.

When I made it to my first period, I held the same jubilant manifestation. Carmelo saw my face when he walked in a little after the bell and started to chuckle. I still held my uplifting look, but was curious as to why he was laughing "What's funny Carmelo?" I said jokingly, so he knew I wasn't trying to start a problem.

"Landon, just call me Melo, bro." He was still his calm, cool, and collected self when he spoke.

"Well what's up?" I wanted to make sure he wasn't laughing at me, but I figured he was.

"It's just funny to see how you're all caught up with this one girl." His response was vague, so I was still confused.

"Yeah? Is that a bad thing?" I had a hint of anger developing, if he planned on saying anything negative about Brooke.

"No bro. I'm happy for you, but what you got going on, definitely not for me."

His clarification made me at ease. Everyone does call Melo a player, but he doesn't seem like it. Yeah, he's a cool guy, but I don't think he would fool around all that much.

Later that day at lunch, Brooke and I made it to our table at the same time. As soon as she sat down everyone at the table started singing happy birthday to her. I joined in with my arm around her shoulder swaying her to the tempo of the song. The pure joyous look that accumulated the covering of her face made me blush. Seeing someone who brings you that much happiness, happy themselves was moving.

I still stared at her as if she were an angel. I was admiring all of her beauty. I could sit and look at her for hours, I was so glad she was in my life. I'm so glad I even have the chance to make her as happy as she makes me. Seeing her have no care in the world in the best way possible. Nothing could bother her, because she knew she was loved, by everyone at the table singing to her. It was all about her, and it couldn't be better any other way.

The rest of my day I struggled to do my work, because I was nervous and distracted thinking about Brooke. I knew how I was going to ask her, but when exactly. When we get to our cars? When we first leave the building? I think the car idea is better, because if she rejects my offer I have an easier way out. I didn't even want to consider the possibility of her saying no. Even though it was her birthday and I'm asking for her to go out with me. It still felt like a privilege to spend time with her. As if being with her was honorary.

When I came into eighth period, Paul and Ryan asked me what my plan was with Brooke. I've talked about it briefly, but I knew they would be supportive. Once I told them my plan on taking her on an evening picnic there was an uncomfortable moment of silence. The whole classroom was quiet as if they were listening in on my plan. After those few seconds passed Paul bursted out into uncontrollable laughter, and Ryan joined in trying to hide his giggling. I felt like an idiot telling my guy friends about this like I expected them to respond any different. Once their cackling was finished I gave them a stern look as if I didn't say what I just said. Hearing it out loud sounded really dumb, but I knew that Brooke would enjoy it, and that's all that matters. It's not like they've ever been in this predicament themselves, so how could they not laugh?

I did my best to ignore what they were saying in their jokes. I was still determined to ask Brooke, but what if it was a bad idea, and I didn't realize it until they started laughing. Sara wouldn't mislead me like that on her best friend's birthday. So this had to be the right idea, and Brooke was going to love to do it.

Once we got out of our eighth period, Paul and Ryan watched me walk off, and were actually showing signs of support. Which is something I could commend them for, we could all joke, but they did really want to see me and her happy together. Pretty mature of them, because sometimes it seems like Sara makes Brooke choose between me and her, but my friends hardly ever do that.

When I found Brooke in the parking lot, I started to tense up. A part of me wanted to just go to my car, and act like I didn't care, even though I obviously did. She also spotted me coming to my car, and began to wait on me. There was no dodging. I had to ask right now.

"Brooke?" I said to her as we became within speaking distance.

"Yes, Landon?" She responded intrigued in what I was going to say. She gave me her full attention ready to listen, but also with a look of being anxious.

"Do you want to-" Before I could finish asking my question that I was forcing myself to say, due to all of my nerves, she interrupted me.

"Yes I will go, Sara already told me." She let out a smile and showed her pearlescent white teeth.

I was initially shocked, because I didn't think that Sara was going to tell Brooke, but I was kind of glad she did. I felt less masculine for asking to go on a picnic, but Brooke really seemed to enjoy the thought of it, so I could care less how I appeared to anyone, but her.

When she obliged, I raced home and got everything that I had for her together. I forgot to give it to her in the parking lot, because I was bombarded with emotions of her saying yes, and Sara telling her. I got ready, and made my way to her house to go pick her up. Mom already knew my plan so leaving without notice wasn't a problem. Upon making it to Brooke's house, the sky started to blanket darkness. It was only five-thirty so it shouldn't have been getting dark this early. The sun was rapidly falling down, and I wanted to at least get to see the sun set.

Brooke came out before I could even go in. I saw her

swiftly shuffle to my car. I gazed at her when she initially got into the vehicle.

"C'mon, we can't miss the sunset." She said enthusiastically, waiting for me to accelerate the car.

I hesitated no longer and started to head toward our destination. The drive there was nice, I got to listen to Brooke talk about all of the things everyone got her. I acted like I was surprised when she talked about each thing she got, as if I didn't already have previous knowledge. It was funny to see how empathetic she felt towards everyone who got her gifts, finding complete satisfaction in each one.

When we arrived at our stop, we hustled out of the car to make it to a suitable place to watch the beginning of dusk. I got all of my gifts for her hoping what I got her wouldn't be so apparent.

We sat down and took a moment to calm down and catch our breath to appreciate the environment around us. I still had slight nervousness thinking that she wouldn't like what I got her, but I managed to give her what I got her.

"It may not be as cool as what everyone else got you, but I hope you find it special." After handing the gift towards her I shied away from eye contact.

I watched her open what I gave her hesitantly. I was wondering what she was thinking. Did I mess up? I thought she would like it, I can't believe I messed up.

"Landon, I love it." She said aloud, as she began to read

the note I wrote her. I was flustered with happiness by her admiration for what I got her.

It was always easier for me to convey my feelings through written words, than speaking. Everything was better formatted and just made more sense. I just hoped my words could touch her the way they were written for. Although my words could never fully unveil my feelings for her. Maybe a sample would suffice until I could find new ways to convey my feelings for her. The simplicity of looking at her, and my problems being dissolved couldn't be worded.

Once she finished the note her eyes became teary. Seeing how much she liked what I wrote, maybe more than everything else, I felt accomplished. She wasn't really one to say fully what's on her mind, but seeing the expression on her face was the only validation I needed.

I did good. All of my overthinking paid off. Everything I did to prepare for this moment was justified. Seeing her happy was everything to me. Watching her reach a state of nirvana like this also brought me to a new leave of ecstasy.

"Thank you Landon, this is the best thing anyone has ever gotten me." She reached over to give me a hug, and my heart felt as if it melted. "If there was a way I could give you the world I would." I responded while I was proximal distance away from her ear.

She let out a deep sigh, but it didn't seem negative like the one she had a month ago. I still thought about that, thinking if there was any animosity building between us. Then we would have times like this and my worries would melt away. I went from overthinking about everything and its details to only thinking about her.

"Landon. I have a question." She said after a couple minutes of silence, and us admiring the view that was presented.

"Yeah, what is it?" I was confused what she could possibly ask right now.

"Out of everyone, why do you want me?" She sounded insecure with her question. I thought I might've done something wrong, but what did I do to make her ask that?

"Because you're Brooke Rose." After saying that she was speechless. We fell silent, and she smiled towards me like only she could do.

The rest of the night was surreal. I was glad I could say undoubtedly I did something good for Brooke. As much as she does for me, even this small token that she appreciated, probably meant more to me than it did her. I loved her, and she knew it without me having to say it. Seeing her happy was a feeling that couldn't be matched. I'm so thankful for her, I wish moments like this could last forever. The image of her smiling was burnt into my brain, and I hoped it would never wash away.

XVII

I couldn't believe it was almost Halloween. Brooke and I have been together for a year. Well it's kind of hard to put a stamp on the year mark, because I met her a little over a year ago. We didn't go on our first date until mid November. All I knew for sure was that Brooke has been in my life for a year now, and it's been the best year of my life.

During first period, Matt and I got on the topic of Halloween. We didn't know what we planned on doing, since Brooke and Sara already had decided to do something with a group of girls. I think Brooke mentioned it would be just a bunch of horror movies.

"What are we gonna do Matt?" He already knew what I was talking about without me having to say it.

"I have no clue, I just want to find something to do." We were in agreement, but had no idea what sounded like a fun way to spend Halloween.

It's not like we could go trick or treating. People would slam their doors in a six-footers face asking for candy. We also weren't very popular so it's not like we could do what Brooke and Sara were doing. Even if we did with Paul, Ryan, and Tony, we would be too childish to finish a movie.

"There's a party, if you guys are talking about Halloween." Carmelo added in. I thought our conversation was only audible between us two, but I'm glad Carmelo heard, because I was intrigued.

"A party?" I was making sure I heard him right, because I've never been to a party before.

"Yeah. Right around Halloween there's always a big party. It's gonna be fun, you guys should come." Carmelo finished his statement with the invitation.

A highschool party. I had a negative notion of the idea initially, but I've never been to one. Maybe it's fun, and Melo turned out to be a pretty cool guy. He wouldn't invite me if he didn't think I would enjoy it.

I read Matt's face and he looked unsure. Why was he unsure? A party sounds fun. I don't think he's ever been to one either so he should want to go. I was all in with the proposal.

"I'll come, where's it at?" I answered, while Matt held his same expression.

"Abby Trickey's house." He responded.

I had no idea where her house was, because she was a

senior and I didn't know many seniors. I had to tell him I didn't know where her house was, but I didn't want to come off as lame. He made it sound as if everyone knew who she was. I had to ask to make sure.

"Where is that at, I've never been." I said hesitantly and nervously hoping to not be judged.

"Oh yeah. I forget you're young. I'll text it to you." He said while calmly chuckling.

We then exchanged numbers so he could text me the address of the house. Once he sent it, all I had to do now was wait. It was only in two days, but it gave me something to look forward to, instead of overthinking about what Brooke could be doing. I knew what she was doing. I was just unsure, because we said a little while back, which she might've forgotten, that we were supposed to watch movies on Halloween. We did briefly talk about it during the summer, but it was something I was still hoping to do with her. This wouldn't be better, but it would be a nice distraction.

Later that day in lunch I wanted to be shy about going to the party, because I didn't know how Brooke would react. Unfortunately the conversation shifted to Halloween, which seemed inevitable. Paul and Ryan spoke on how they were going to go trick or treating regardless of their age. Brooke and Sara spoke more of their plans, and Matt looked at me before starting to speak.

"Well Landon, Carmelo, and I are going to a party."

Matt spoke boldly, but I cowarded away once he finished his statement. I didn't even think he planned on going.

"Carmelo?" Brooke said passive-aggressively while looking in my direction.

"Yeah…" My mouth remained open trying to find words to say, so she wouldn't become upset.

"Sounds like you're going to have fun." Brooke spoke sarcastically, and was visibly upset. I peered over at Matt to give him a stern look.

"It won't be as bad as you think. Melo is a cool guy." I was trying to justify my choice.

"Melo? Oh so you guys have nicknames now?" She was starting to get riled up, and I didn't want to keep pushing her buttons. What should I say, I couldn't lie to her.

"We're friends, but he's not as bad as you think." I was becoming very concerned with what seemed like a likely outcome.

"Okay. I believe you." She responded and gave a genuine smile to reassure me.

I'm glad she trusted me, it made me feel more secure. She knows I wouldn't do anything to intentionally cause problems between us, so she was very lenient of what she was comfortable with me doing. It's not like I did anything very often. If I ever do anything I usually let her know, so if she were to text she would know I'm busy and not ignoring her.

The rest of the day was pretty routine, besides me being

stuck with my lingering thought of upsetting Brooke. This would be my first party, and the situation was unlikely, but I wanted to have fun nevertheless.

The party was in two days, but I couldn't get my mind off of it. What was I gonna do there? I've never drank before, or anything like that. Is it a costume party? Do I need to wear something so I don't look out of place? I was nervous even though the point was to have fun.

The next day at school I was energized early in the morning. I couldn't wait to ask Melo about the party. I didn't want to keep harping on it, but I wanted to be in the loop, so I'd know what to expect.

"Hey Melo!" I called out to him as he was walking in. The bell rang as soon as he came in.

"What's up Landon?" He laid down his backpack and plopped down in his seat.

"Is the party a costume party?" I tried to not sound dumb, so he wouldn't make fun of me. He liked to joke around, and although we weren't the closest of friends, I knew he was always joking. He never tried to be malicious with his words.

"Bro...It's Halloween. What do you think?" He was light hearted even though his words sounded condescending.

"Yeah, my bad." I laughed a little, acknowledging how dumb my question was.

"Speaking of the party, can you give me a ride there?" He asked as I was about to turn to my school work.

"Oh yeah for sure." I responded nicely.

He recognized my answer, and nodded his head. After that there wasn't much said. Carmelo wasn't really one to speak first. We were kind of similar in the aspect of being reserved, and not being outspoken.

Well now that he answered my question, a new one arised. What was I going to wear? I should've asked Melo when I had the chance. Luckily I had lunch time to ask Matt.

In Mr. Owen's class Paul asked about the party. I told him that it was at Abby Trickey's house and he seemed amazed. He seemed shocked, but I don't know why.

"How did you manage to go to one of Abby's parties?" He asked in a whisper so we wouldn't alert Mr. Owens.

"Carmelo." I said back while shrugging my shoulders.

Was this supposed to be a really good party? The face that Paul displayed made me think that I was invited to something only the "cool kids" went to. If that's the case, why would Melo invite me? Did he really see me as "cool" enough to go to one of these parties? I've always thought I was just another kid. People knew my existence, but I didn't think anybody thought about me more than that. I'm probably not going to know anybody that's there, so it's gonna be awkward for me since I'm not very good at socializing.

After school ended I went to the store to buy a mask so I could hide my face. I wasn't going to get a full costume, but I wanted something. A mask seemed like the best median available. In the store they had an entire section strictly related to Halloween. I wanted to hurry because I didn't like being at the store alone. I always got a weird feeling being there without someone I know. I scurried through the main aisle of the Halloween section looking for a mask. I stumbled upon a mask from the horror movie "Scream". I knew nobody would be able to see my face, and the guy with the mask in the movie was quiet. Meaning if people questioned why I was quiet I could just pretend as if I'm playing the character.

When I got home my mom heard the ruffling of the bag I got for the mask, and asked what it was. I didn't want to tell her, but I had to so I could go to the party.

"I went to the store to get a mask for the party." I was trying to lightly add that I was going to a party so she wouldn't think much of it.

"What party?" She saw right through my attempt and asked about it immediately.

"Just a little Halloween party, nothing much." I noted, thinking that she wouldn't keep asking about it.

"As long as you're with one of your friends, have fun." I was surprised by her response. She really wasn't bothered by the thought of me going to a party. She probably thought it was just a small get together with my friend group, but I didn't want to ruin any chances of me going so I stayed quiet.

I sat in my room contemplating the party and what could possibly happen. I kept my room dark, planning to sleep on my ideas of what could occur. It would be weird with Brooke not being there, but it's not like I was going to be trying to entertain any other girls. I think that's why Brooke was so relaxed about me going, or at least more than I was expecting.

Halloween came around, and I was anxious to go to my first party. Here it was, a highschool dream. Dream may not be the right word, but this was the kind of thing to happen in movies. I didn't think I would ever be in a position to ever have a real experience of these things. I still had to act cool about everything, so I didn't seem strange.

During the first period, everyone knew that it was Halloween on Friday. Every time this would happen something fun was bound to take place. Carmelo walked in with a smile on his face when seeing me. He thought it was funny that I was so enticed by the party. I feel as if I'm making too much of a big deal about it, but I've never experienced this before. With my millions of scenarios I came up with, nothing turned out to be bad.

I went through the day normally, as I usually would. Trying to be cool about the situation, knowing that talking to Brooke about it would bother her. Even though during lunch and sixth period she was only talking about what she was going to do tonight. Her and her friends. I didn't know how she could continuously go on about watching movies. It made me think that there could possibly be doing more than that. I tried not to let it bother me too bad, because of the trust we've instilled in each other. I knew she didn't plan on doing anything, the same way she knows I'm not going to do anything to jeopardize what we have. I never would.

After school I met Camelo in the parking lot to ask what time I should pick him up. He was with Abby talking about the party, and she didn't know who I was. So that made approaching the two of them kind of awkward. I felt out of place upon arrival, seeing how these two were some of the coolest people in the school, and I was just me. Landon Morgan.

"What's up Landon." Melo made me feel welcomed with a simple dap of our hands. I gave a small grin, and was going to listen to them finish their conversation, before I say what I need to.

"Who is this?" Abby said with a small look of disgust on her face. It hurt a little to see how rude she was about seeing me, but I couldn't really blame her. Compared to her I really was a nobody, but I didn't think I was flat out disgusting.

"Hi I'm Lan-" Before I could speak Carmelo interrupted me to introduce me to her.

"This is the coolest dude ever. His name is Landon and he's taking me to the party tonight." After he said this, there was a look of surprise on Abby and I's face.

Did Carmelo really think I was cool? I honestly thought he was just tolerating me, so I would take him to the party. He seemed genuine though, like he actually liked my presence. I wasn't just some weird kid to him, but I held a certain amount of value.

"Well it's nice to meet you then Landon." Abby said while reaching out her hand to shake mine.

I accepted her handshake, and was glad to be accepted by the two of them. I felt like the social barrier between us was fully broken at this point, seeing that Melo was willing to introduce me in a good light.

"Hey Melo. What time do you want me to pick you up tonight?" I asked, so I could get ready, and be on my way.

"Uhh, probably around nine to nine-thirty should be good." He said switching his tone to slightly more serious so he could relay he was being sincere.

I simply nodded and went to my car. I was in a blank mind space on the way to my car. That was until I was approached by Brooke, who was looking a little distraught.

"Hey Brooke! Is everything alright?" I was concerned while reading the look on her face. She looked as if she was built up with anger.

"Why are you with Abby Trickey, and Carmelo May?"

She was trying to keep her voice down and not let the anger speak for her, from what I could tell.

"I was just asking about the party tonight. That's it." She took in a deep sigh after hearing my words. I thought she was becoming more calm, but she still held a stern face after her sigh.

"What are you even going to do at this party?" She sounded prissly as she spoke.

"I-I don't know." I shrugged, because I really didn't know what to expect for tonight. I thought she knew I wouldn't do anything to harm our relationship.

"Ha. You don't know?" She was getting more irritated with my responses. I was being truthful, so I didn't get what the problem was.

"Do you not want me to go?" I was trying to get closer to her, but she kept her distance away from me.

"Nope. Just do what you want." She walked off after her statement, and I was left standing there confused.

Would she really be mad if I went to this party? She knows I only talk to the same six people everyday. I'm just confused about what is so wrong with Carmelo, he seems like a good guy. I just need to go home and clear my mind until nine.

When I made it home I went straight to my room and laid down to think about what could be a possible outcome of me going to this party. I've been anticipating it for a week now, and Brooke is doing her own thing. So it's not fair that I can't go to a party, but she gets to do what she wants. I still don't want to cause problems, but it seems fair for me to go if she goes with her friends. It wasn't that I was trying to be petty, but it would make sense that I get to do what I want if she does.

While thinking to myself I drifted away to sleep. After a couple hours I woke up delirious thinking that I could be late, but luckily for me it was only eight-thirty. I checked my phone to see a message from Carmelo. It was his address. He only lived around five minutes away from me, so I had a decent amount of time to get ready.

After getting ready I let mom know that I was leaving, and I hugged her goodbye. Once I made it to Carmelo's house I told him I was there, and waited for him to come out. Then I waited a little more. Then waited more after that. By the time he came out it was nine-forty-five. I got to his house at nine-ten. Melo entered the car with a smile on his face, acknowledging his belatedness.

"My bad man, I was getting everything together." He dapped my hand, as I was checking out his costume.

He was dressed as a mechanic with a scary mask, and a fake knife. I had my mask in the back, but it didn't compare to Melo's outfit. Melo looked around my car inspecting everything. He turned his attention to my auxiliary cord.

"Can I play some music?" Carmelo said as he was reaching his hand to the auxiliary cord.

I obliged to his request with a nod of my head. He grabbed the cord, and plugged in his phone. As he started playing music, I was stunned by the eroticness of the tunes. It was loud and sonorous. I liked it. I didn't know what they were saying, but I was jamming out to the words I could make out.

Carmelo and I were enjoying his music all the way until we got to Abby's house. Melo seemed pumped up, which was a surprising sight as he usually stays calm. He was really excited, and that made me excited. Seeing someone who is usually in a shell break out of their shell. I wasn't the same way, but I enjoyed the energy Carmelo was putting out.

While going to enter Abby's house, which was a really nice four thousand square foot house, I heard a lot of mixed voices talking over each other in a crowd. I saw strobe lights emitting from the entrance, and knew that had to be the entrance. I put on my mask, and followed Carmelo closely until we were inside. Everyone seemed to know Melo as they would come up to him and greet him. One person after another. He might've said hello to about twenty people before even going inside.

When we did get inside, I tried to stay close with Melo, but I lost him within five minutes, because of all the people swarming inside. There must've been at least two hundred people. I had to maneuver around everyone just to get where I was going. Once I realized I lost Carmelo, I found a couch and sat down trying to recollect my thoughts. Was this really the right choice? I have no idea what I'm doing. I'm just here. After sitting for a while and bobbing my head to the music a girl approached me.

"Not having fun?" She asked me, as she was looking down at me from a standing position. I had no idea who this girl was, so I was surprised by being approached.

"I'm having fun I guess. Just relaxing." I lifted the mask that I had on and moved it to the side.

"Ah. Relaxing? Well you want to dance?" She reached out her hand to take mine.

I shouldn't dance with a girl, that would be wrong. Although it's not like she was dancing in any sexual way. I thought we would just be having a good time.

I reached out and took her hand to get up and dance with her. The girl and I were moving to the music. I wasn't much of a dancer, so I didn't know what I was doing. I was having fun, but was thinking about if Brooke would approve of this. I didn't even know this girl's name.

"What's your name?" I asked her in the middle of dancing.

"Alana. What's yours?" She stopped dancing to notice my greeting and I was stuck looking into her eyes. I wish they were Brooke's eyes.

Alana wasn't a bad looking girl by any means, she just wasn't Brooke. Alana had long brown hair that matched her brown eyes. She was dressed up as a cowgirl for the party. Her costume was a little revealing, but I could tell what she was going for.

"I'm Landon." I put my hand out to shake her hand, and she matched my gesture while smirking.

"It's nice to meet you, Landon." She responded and was getting ready to start dancing to a song I could tell she liked. Before she could really get into the song I stopped her.

"I have a girlfriend, and I don't know if this is wrong." I wasn't trying to completely distance myself from Alana, but I wanted to respect Brooke's unwritten boundaries.

"Where's she at?" She started to look around the compact house until I pointed her out.

"She's not here." I said with a little bit of sorrow.

"Hey, don't feel bad. Just have fun, I'm sure she wouldn't mind you having fun. It's not like I'm going to bite." She said with a careful sound for my situation.

It was obvious that Alana had my best interest in mind so I continued to dance with her. We danced for a couple more songs, until she told me that she had to go. As she was about to leave, she asked for my number. I was hesitant in giving it to her, but it's not like I had to respond to her the way I do Brooke. So I gave her my number and watched her leave.

"Alana Thompson?" Carmelo said as he came up from behind laughing.

"I was just being polite." I responded. He didn't take what I said seriously.

I noticed he had a bottle of alcohol in his hand, so he was probably intoxicated. I looked at the bottle to read the label. "Seventy-five percent alcohol." Carmelo was definitely drunk.

"Do you want some?" He asked while reaching the bottle out to confirm his offer.

"I'm good man, but thank you for offering." I put my hand towards the bottle to push it away.

"Try it. Trust me it's really good. It's not like one drink is going to kill you, I just want you to get a taste." After saying that I took the bottle from his hand and took a drink.

It tasted really bad, but I could tell there was a hint of watermelon flavored masked behind all of the alcoholic contents. After removing the bottle from my lips I had a face of disgust. It felt as if it was making my hot breath and burning my esophagus. I hated it, but Carmelo was excited to see me drink it.

"That's it? Drink a little more." He declined me trying to give him the bottle back.

I took another small drink, thinking that it wouldn't taste as bad this time, but it tasted worse. I absolutely hated the taste. I forced the bottle back Melo, so I wouldn't even be tempted to take another drink. I still had to drive home after all.

People started leaving, and Carmelo asked if we could go which I was perfectly fine with. I was just enjoying the music, feeling more free than I have my whole life. I was rocking and swaying with the music, and didn't care what anybody thought of me.

When we started to leave Carmelo and I started laughing together, with no words even being said. This was fun, I felt totally at ease. I finally wasn't stressed about anything. I didn't care what anybody thought, not even Brooke.

XVIII

Christmas was around the corner, and I never told Brooke what happened at that Halloween party. She doesn't seem to be mad at many in any factset, so I'm not going to test my luck and talk about it. Alana also has been trying to text me, but I always give her overdue answers. I try to politely tell her that I'm not interested in her at all.

We're currently in the middle of our winter break, and it didn't seem as much was going to happen. Brooke and I have been a little more distant, but mostly because I feel guilty. I wasn't being fair to her at all, but I put myself in a bad predicament. I needed to do something to get my mind off of things. The days felt lifeless, and meaningless. What was I supposed to do? Especially if Brooke didn't want to do anything.

Not being able to see Brooke that often has been bothering me, because she had become a part of my routine. I loved having her around, and I loved the connection we have. Had? I don't know, I'm so confused about what's going on between us. It couldn't be all my fault, because she went and did her own thing, and I just so happen to do the same.

Christmas lost its taste. I tried to invite Brooke over, because I got her a present again, but she didn't sound as if she had any interest in coming over. Not because she was mad, but because she was already doing something with her family. Maybe she was mad at me, I truly don't know.

As Christmas passed, mom tried to fill my emptiness I was feeling, but it didn't work. I was looking at the year in retrospect. Thinking about all the things I've messed up; Jackson's Family, the bond in my friendships, and now Brooke. At least that's how it felt.

Luckily for me Carmelo texted me asking me if I was interested in a New Year's party. I was interested, but I didn't want to go unless Brooke could go. I asked Brooke if she wanted to go a little after being asked by Carmelo. She actually sounded excited. I couldn't read her tone through a text, but she seemed intrigued by the thought of going to a party with me. This would be the first time I've seen her in person in a week, so I was really excited as well.

I laid around my house waiting for the days to pass until it was eventually New Year's Eve. Waiting felt like it took forever. Alana asked me if I planned on going to the party, which I told her blandly I was. I was hoping that if she saw Brooke and I together, she would stop talking to me.

Even after the party I didn't see much of Alana at school, so I was confused as to why she kept trying to text me. It's not like I was that good looking or anything. Maybe she was just trying to be friendly and I was reading it wrong. If I tried to explain all this to Brooke it would be awful, so I'm just going to shut my mouth until the party.

I told mom my plans of going out, and she noted that she wanted me to come home at a reasonable hour, because I didn't come home until three in the morning from the Halloween party. She never made a big fuss about it, and I also never mentioned what happened.

The party was at Abby's house again, which made me think Brooke would be mad about that. At least if we were both there together, we would be able to monitor what each other was doing. So nothing could go wrong tonight.

Night came faster than I thought it would, and before I knew it it was time to get ready for the party. Paul ended up wanting to go so I was expecting to see him there as well. Melo made it sound like an open invitation so I didn't have a problem with inviting Brooke or Paul. I got myself together, and took in a deep breath before walking out the door.

"Be safe!" My mom called out to me before I finished walking out of the house.

I didn't give an answer back because I was afraid of

the things that could happen. I wasn't picking up Carmelo this time, so I was riding all the way to the party alone. I decided to play the music that Melo was playing on Halloween, because that really got me amped for that party. It did make me a little more ready, but listening to it alone amplified that empty feeling I've been having.

I made it to Abby's house about fifteen minutes after the party started. I saw no signs of Paul or Brooke's car anywhere. Luckily I saw Carmelo near the entrance, so I got out of my car and made my way to him. He was talking amongst a group of people. I was hoping I could slip into the group without directing any attention towards myself.

"Landon!" Carmelo said, interrupting whoever was talking. He looked happy to see me, and that made me feel more comfortable.

He walked across the group to give me dap. I smiled a little seeing how I was accepted by everyone he was talking to, just because I was accepted by Melo.

"What's up Melo!" I spoke a little louder than I usually would, but I was trying to match his energy.

"Come inside, I got a drink with your name on it." Melo said while laughing. There was a hint of alcohol within his breath.

"I think I'm gonna wait till it's closer to midnight." I told him as we were walking in regardless.

"Ahh smart, go into the New Year with a BANG, huh?"

He was really enthusiastic which I thought was funny. Carmelo at school was way different from Carmelo now.

When we were inside near the kitchen I saw Alana. After seeing her I tried to act as if I didn't see a glimpse of her. Although out of the corner of my eye I could see her approaching me with a bottle of alcohol in her hand.

"Hey Landon." She spoke seductively and with a little bit of a slur. I had assumed that she was drunk.

"Hey Alana." I responded blandly, but politely so I wouldn't come off as rude.

"I've missed you." She said while wrapping her arms around me. I was very uncomfortable as she started squeezing me tighter.

"Yeah…" I patted her back hoping that a small amount of physical touch would get her off of me.

Once she got off me, I tried to distract her by asking me to get something I heard Carmelo talking about. I didn't know much about alcohol, or anything, but I hoped it would buy me time away from her.

As she went off I saw Brooke walk in followed by Paul. She looked timid, not wanting to involve herself with anything. Paul looked a little excited to be at the party. Neither of them were the types to go to parties so this was a new experience to them. They spotted me, as I was a taller person and easy to spot. After seeing me they came up to me.

"Hey! how are you guys?" I said as they came up. Brooke didn't look too happy, so I gave her a comforting hug.

They were speechless just looking around observing everything. I didn't know how to lighten the mood, as it was very awkward. The three of us got caught just looking at each other with no words. I haven't seen Brooke in a week. I don't even know what to say. She's so beautiful. Everytime I see her it's like I fall in love with every detail on her face again. I just looked at her with a soft smile. It's like she read my mind, because she started to smile back.

Shortly after Alana came back with the drink I asked for. She was giggling even though nothing happened. Brooke and Paul looked at her crazy.

"Here you go, Landon." Brooke looked at me confused, and I felt the uneasiness of the circumstance.

"Oh Carmelo was the one who asked for it." I said quickly and nervously.

Unfortunately Carmelo walked by, and took the bottle out of Alana's hand. After giving the bottle to him her attention turned back to Brooke, Paul, and I.

"Who is this?" Alana asked while pointing to Brooke in a look of disgust.

"I'm the girlfriend." Brooke said before I could even answer. This was escalating quickly, and I didn't like the look of it.

"Oh, he was talking all about you when I first met

him, it's nice to meet you." Alana reached her hand out to shake Brooke's.

Brooke had a surprised look on her face. Did she think I was cheating on her? If so I'm glad Alana said what she did, because I would never do that to her. After their small interaction, tensions seemed to cool down.

Time passed and we all started to enjoy the party more. I was dancing with Brooke, Paul, and Alana. I was surprised that Brooke wasn't bothered by Alana being around. At least she acted like she wasn't.

Midnight was coming, which meant the New Year was near. It was about eleven-forty-five, so we had fifteen minutes until the clock showed a new year. I was kind of nervous. I didn't want to go into a new year with any problems between Brooke and I.

"Brooke. Is there anything wrong between us?" I asked hesitantly, scared of her answer.

"I thought there was, but I guess not." She still kept a stale voice.

There was a hint of uncertainty in her sound, which I didn't like.

I didn't know how to react her response, because I kept getting lost in her eyes. I missed her security, and company. Nothing was worth losing her over.

Midnight was getting closer, and I was getting more nervous. Wasn't I supposed to kiss her? That's a thing that couples do on New Year's I'm pretty sure. If that's the case why did she walk away? As Brooke walked away from me, Alana came to me.

"So how long have you two been together?" She asked as she danced her fingers on my shoulder.

"Uhh-A year. And three months." I was feeling really uncomfortable, but didn't know how to get her off of me.

"Oh that's not too bad." She said blatantly while looking deep into my eyes.

"Wha-What do you mea-" Before I finished she puckered her lips and kissed me.

I pushed her away and looked at her in disgust. In pushing her away, I tipped over the music box, and caused the music to stop. My face was red hot. Brooke looked at me with a face of terror. I saw tears building up in her eyes. Brooke stormed out of the house, and Alana stood looking at me in confusion.

"What the hell is wrong with you!" I screamed at her, causing a scene. I didn't care what I looked like to other people. I was furious that Alana would do that knowing I was in a relationship.

"Woah woah, what's going on?" Carmelo came in and intervened, so the situation wouldn't progress more violently.

"This skank just kissed me, knowing I'm in a relationship." I said while pointing at Alana. She looked like she was about to cry, and fought back her tears.

"Calm down man. Let's go outside and cool off."

Carmelo led me outside away from everyone, while fixing everything back to normal.

I was struggling to catch my breath, because of all my built up anger. I could punch a hole through the Great Wall of China. I saw Brooke in the distance, and ran to her.

"I'm sorry, she kissed me. I don't know why she did that." I said while approaching Brooke.

"Leave me alone!" She yelled back at me. I was hurt, just as bad as she was. She might've thought that it was a mutual kiss, but I only wanted to kiss Brooke.

Paul came to calm the both of us down. He had his arm around Brooke which fueled my aggression. Why did he have his arm around her?

Why did he go to her first?

"Get your hands off of her." I said to Paul sternly. Anger flooded my mind, and I was starting to see red.

They both looked at me like I was a monster. What if I am the monster? What have I done? My hands were shaking. I didn't mean for any of this to happen. I only wanted to rekindle the spark between Brooke and I, because it felt as if it was going away. Now I'm alone. I messed everything up. Like I always do.

I left the party and rode home in silence. When I made it home, mom was still up waiting for me to come home I presume. She reached out her arms to give me a hug. I fell into them and my eyes started pouring out tears.

"What's wrong baby?" Mom said while caring for me to make sure I was alright.

"I messed everything up. I mess everything up. Why do I mess EVERYTHING up? Why can't I be enough? I love her mom." I tried to say what my heart was thinking through my tears.

"She loves you too. It'll all be okay. Whatever you did I'm sure you'll fix it. We all love you." Mom spoke softly trying to calm me down.

I continued to sob knowing that this is going to be the end. All of my trials and tribulations to make this work amounted to nothing. I let some random girl I don't care about kiss me. I am hurt, and the only person that could heal me, would be disgusted to look at me.

XIX

Everything changed because of me. Brooke would give me minimal communication. Not even a chance to explain myself. A couple of months have passed since the New Year's party. It was almost my birthday, and the memories of what occurred last year in Texas were torturing my mind. A constant reminder of my continuous failures.

Brooke moved tables from me, and created a rift between Sara and Matt. It's not fair that I'm the reason that Sara and Matt might not stay together. I remained quiet around everyone. Brooke still let me sit by her in sixth period, but I knew she didn't want me to. I was too selfish to let myself leave and let her go.

Paul did his best to comfort both Brooke and I. He told me that he understood that it really wasn't my fault. I couldn't help, but to think it was, but why would Alana even be that comfortable to do that. Did I give her subliminal signals? What did I do wrong? Sure she was drunk, but still what in her mind would make her think that I was okay with that? I must've done something wrong. I just didn't want to lose Brooke over that.

My birthday rolled around, and I spent it alone. I thought back to how everyone surprised me for my birthday. Seeing Brooke and all of my friends together, so thankful for me, and being appreciated. Now, I'm isolated. I barely got acknowledged for my birthday. Even though I wasn't really recognized, her voice telling me happy birthday remained tattooed on my brain.

I was struggling. I needed Brooke, but I knew she wouldn't come back. I regressed all the way back to how I was at the beginning of my freshman year.

The rest of the year was basically the same, nothing memorable happened. Nothing worth talking about, or enough that felt meaningful. Mom was trying to help me cope with my loneliness, but that wasn't helping. I was glad she tried to help, but I just needed to find a way to get Brooke back.

Carmelo and I still stayed pretty good friends, and I continued to go to parties thinking that would be helpful, but it wasn't. At the parties I went to I found myself sitting alone. People would try to talk to me, but I would give them minimal conversation. I just found it as an excuse to be out of the house, and a chance for me to drink. At least when I drank I didn't think of it. It would be difficult to drink and drive, but I would still do it. I didn't care that I could crash, I didn't care about any of the repercussions. I just wanted to escape.

Carmelo tried to talk to me about my drinking habits, but I ignored it as long as possible. Everytime he would point out that I do it an excessive amount, I would note how he does the same, and to not worry about me. He was just trying to help. I don't know why I pushed him away. I didn't know why I watched the seasons change alone. I could've listened to Brooke to begin with and there would be no problems.

I kept digging myself into a darker hole in my mind until there was nothing, but darkness. I thought the darkness was comforting in a way, seeing as though nobody could get to me, because of how deep I decided to dig my hole. The only thing I covered the hole with was my issues, all the things I blamed myself for, and the alcohol that helped me escape my natural thinking. Anything so that people couldn't get to me, and so that I could leave my sober thoughts away. I needed help, and the only person that could help me wanted nothing to do with me.

With summer coming up, I hoped that there would be a way for me to get a chance to talk to her. Maybe a chance to win her back. I didn't want to think of the possibility of her moving on. I needed her in my life.

I texted her the week after the end of our Sophomore year, asking her if there was anything I can do to see her.

Give my full side with no excuses. She's always understood me the best so maybe she would be willing to hear what I have to say.

After texting her I sat covered in the covers of my bed waiting for her to reply. I refused to go anywhere else while I waited for a response. It took hours, but I didn't care, I had nothing else to do. I never did, so I could've sat in my rooms for days if I had to.

When she did finally respond, she simply said sure. A monosyllabic answer was good enough for me, but I still wanted to hear more from her. I texted asking when I can see her. The response only took half an hour this time. She said that she would come over tomorrow, because she misses my mom. I was glad she held nothing against my mother, but it made it sound like she had no care for me at all. Which I can understand, but still hurt regardless.

After telling me that I poked my head from out of the covers. I took a deep breath. Breathing clean air for the first time in hours. I looked around my room to see the mess that has accumulated over time. I decided that since Brooke was coming over that I should clean everything, and make the house look presentable. Which mom kept the rest of the house clean, she just let me have my distance, and didn't really converse with me until I was ready to speak.

I got up and fixed my bed, tidying it up. I straightened all the wrinkles out, and cleaned out any trash I found on the bed. I also picked up all the trash that was on the floor. I did this all in the dark, not comfortable with the light quite yet. Although when I was transferring the trash from my room I expected it to be light outside, but it was already pitch black outside. The lamp that was the only thing emitting illumination in the living room punched my eyes with pain. It was the first bright thing I've seen in what felt like a week. Navigating throughout the house made me feel like I was exploring uncharted territory. A place I've grown used to, now foreign. Every place I looked out gave me a memory of Brooke and I. I stared at the couch for minutes remembering when she came over for Christmas and we exchanged gifts. I would do anything to have moments with her like that back. The entire house felt lifeless, haunted by the memories she left me with.

I went back to my own room after throwing my trash away, and turned on my lamp. The snow globe she had gifted me that Christmas was sitting on my dresser. I picked it up and shook it. While it was shaking I became teary-eyed. I missed her. I missed her more than anything I've ever lost. All of my childhood toys that I lost, and the childish pain from losing those, couldn't compare to the pain of not being secure in our relationship.

I held back my tears, replaying the image of the text she sent in my mind. She will be here tomorrow. Everything will be okay. What if she's only coming over to see my mom? What if she doesn't even talk to me while

I'm here? What if I mess things up even more? Thoughts lingering in my head, while I sat at the edge of my bed. I couldn't help but to think of the negatives that could happen. I wish I could drown my emotions in alcohol, but I didn't have any to do so. I had to stay sober and fight my conscience about the things that were more than likely going to happen, because I inevitably mess everything up.

This is not at all how I thought the rest of my Sophomore year would be. I thought it would be something memorable, and a fun experience. It ended up being the beginning of what felt like the end. A year where I clouded my thinking, because of my own mistakes. I hoped I could at least make my sophomore summer better than what the year had to offer. I didn't know what to expect at this point. I just wanted Brooke back.

XX

Brooke was coming over today. The thought of seeing her seemed surreal. I longed for her for such a long time, that even the chance to recuperate mishaps was something I looked forward to. She might only be coming to see my mom, but at the very least this would be a chance to see her this summer. Even if it was this one time, I would cherish this one moment for the entire summer.

I told mom that she would be coming over and she seemed excited to see her. She sounded like she thought we were back together. We never broke up "officially", but we weren't together. I didn't want her to think otherwise, so I let those thoughts stay with her. She would be disappointed to hear that she was coming over just to see if we would fix things. I still don't know if things are fixable, seeing how I messed up so bad.

I was a nervous wreck, waiting for her. I was

trepidatious thinking of what I would say, or what I should say. I wanted to shake all of my nerves, but I know that I would tense up regardless of my preparation. I couldn't stress enough of how much I needed her in my life. This talk was going to be everything to me.

After a couple of hours pacing around my house waiting for her, there was a knock at the door. My heart was racing, I felt my hands shake, and my knees shaking uncontrollably. I started walking to the doors, with every step feeling like a mile long walk. I felt myself becoming smaller as I got closer to the door. I was internally panicking, but I refused to show it externally. Why was this so hard? I wanted this with everything in me, but now that the moment is here I was freezing up like I knew I would. I could see her silhouette through the door. My hands felt like they were being held down by anvils. I started to breathe quickly as my hand made contact with the handle of the door.

I started to turn my hand to the handle, and Brooke finished opening the door on the other side. She hurried and opened the door, and fell into me with a hug. I was stunned and confused. She was hugging me after everything I did? I didn't want to complain, because I missed her. I was only confused, because I didn't think I deserved it.

"I missed you, Landon." Her eyes became full of tears

and voice started to tremble and she stayed clinched on to me.

I was speechless. I just hugged her with the intent of not letting go. I didn't want her to walk away again. Did mom say something to her before she came? Was there something wrong? I didn't know what to say, so I just closed my eyes, and said whatever formulated in my head.

"I love you. I'm sorry for everything that happened. I-I don't know why I didn't tell you sooner. I should've listened to you, I'm sorry." I was feeling a full range of emotions, not knowing how to control myself now that she's finally here.

She had every reason to be mad, but wasn't. She didn't ignore me like I thought she would. She came straight to me first. I missed all the time we wasted being upset at each other. I was tired of the hole I was digging myself without her. I was mad that I didn't listen to her when she tried to warn me. Why has everything I planned to say to her for the past five months suddenly disappear from my thoughts? All of the things I said I would say, if this moment would ever come. I guess I never thought it really would happen, but here it was. I wondered what she's been thinking about our relationship these past months since we haven't been together.

Obviously I felt empty, and like nothing mattered, but she looked unfazed by it. That bothered me at first, but there was some comfort in knowing she was still happy with her friends. Even though I was in such a dark place seeing her smile from a distance was good enough for me.

"Brooke, can we talk?" I asked as we continued to stand there holding each other.

"YES! Just let me say 'hi' to you mom first." She said while she was wiping away the built up tears in her eyes.

I let her go into my mom's room, but the feeling of emptiness immediately raced back as I let her go. She was like the missing puzzle piece I needed. My chest felt caved in, as if she took it with her. She was only steps away, but it felt so far away, because of how long I was waiting for this moment.

She came into my room, and sat on the side of my bed. I followed her in and sat from a distance scared to intrude on her space. She grabbed the snow globe that she gave me two Christmases ago. She shook it to watch the snowfall, the same way I did when I was reminiscing about our times together. The snow was falling slowly. As it was falling, a smile on her face began to form. I got to see her happy again, and it was with me. I missed all of the little details I would realize with her. The way she would ease up the tension in her shoulders when she smiled. How she would start with good posture until she felt comfortable enough to slouch.

"I've missed you so much. I need you with me." I muttered to her hoping that I wasn't pushing any boundaries with my words.

"Life hasn't been the same without you. I'm sorry I didn't listen to you." She put the snow globe down and positioned herself towards me, to direct her attention.

"Please don't apologize, it's all my fault." I spoke with sorrow in my voice. I didn't want to pity myself, but I wanted her to know that I was sincerely sorry.

"I know it's your fault, but I wasn't fair to you regardless. We could've talked about things, because I know what happened wasn't your intention." Her response surprised me, but she knew how to shock me with her words like nobody else did.

"I don't know what else to say other than I love you. I wouldn't do anything to ever intentionally hurt you, or jeopardize our relationship." I moved closer to her. I was seeing if she was comfortable with me closing the distance between us.

"Just don't ever do anything like that ever again." She moved her hand towards me as she spoke.

"I promise I won't. I want us to last forever." I moved my hands closer to hers.

"Forever?" She asked with a confused tone.

"Yeah?" I thought I might've been asking for too much with that, but that's really what I wanted. I couldn't imagine living without her around.

We looked into each other's eyes, the same we did when we were at that park. Reminding me of the first time we confessed our love for each other. This moment was picturesque to what I had imagined in my head, while I isolated myself. I missed being this close. The feelings, alcohol I would drink to supplement this feeling, couldn't compare.

She closed her eyes and moved closer to me, and I reciprocated the motion. We shared a kiss, the one I wanted to share at that New Year's party. All that time, I was waiting for this, all of this. Things were perfect again. All the time we lost felt as if it was being restored with this kiss. She could never understand how much I truly loved her, but I was going to do everything I could to show her how much I did. To show her how much I don't care about Carmelo, Alana, or alcohol. None of those things could ever compare with how I felt with Brooke. She was my peace, and my peace after these long gruesome five months has been restored.

I felt blended with her, and even after this kiss was over the feeling remained. I had her back when I never thought this would happen again. I wanted her to stay with me. I wouldn't do anything to risk anything close to Brooke and I's relationship coming to an end.

XXI

It was late July, and things felt as if they were back to normal. Brooke and I started spending time together routinely again. Summer was fun again. Paul was in Colorado for the entire break, so I actually got to spend time with him, and the rest of our friend group. I stopped going to parties, which in turn got me to stop drinking so heavily. I didn't need those supplements when I had all of my friends, and most importantly I had Brooke again. I no longer felt as if there was a void to be filled.

Mom could tell I was a lot happier. She didn't want me to get as low as I was. I don't know if she knew about my drinking problems, or anything.

I figure not or she wouldn't continue to let me go out so late all the time, like I was. I was good at hiding the fact I wasn't sober when I would come home drunk. Usually I would poke my head inside mom's room to say "hi" and then go back into my room. She obviously didn't like the minimal communication I would give her, but I don't think she wanted to cause anymore damage.

Mom would invite Brooke over a lot more often. So Brooke and I would usually find things to do around my house. Although there wasn't much to do, we would usually settle for watching a movie. That didn't really bother me at all, because at least I got to be with her. We usually wouldn't even get halfway done with the movie before we started talking, and making out a little more.

The summer was a lot more fun than I thought it was going to be. School was also right around the corner, and getting schedules was about to be a priority. Now that we would be juniors, that could drive, we were going to get our schedules ourselves. Brooke and I planned on going together to get ours.

When going to get our schedules we were surprised to see that we had four classes together. The first three classes of the day and then our seventh hour was the same. Seeing how similar our schedules were, I could care less who else was in our classes, because we were going to find a way to sit together regardless of who was in our classes.

I did check with Paul, Ryan, Tony, and Matt, to see what classes they had. Matt had a widely different schedule from the rest of us, because he was a senior. He also had most of his credits, so he was just taking a bunch of different electives he thought would be easy. I couldn't believe that he was going to graduate soon, and it would just be Tony, Paul, Ryan, and I left. It turned out that Paul and I had one class together, which was the seventh hour with Brooke and I. Tony and I had our second hour together with Brooke. While Ryan and I had no classes together.

The scheduling was vastly different from last year which gave me hopes that this year would be a lot more contrasting compared to last year's schooling. School itself is easy, it's just stressful with the added drama that occurs, and the constant routine we're expected to grow accustomed to.

The school year was approaching, and before I could fully grasp the reality of it, the first day was here. I lost my admiration for the new year. It felt like any other day at this point, especially now that I'm an upperclassman. It's not like anything about the school was going to catch me off guard. I already knew a good amount of people, because of going to parties and just being at school. I wasn't going to think much of the first day, because I was really losing my care for school in general. Nothing about this felt special anymore, just another task to complete.

When getting to school Brooke and I got our former parking spots reestablished. She now had a license obviously, so now she wouldn't be driving illegally. We walked in together talking about the movie we were "watching" about two days ago. We joked about the plot of it, knowing that neither of us actually watched it. There wasn't much to really say as our class was somewhat close to the entrance of the school. When we got to our class we immediately put our bags down, and sat shoulder to shoulder. We sat quietly as we watched everyone else walk in. Seeing that we didn't know anybody else very well in the class, we began to talk again.

I don't remember anything that the teacher was saying. I was concentrating on what Brooke was talking about. Her words were very poise, and I missed the conversations we would have in class. I liked being quiet, but talking to her made time go by a lot faster. We spoke in a whisper the whole time so we wouldn't bother anybody in the class.

The next class, Brooke and I walked there together carrying our conversation that started in the previous class. When we made it to our class we saw Tony sitting at a table alone. We went to sit by him, and he didn't acknowledge us at first when we sat down. We thought it was odd how he didn't even look up.

"Hey Tony. Are you okay?" Brooke asked with a level of concern that showed she actually cared for how he was feeling.

"Yeah…I'm alright." Tony responded slowly and with sorrow it sounded like.

I sat down and spoke to him about random things I knew that he liked. He always seemed so down, but anytime we would ask if he was okay, he would say he was. I'm sure if he wanted to talk about anything that was wrong he would.

Even this summer whenever our friend group would hang out together, Tony would always look sad. It was odd, because it was rare for him to carry a smile after we would all go our own ways after hanging out. I would try to make sure he was to the best of my ability, but usually I was met with silence. The same silence I was stuck with in class while looking at him. It was a cold and loud silence.

The class ended, and before I could call out to Tony he was gone. He turned around the corner quickly. Brooke and I looked at each other hoping the other would know what was going on with him.

"Is he alright?" Brooke asked me, while looking at the last spot we saw Tony.

"I-I don't know." I answered generically, but I had no good answer for her.

We walked to our next class conspiring what could possibly be wrong with Tony. He was our good friend so we wanted the best for him in all aspects. When we got to our third class together I rolled my eyes when I saw who was in there. Of course Brooke was giddy, because sitting in class looking air-headed was Sara. She was oblivious to everything going on until she saw Brooke. When they saw each other they both made the same high-pitched squealing noise. I knew how this went last year, and I assumed it would be the same now.

Sara looked at me with the same look of disgust she did last year when we came back from winter break. I saw the mean snarl she was directing towards me, and avoided eye contact. She probably didn't know that things between Brooke and I were back to normal. I still followed Brooke to the table with Sara. I sat across from Brooke, while she sat next to Sara. The same way it was last year.

"What are you doing here?" Sara said to me in a prissy voice, with the same look of disgust on her face.

"Sara! Don't be mean to him, everything's been resolved." Brooke stopped me from responding to her, and butted in.

I sat back looking at the two of them holding my silence. I didn't want to cause any problems, so I decided to remain quiet. I hoped that would resolve the conflict between Sara and I, so I wouldn't have to.

"Oh...I missed a big part of the story, didn't I?" She said rhetorically, oblivious to what happened at the beginning of the summer.

She rested her anger towards me, and looked at me with the same bitter face she would usually have. The rest of the class was normal after those few words that needed to be said. I was glad I didn't really have to say anything.

Later at lunch, Brooke willingly came and sat at the table with my friends and I. They all were shocked at first. Looking at us as if they missed something, which they did. Sara sat next to Matt knowing that there would be no division between her and Brooke anymore. I was happy to be with Brooke again, and things seemed to be back to normal. Even though, when we tried to talk to Tony he seemed as if he was shutting down.

We tried to engage him to get him to talk, but he spoke defensively not wanting to be bothered by anybody. We were all pretty confused, because we weren't trying to cause problems. We just wanted to know if there was anything wrong, so we could help. No response, only silence.

Whenever Paul, Brooke and I got to seventh period we mentioned how Tony's behavior was strange. We couldn't really come to any conclusions, so we started talking about other things.

Thoughts of Tony still lingered in my mind, but I was worried about so much. I didn't want to mess things up with Brooke again, so I remained conscious of things I did thinking of how she would perceive my doings. I thought about how Tony was feeling. I had no clue what to do, or if I should do anything at all. I was probably overthinking like I often do.

Once class ended, I walked with Brooke, but I was quiet. Not because of her, but because I was thinking. Thinking about how Tony was when he was scared to go home at the end of our freshman year. He ended up getting better after that, but what caused that to begin with. I could never find out. He knew that if he ever needed anything that he could contact me, and I would help.

School ended and it started to rain when we were leaving. It was August, the only month there was supposed to be no rain, but it rained. I hustled to my car with Brooke. As we both tumbled into my car we laughed about getting wet. During our laughter I could see Tony in the distance walking with his hood on. Before I could think of offering help to him, Brooke pulled my attention away, so it would be more directed towards her.

She asked me if I wanted to do anything, but I was speechless in response. It's not like I didn't want to be with her, I was just becoming more concerned with Tony. This was getting extremely odd. Why was he like this? How should I help him? Should I even try to help him? There could truly be nothing wrong, but I don't know Brooke took my empty response as a sign to leave. She began to get out of my car looking annoyed. Before she could fully get out I grabbed her hand and told her to wait. She came back in and waited for me to speak.

"I'm sorry, I'm just really worried about Tony." I told her after a few seconds of quietness.

"It's alright. Everything will be alright. You're a good friend." She put her hand on top of my to reassure me.

I believed her, and fell into the comfortable space she provided. I invited her over, and she obliged. She asked if I could just drive, so I did with no hesitation, putting the car in drive. We ended up driving past Tony, and it looked like he could've cried. I couldn't help but to feel terrible. I wanted to stop the car, but I just kept driving.

By the time we got to my house it was pouring down rain. I only thought about if Tony was somewhere sheltered. The look of concern rested on my face.

"He's okay Landon, you don't have to worry." Brooke told me, when we went to my room.

I tried believing her, but I still carried my concerns. That was one of my closest friends, I only wanted the best for him. Brooke did her best to make sure it didn't bother me too heavily. I started to let my worry go the more she spoke to me. I didn't have to be with her. If this were to happen only five months ago, I don't know what I would do. The amount of security I felt with her, was all I needed to feel safe.

As her time to go back home came near, I began to think about Tony again. When taking her to her car, which was still at the highschool, I saw where I last saw Tony and wondered where he was. When we got back to her car, I reimagined him walking looking upset and being alone. Why did I get to have someone, and he didn't. It just wasn't fair. I wanted him to be as happy as I was.

"He's okay Landon! Stop worrying." She exclaimed.

"I can't, it's not that easy. He's one of my closest friends, I don't want him to feel alone." I responded with the built up worry I've held all day.

"I know, but he'll get better. Have more patience than panic." That last sentence resonated with me.

I held on to what she said as she left, and while I was making my way back home. I could only worry, but I tried my best not to. Even as I made it home and I layed in my bed, I repeated Brooke's phrase to myself: "Have more patience than panic."

XXII

It was a gray cloudy October morning, and no part of me wanted me to go to school. I sluggishly rolled out of bed with my eyes half open. I didn't feel like I was awake, and I had a stinging headache. School was already getting to feel like an endless routine that needed to be done. Everyday was losing more importance. Brooke and I had no problems still, and the year was looking pretty good overall.

Whenever I convinced myself to get ready for school, I looked in the mirror to see myself looking like a mess. I did my level best to look presentable quickly so I wouldn't be late for school. Although school is starting in fifteen minutes. I made sure I didn't smell bad, and headed out the door swiftly.

The weather has been pretty poor recently, and it seemed unexpected. Last year the weather didn't seem this way until January. Not because it was cold, but more so because it was so gloomy. Obviously days are shorter around this time. Just seemed kind of peculiar that the weather was getting this way so early.

School was pretty normal when I ended up getting there. I was only about five minutes late, which was impressive knowing the kind of day I've had. When I made it to class Brooke looked confused as to why I was late.

"Did you not see my text?" She asked as I was setting all of my things down.

"Oh yeah my bad, it was a rough morning." I responded jokingly, while looking at the text asking where I was.

I played catch up for the rest of class. I was trying to hold a conversation with Brooke while simultaneously doing my school work. She took it as me ignoring her, and became quieter as we headed to our next class. I reassured her that I was only doing that to make sure I wouldn't fall behind. Our conversation was put to a halt when Tony came in with a bright smile on his face. He started talking about a bunch of random things nonsensically. Brooke and I were visibly confused, as this was nothing like Tony. I wasn't complaining, because he appeared happy, and I didn't want to take it away from him.

The more he talked the more my happiness for him faded. The only reason being I smelled a hint of what seemed like marajuana. Was he doing drugs? Was his resort to his pain being high? I asked Brooke after class to see if she smelled the same thing I did. She told me that she did and I instantly knew why he was so open. I was disappointed that he went about creating bad habits to handle his problems, but I sound hypocritical. I did the exact same thing with alcohol when Brooke and I weren't together.

The only real reason I stopped was because I got Brooke back in my life. So could I help Tony in this scenario? I felt as if I had to do something, so this wouldn't be a constant thing, where he wasn't sober.

Later at lunch the smell was still being emitted from Tony. Everyone was shocked to hear him speak so frequently. They also could smell the odor that came from the marajana he was using. Although nobody said anything. Why didn't we say anything? I guess I didn't feel the need to make a big deal out of it, but he came to school this way. Who knows what he does after school, if he's willing to come to this environment under the influence.

Paul, Brooke, and I spoke briefly about it in our seventh hour. We didn't know if this should truly warrant concern or not. Is this even okay? He's happy and socially open, but it's obviously not a good habit to start. It was hard to know what to make of the situation without knowing all of the details. I didn't want to assume too much, but I also didn't want Tony to go down an unrecoverable path.

Tony was like this for the rest of the week, until we

asked him about it Friday. We all gathered at the lunch table inquiring about his health decisions, and why he was choosing to smoke marajuana. We all were becoming more concerned by the day, because even in this state of not being sober, he was continuing his patterns of not being able to portray happiness.

"Tony. What's going on man?" Ryan asked at the lunch table as we all huddled together to see his answer.

"Nothing, I'm perfectly fine." Tony responded with a nonchalant tone.

"Then why do you come to school high all the time now?" Paul said right after Tony finished speaking.

"I...Why are you trying to ruin my high?" He was trying to keep a joking demeanor.

"Cause this isn't okay, we're worried about you." I butted in stressing my concern.

Tony looked at us as if we were villains. We were all in agreement that we wanted the best for him. It was hard to see how he wasn't insightful and that he was oblivious to having a problem. The air was becoming thick as tension continued to arise between Tony and all of us. The silence overtook the table and nothing was said. We just left without any problems being resolved.

When seventh period rolled around that day it was hard to speak without thinking about Tony's situation. Why did I become so obsessed with this? It's not like I'm helping as is, so why am I so involved. Paul could sense the distraught I was feeling and tried his best to comfort me, but I was stuck in this mood. I wanted him to feel better. I want Tony to not have these problems, but I don't know how to help. I was lost and felt as if time was running thin for me to do something helpful.

Before leaving school I saw Tony still in his unsober state, and he approached me. I looked appalled to think that one of my childhood friends was turning for the worst. Although he looked happy, was this worth it?

"Hey Landon!"

"Hey Tony."

"I hope everything goes well for you." He said while walking away from me.

"What? What do you mean?" I called out to him, but I got no response.

...

The next monday Tony didn't come into second period that following morning and instantly I was filled with fear. Brooke read the melancholy tone on my face. She became quiet during the class period. What was there to say? I was so worried for Tony. He didn't text me back over the weekend when I texted him Saturday. He usually didn't text back until later anyway, so I didn't think too much of it. I guess I should've because now he's not even at school. Where could he possibly be if he wasn't here? I could hardly focus on what we were learning, only thinking about Tony's whereabouts. I was fearful that something happened. These patterns of uncertainty in his life had become too prominent.

He wasn't at lunch either. Nobody even thought about it. That was until Paul asked if something was missing. Brooke looked at me to see my grim facial expression.

"Tony." I said bluntly, loud enough for everyone to hear.

"Yeah. Where is he?" Matt said back, not having a real concern about him.

"I-I don't know." I was doing my best to not break down in front of them, because I didn't want it to seem like I was overreacting.

Although I was around everyone I isolated myself from everyone, seeing that they didn't care about him as much as they should. Why are they not scared like I am? They're all still joking and laughing, but Tony isn't here. Why aren't they scared like I am? Maybe because my concern was too high. I thought it was warranted. I thought the way I was feeling had justification.

The rest of the day passed, and still no sign of Tony. He wasn't there Wednesday either. Yet I was the only one that was truly worried about what could possibly have happened to him. I tried calling and texting, but I got no response. I asked everyone in the friend group to check on him, but they also got no response. Brooke would keep telling me everything would be alright, and I wanted to believe her, but I couldn't, something had to have been wrong.

Unfortunately I was right. I came into class hearing horrifying rumors. The teacher came in with the same grimson look I've carried the whole week. She had an envelope, and it opened it up after the bell rang. I was confused as to why the teacher looked so sad, but I didn't want to seem as if what she was about to say was unimportant. Brooke was equally as confused as I was.

"Class...I'm sorry I have to read this, but uhh... administration asked me to, because they felt as if it was your right to be aware of what has happened." Her voice was trembling, and I still held my same confusion.

"What do you think happened?" Brooke asked.

"I don't know." I responded.

"There was a student that...committed suicide." The teacher said doing her best to hold herself together.

The room became silent. I prayed and hoped that it wasn't who I thought it was. I looked at Brooke and she held the same scared expression I did.

"Anthony Sims was the student. We're aware that you might have been friends with this individual, and we're here for you while you deal with this loss. We want to let you know that we take each and every student's mental health seriously, and that you're never alone. If you ever need someone to talk to, never feel embarrassed, your supervisors are only here to help you. I'm sorry."

As the words left her mouth my heart sank more and more. I was mortified. This had to be a nightmare. I put my head down on my desk, and as the thought of this being a reality settled in I began to sob. I was uncontrollably weeping in front of my peers. Brooke and my teacher put their arms around me as I continued to cry. I was so angry, and so sad, but I didn't know the right way to express myself. I just let the tears flow from my eyes like a river. I was hurt. Why? Why Tony? What happened? I loved him like he was my brother. Everyday he was silently crying for help, and I didn't help him. How could he be so selfish to go? Why was I so selfish to not help him? The image of him in the rain alone was burnt into my brain. This was all my fault. He's gone. I could've thrown up from the tears that kept pouring from my eyes.

Brooke helped me up and walked me out of the class. I didn't want to be an interruption, but I couldn't grasp on the idea that Tony was gone.

Why? Why was nobody as concerned as I was? Why were we all such bad friends? He deserved so much better than us. Why do I now have to speak about him in past tense? I couldn't even move, the pain the news brought kept me anchored to the ground, even as the bell rang. Brooke stayed by my side, and helped me get to my next class.

The halls were silent, only filled with the sounds of my whimpering. I thought about every moment I had with him. How could I have missed the signs? My heart felt like it was being digested by my stomach, because of the distance it sank. He's really gone.

The next few periods, my tears became more controllable, and my emotions turned more towards anger. We eventually made it to lunch and everyone was quiet. I looked around at everyone's face to see them sad. It took Tony dying for them to not joke around. Why do they care now? I couldn't stand the silence. It felt as if the whole cafeteria was empty.

"So now you guy's care? It took him to DIE FOR YOU TO CARE?" I started yelling knowing everyone in the lunchroom could hear me.

Brooke grabbed my hand to try to calm me down, but I still held the anger throughout my body. Nobody cared like I did. Why did we let this happen? I looked at Brooke, and fell apart wishing there was some way for Tony to hear me. Hear me fighting for him like I should've done when he was here. He was gone.

I stayed silent for the rest of the day, not wanting to act irrational in front of everyone. It was difficult, but I managed to make it through the rest of the day holding back the emotions I was feeling. Although when I came through the door I fell to my knees and continued my weeping, until mom came in. I didn't want her to see me like this, or for me to tell her, but I couldn't control myself.

"What happened?" She came down on the floor with

me to attempt to comfort me, like everyone has tried and failed to do today.

"Tony...died." I said fighting through my tears to mutter.

"What?" Her shock was audible, but I couldn't see because my eyes were so full of tears.

"Tony died mom. He's dead." I could hardly breathe, because of the amount I was crying.

Mom began to bawl her eyes out with me. She knew how much I cared about him, and she cared for him just about as much as I did. She was hurt, even though I could tell she was trying to stay strong for me, but it was hard when it was so easy to fall apart with each other. Someone who actually understood what I was going through and felt the same. He was gone.

Mom took me to bed, and tucked me in as her crying became controllable. I didn't know I was even capable of producing this many tears. I knew it was all my fault. I grabbed my phone after hearing a notification. I prayed that it was Tony texting back, telling me that today was a big hoax, but it was Brooke asking if I was okay. Obviously I wasn't okay. I wasn't going to be okay anytime soon. I lost one of my closest friends, when I was supposed to be there for him. I failed him. I saw his name near the top of my messages, and decided to text him. I texted thinking there could be some way of him seeing it saying:

I'm sorry Tony. I failed you. You were one of my best

friends in this whole world. I can't believe that I have to be here now without you. It doesn't seem right or fair. You deserved so much better than any of us could have ever offered you. I wish there was something I could do to bring you back, because I don't want to finish life without you. You were so important to all of us, and I loved you. I'm sorry.

I kept sobbing as I typed out the text for him. I couldn't believe this.

He was gone.

XXIII

Months passed and it still didn't get easier to deal with. All I could do was blame myself for what had happened. I still text Tony every night, and tell him what happened throughout the day. It's gotten a little bit easier to accept the fact that he wouldn't respond, but it was still all pretty unbelievable. I still want to know what caused it, because we found out there was a suicide note, but there was no way for me to obtain it. I didn't even know if I would have the strength to even read it after all these months. Our table at lunch felt as if it had a hole in it. It did, he was gone.

The school made a small memorial for him, so students wouldn't forget, but how could we. It wasn't something I wanted to see everyday, but I was glad they wanted to put him in a positive light. Some students would leave notes, flowers, or other things to accommodate for not being there when it actually mattered.

I've never experienced anything like this. No matter what I could do he could never come back. The whole school felt his loss. Even though he wasn't friends with that many people we could all feel the change in the school's atmosphere.

An empty void was forming inside of me because of his loss. I couldn't help but think that I was a reason that he did it. I should've helped him. Why was I so selfish? All the signs were there, but I just ignored them like he wasn't one of my best friends. Now the only time I see him is when I replay memories in my head.

The only person that seemed to fill the hole that was formed in me was Brooke. She was like an addictive drug I couldn't get enough of. I felt bad for obsessing myself over her, but I wanted to do anything to get Tony's death off my mind. I couldn't really tell if I was bothering her, but her being around was the only way I could heal.

My school work felt meaningless, and I didn't have much energy to do anything. Maybe because Paul, Matt, Ryan and I got a little distanced after the incident. I blamed them and myself for what happened, and it seemed as if we all turned on each other. It wasn't easy for anyone. How could it be? We lost our best friend. No matter what any of us did, we just had to live with that.

I tried my best to. I didn't start drinking again, although I was tempted to do so. Brooke convinced me that wouldn't be a healthy way out. Obviously it wouldn't be, but it would stop the pain from overcoming me. I just aimed to not disappoint or let anyone down anymore. From ruining Jackson's life, to almost losing Brooke, to losing Tony. Life was overwhelming me, and I didn't know how to cope with my emotions.

The last time our friend group was all together, besides lunch still, was when his visitation happened. No words were said amongst each other while we were there. The hurt we felt was shared and we were all equally speechless. I remember Brooke holding my hand tightly squeezing it to let me know she wouldn't go. I don't know what I would do if this ever happened again. The feeling of loss was unbearable. I was still angry. Angry at myself, angry at my friends, and angry at Tony. Why did I let him go? Why did any of us let him go? Why did he let go?

As the first semester was coming to a close, and the weather was getting colder my emotions became cold with the climate. I only talked to Brooke and hardly talked to Paul anymore. I didn't know how to. Nothing changed between us, but everything changed around us.

The last day of our first semester, the school knew that the environment of the school was depressing. So they tried to do something fun for the students. They let us double down on our "senior prank", but let every grade participate. I didn't really get involved in it all. Everyone prepared for this prank for a week, and I couldn't care less. I just wanted to get through this day and then isolate myself away from the school. I hoped that this prank wouldn't disturb me in any way, but I still prepared myself for anything. I was conscious that any possibility I made up in my mind would occur.

I can say this is the first day since Tony passed the halls that didn't feel completely empty. I saw people smile and snicker. I had hoped that this might be a good thing to happen to us. I tried to eavesdrop on people's conversation so I could get a hint at what I should expect to occur. Nobody was talking about it. This was strange, and I was becoming antsy. I wanted to know what to expect.

By the time lunch came around, talk about the prank started to spark up. While walking to my table I was hearing a bunch of different things that were expected happen. I couldn't tell in depth what they were talking about. I was going to still stay to myself no matter what.

"Have you guys figured out what they're doing for the prank?" I asked the table.

Everyone stared blankly at each other waiting for someone to respond. Did this mean they knew or did they not? I sat for a moment just waiting for an answer, but nobody gave one. I didn't even really like talking to them anymore. Everything they said seemed ungenuine, and it seemed as if we were forcing ourselves to continue to sit by each other.

Lunch ended with minimal conversation. Although I could tell the prank was about to happen. There were a bunch of students standing by Tony's memorial. Anger filled me thinking they were about to do something to dishonor him. So I stood with them to intervene in any way, to stop something negative that could potentially happen. Paul joined me with the same disgusted look I had as we both anticipated the worst to occur.

After a couple minutes the bell rang and nothing happened. More students were surrounded by the memorial to the point where it seemed as though half of the school was here. I was becoming more anxious with the more people there were. Paul and I got closer together fearing what could happen. Our principal came to where we were and confronted us.

"Why aren't you all in class?" He questioned firmly.

All the students pulled out a utensil, and pricked their fingers. A single drop of blood came from their fingers. After that the students who were the closest to the memorial formed a line. Nobody said anything in response to our principal, but all executed movements in unison. I was shocked to see. I was politely shoved out of line. I felt guilty because I didn't have anything to prick my finger. Neither did Paul, so the both of us spectated everyone. After they finished.

Jayden Culvert of all people spoke, "Our mental health matters, and we will do anything for our silent voices to be heard. No need for the student body to feel as if we're drowning alone."

Everyone started clapping for him. Paul and I followed suit. I was surprised by how powerful his words were. It was like he truly cared. He didn't know Tony, but he said exactly what I was thinking. I was touched. I thought I was the only one who was affected by this immensely. They took the occasion for a prank and made it an opportunity to empower our voices.

I was really grateful. I had it planned out in my head something bad would happen, but our school showed that people aren't always that bad.

Paul and I embraced each other. He began to tear up as he told me he was sorry. I didn't know what to say in response so I held him as a best friend would. The same way I wished I could've reassured Tony. I've never seen Paul cry, so I knew he meant his apology. I felt terrible that he thought the need to apologize to me. It made me realize the selfish mind I had, and used other people to cover my own insecurities. I lost Tony, but he wasn't gone. He would never be gone.

That was the best way for the first semester to end for me. It improved my mood slightly, and put me more at ease with what happened. Still, it was difficult to fully come to terms, but it helped to know that I wasn't alone.

Christmas came faster than expected, but it felt like any other day. I was sixteen almost seventeen, there wasn't anything that could've made it that more special. Brooke and I agreed to meet somewhere the day after Christmas, because she would be occupied by her family. Mom and I hung around the house Christmas day. I was just waiting for the next day so I could see Brooke, and get out of the house. The day felt long, and it was freezing so I did my best to bundle up with blankets I found around the house. I waited to pass watching every Christmas movie imaginable.

Finally the day passed over. We agreed on going to a burger place and I enjoyed. I didn't think there was any special reason other than seeing each other. I brought a gift I prepared for her. My gift to her was a funny shirt as well as a big stuffed animal. She mentioned how her dog tore up her other stuffed animal, and how it saddened her. I wasn't really expecting to get anything in return. I just felt the need to get her something, because of how much of her time she's given me.

Upon arrival I saw Paul's car there. At first I just thought it was a coincidence, but when I looked in the window of the restaurant, I saw Brooke ordering with her belongings at a table that Paul was already seated at. Did I miss something? I thought this was just supposed to be a one on one date with Brooke and I. Not that I was mad that Paul was there, I was just confused. I figured there was some sort of probable cause that he was here.

I walked in and sat down next to Brooke's belongings. I didn't have much of an appetite, so I wasn't worried about ordering. I looked at Paul who was already looking at me.

"Why are you here?" I asked him. I thought I sounded snappy as the words came out, but I didn't really care.

"I missed you." He replied.

"So did you set this up? And if so, why didn't you just ask to meet me somewhere?" I was becoming more confused by the minute.

"I didn't think you would come if I asked, so I asked Brooke to invite you." He started to avoid eye contact. He was embarrassed with his words it seemed.

"Paul...I would've come if you asked. Do you think there's a problem between us?" I was starting to become concerned with his feelings.

"I thought there was. I thought I lost my best friend. When we were at Tony's memorial that last day of school, we hugged each other. It was like I got a glimpse of being your friend again." He got quieter as he spoke.

Paul wasn't really a confrontational person, so I understood why he was speaking the way he was. I felt bad, I knew I was distant, but I didn't know I was causing problems.

"I'm sorry...I know I've been distant. It's just been so hard, because it felt like I was the only one there for Tony until the end." I was aiming to give him a good response without starting an argument.

"I was there for him. Everyday after school I would take

him home. He would tell me how you were with Brooke after school, so I thought the same thing about you."

I started to feel sorry for myself. I was really the problem. I know that it wasn't his intention to make it sound that way by what he said, but I felt like it was my fault. I could've done more. I've healed so much since then, and I didn't want the thought of my own wrong-doing to open the wound back up.

"I know. I know it's my fault. It hurts me every night, and I was starting to deal with it better, but don't put everything on me." I told him sternly.

"I'm sorry I didn't mean to make it sound that way. It's all of our fault, but…"

Brooke walked back to our table, and the both of us fell silent. She began eating her meal. After a couple bites she began to slow down her chewing, realizing the awkward feeling that was at the table. Brooke glanced at me, and then looked at Paul. Paul was shying away from eye contact, and I only looked at Brooke.

"Is everything alright?" She asked while there was still some food in her mouth.

"Yeah." Paul and I said simultaneously.

"Well…are you gonna tell Landon what you told me?" Brooke asked Paul while looking at me.

"I'm sorry Landon." Paul told me. He held a sorrowful look on his face.

"There's no need to be anymore. We can't change what happened." I responded as if I had no care.

I wanted all of this to be over. They looked at me as if I was crazy. It felt as if the roles had changed. They care too much, and I acted as if it didn't matter. Why should it matter? He was gone and it was becoming easier to accept over time.

The restaurant became empty. Only Brooke, Paul, and I remained. They started giving me antagonizing looks, because of my previous comment. I thought being blunt and harsh would be the only way to get out of this talk. Paul should've known we're still friends, so it was somewhat disheartening that he thought so little of our relationship that we've built.

I wanted to say more, because this was the first time in a while that I've really spoken to Paul. Although my mind became empty thinking of what I should say. Being here started feeling forced, as Brooke was now finished with her meal. As silence grew louder, Brooke took initiative to initiate some kind of action.

"Well I think I'm going to go home, you guys should stay in talk if you have time." Brooke said as she was gathering her things to leave.

I didn't even have time to fully say my goodbyes to her as she left. There still stood silence when she walked out of the door. Paul and I looked at each other with blank faces. What was I supposed to say? Things didn't change, but they were obviously different. I didn't know what words to say to make this interaction easier on the both of us. I also didn't want to just walk out on him, because he deserves more from me. The way I've been acting is understandable, but isn't fair to the person who's always been there for me. It's always been Paul and I together for as long as I've lived in Colorado. Now it feels like there's a mountain between us. It was unbearable. I felt miserable that he was even scared to approach me.

"I love you Paul. Nothing's ever going to change that." I said after a few more moments of silence.

"I love you Landon. I just don't want to lose you too." Paul was becoming teary-eyed again.

I didn't know what words would comfort him. I stood up with it being only us two in the restaurant now. He stood up as well and we hugged each other. The same way we did at Tony's memorial. The same way we should've at Tony's visitation. The same way I could only hug my best friend.

After embracing each other, I left. While I was leaving it still felt as if I had a gaping void in my chest. The same one from the day we lost Tony. Slowly it was being filled. Ignoring it wouldn't help. Destroying the relationships I have with people wouldn't help. I realized I wasn't alone.

They were here for me.

XXIV

I spent most of the beginning of the new semester doing my best to rekindle relationships that felt as if they had fallen apart. Ryan and I reconnected easily, because of his kind and patient nature. Matt and I took more time as he was focused on getting ready for college seeing that he was a senior now. It was pretty unbelievable to see how much time had flown by, and I was wasting it by isolating myself.

When fixing my relationships with my friends, it started to seem as if I was neglecting Brooke. That wasn't my intention at all, I was just making sure I didn't make the rift between me and others not widen beyond repair. Although she didn't make a big deal about it. I was slightly confused by that, was I spending an extended amount of time with her before? Did she just not want to be with me as much anymore? I don't know what I did, but I was doing my best to balance me and everyone else. Maybe

I should be prioritizing her more, but she really doesn't seem bothered by us not spending as much time together. I was overthinking about Brooke and I again. We've been together for two years now. I shouldn't continue to have these doubts, but it was hard when my mind was blocking the truth with my own insecurities.

It was the week of my birthday, and most things seemed as if they went back to normal. Even though I know they would never be the same again. I used my birthday as an opportunity to ask to hang out with Brooke, because we haven't seen each other outside of school in weeks. It wasn't normal for it to be that way, and I really missed her. So that Monday at school I decided it would've been a good idea to ask her.

"Hey Brooke, do you want to go get food for my birthday? I'm not saying it as if you have to get me something. I just want to eat with you." I was hesitant to ask her, fearing she would say no.

I didn't think I gave her a reason to say no, so ultimately I wasn't too worried about her saying "no." I only had lingering thoughts that stuck with me. It was just strange how she was subtly becoming more distant. I wasn't sure if the time I was spending trying to recuperate my relationships with others took away from what we've already built, and established.

"Yeah...I really would Landon, but my parents and I already have something planned. Can we do something this weekend?" She seemed as if she had been avoiding this conversation.

There was now awkward tension between the two of us. We stood not really knowing what to say. As if we had become strangers. I had to say something, I couldn't just stand here.

"Oh I- this weekend works…" I wanted to continue talking, but nothing would come out.

I felt defeated after talking, so I kept quiet for the remainder of our time together. What did I do? Why doesn't she not want to be with me on my birthday? I was hurt. I felt as if I messed up something without knowing. Maybe she only avoided the conversation, because she truly had to do something with her parents. Why wouldn't she have told me earlier? I wanted to act as if it didn't bother me, but it was obvious that it did.

I spent my birthday with Paul, Ryan, and my mom. It was a good time spent with them, but I could only think about Brooke. She should be here I thought to myself. I was also glad that everyone was willing to be together again. It did feel slightly empty without the presence of Tony, but we were getting able to handle things better. We handled things together, rather than alone, which made it easier.

…

A couple months have passed, and the balance

between me, and everyone else was good. Matt was about to graduate, and had asked that we all come to his graduation. We all already planned to go, so we accepted his offer simultaneously.

Brooke and I were a little better, but we were no longer at the point where we would spend everyday after school with each other anymore. It was different, but it was okay, because I still had Matt, Ryan, and Paul. I guess this was the new normal, and I had to deal with it. As long as I didn't permanently lose any of them I was okay.

Graduation day for Matt was here and we all went to the football field to be there for him. Sara sat by Brooke, who sat by me. I left an open space for Tony, because even though he wasn't here physically, I felt as if he was owed to watch this moment in some way. On the other side of the gap was Paul who understood the meaning of the gap. Paul sat next to Ryan, and we were ready to see Matt get his diploma.

Everyone complained about how long it was taking things to get things going, but I was just staring at Brooke the whole time. If the time was long I wish it could last forever, so I could remain next to her for as long as possible. Every time I saw her it was like I was falling in love with every moment we've experienced all over again. I fell in love with every detail of her face all over again. She was beautiful, and even though this occasion wasn't about her. My mind wouldn't let me take my eyes off of her. I wondered if she still thought the same about me. I became a little more worried about us everyday. I knew we weren't holding on to a thread, but I miss spending all of my time with her. I was just being selfish, and I was aware. Nobody could understand how much I needed Brooke with me. I felt incomplete without her.

"Matthew Gordon." Announced our principal, and we exploded with cheer.

Our cheer was led by Sara, and Matt's parents who sat a couple rows away from us. We were all in unison with our cheer as we watched Matt get his diploma. He showed the piece of paper to the crowd and we continued our applause for him.

Once the graduation was over we met Matt on the field. We all rushed him and gave him a group hug to show our honest congratulations that he made it through school. It's been hard, for everyone. After we let go of him Paul decided to ask him a question I'm sure we were all thinking.

"So now that you're done with school what does that mean?" He asked him as we all laid our eyes on him.

"I'm still going to be around, for all of you guys. Sure I'll be around a little less, but I'll never leave you guys. I love all of you." I smiled, taking his words directly to my heart.

Just the thing I needed to hear. I didn't want to never

see him again after this. I didn't need to lose two of my best friends in that short of a time period.

When I got home after Matt's graduation I felt alone. The house felt empty. I had come to terms that I wouldn't see Matt that much. Still there was no Brooke, and it still seemed off that we weren't hanging around each other as much. Still there was no Tony, and he couldn't come back no matter what I did. I felt alone. I sat in my room isolated in a melancholy state.

The only person that came was my mother. That's all I really needed. She could tell I was feeling down, so she sat beside me, and gave me a comforting hug. I needed this hug. I wanted it from either Tony or Brooke, but I was glad I could get one from my mother regardless.

"I know you've been dealing with a lot recently, and you've been the strongest soldier I could have ever asked for. So guess what?" Mom said to me.

"What?" I responded confused as to why she was proposing anything to me at this time.

"We're going back to Texas at the end of this school year." After she finished her sentence my eyes lit up.

I've kept in little contact with Jackson. He was really busy with football, and I didn't want to get in the way of that in any way. Also because I was scared, because I still felt as if I ruined his life. At least I get to see him and Grandpa. Since Brooke wasn't around as much I guess this was the best thing for me. Regardless of the situation I knew that Grandpa and Jackson could make me feel the comfort I needed. I guess I was going to get that comfort soon.

XXV

The end of my Junior year came, which meant mom and I were going to Texas. A big relief I needed, knowing I didn't have to worry about anything going on in Colorado anymore.

I already had a bag prepared, so I was just anxious to get out of the state. I was excited to break out of the continuous cycle I was becoming accustomed to. Even with the thought that my senior year is right around the corner and I wasn't prepared for the real world at all. Would my friends and I be close after highschool? I mean I've heard from Matt, but it's not the same. Not that I expected it to be, it's just so different. Would Brooke and I still be close? Something I only doubted in my mind was becoming more and more probable with each passing day.

That night I could barely sleep, knowing that I was going to be able to get away from everything. I was so excited for something new. Although I still worried if things would be hostile between Jackson and I, because I ruined his life. It took me passing out for me to finally go to sleep that night, as I fell asleep with every thought still on my mind.

The next morning mom woke me up gently. The sun wasn't even up yet, and I was confused as to why she decided to wake me up so early. I slowly woke up, yawning every other minute it felt like.

"Why did you wake me up so early?" I asked her, as I was still rubbing my eyes.

"Do you not want to go to Texas anymore?" She responded, sounding aggravated.

Neither of us were morning people, so I just complied and got out of bed. I gathered my things that I packed and threw everything in the back of the car. I didn't even want breakfast, I just wanted to go back to sleep. I flopped myself into the passenger seat and laid my head against the window to go back to sleep. Mom came out shortly after and started up the vehicle. I slowly dozed off knowing that the drive to the Denver airport could at least get me about another hour of sleep.

At least that's what I thought, because when I woke up we were still driving. Surely I was asleep longer than an hour. When I fully regained my consciousness I looked around to see we were seemingly in the middle of nowhere. I was confused initially, until I put it together that we were driving all the way to Texas. I've only had to do this drive three times in my lifetime and I hated it every single time. The drive was over thirteen hours. It was a cruel drive that seemed like it was at least halfway over.

I looked at the navigation and I was right we only had six more hours to go. *Only.* I hated this, and this meant we had to drive back, because I'm almost positive we're not moving there. Mom saw that I was awake, and asked if I was ready to drive. I wasn't ready at all. I wanted to fly there, and fly back. I guess I had to be, because she told me I was driving at the next exit. The car was in dire need of gas as is. So it would be a good opportunity to stretch, and get snacks. Mom looked like a zombie. She was visibly exhausted.

We took the next exit, and found the nearest gas station. I was glad to finally get my "morning stretch". I couldn't really tell where we were. It just looked like a barren wasteland. Maybe we're close to Amarillo, because even though I have not taken this drive in years, I can remember the emptiness that city mostly had to offer. If that was the case that indicates that we are almost there.

Once I started to drive, mom almost instantly fell asleep. I just turned the radio on something I knew would keep me up until we got there. There was nothing to look at while driving. Just farmlands, and livestock. It was really boring to just watch the road and the animals pass by. Eventually we made it there, after what felt like forever.

Nerves struck me as we approached my grandparents house. It's been two years, a long two years.

I didn't know if Jackson hated me, or the full extent of grandpa's condition.

When we made it to the house, and I put the car in park, mom woke up like she was alerted of our arrival. She was aware of the situation, and got out of the car to grab our bags. We only planned to stay a few days so we only had two bags in the trunk. Mom grabbed her bag, and I grabbed mine right after her. Mom walked up to the door, and as she did so I could feel the nervousness and anxiety build in my gut.

My grandma was waiting for us and opened the door fairly quickly. I stood a couple feet away as my mom and her mom conversed a little bit. Once she went inside, I was hesitant to follow, but I did so. Once I entered I looked around for Jackson and his mom. There was no sign of either of them. I then looked around for grandpa who was watching television with grandma. I was really excited to see him, even if he will eventually forget me I will love him regardless.

"Hey grandpa!" I said enthusiastically, while walking up to him to be in his line of vision.

"Oh, hey Rachel. Hey…Landon." It seemed as if he was trying to take everything in still.

I didn't know what to talk about, because I wasn't sure of what he remembered. I wish there was something that could fix him. I don't know what I would do if I lost him. Although that was looking like something I would realistically have to come to terms with.

Jackson came into the room soundly, because of his large stature. A rush of nerves flooded my body when I first saw him. He surprised me by smiling when he saw me. Was he not mad? Mrs. West was right behind Jackson as they both came into the room. Mrs. West was giddy to see my mother, but I was still in a state of shock. Traumatized by what happened two years ago. Jackson came up and hugged me. I was stunned by his welcoming gesture, not reciprocating the hug at first. Once I realized that he really wasn't mad I gave a hug back. This has been my best friend forever. Even with me essentially ruining his life, he is still friendly towards me. The hug meant so much to me, and he probably had no clue. It felt like forever since I've seen him. I always imagined I would have to dodge a hurling first coming to my head if I ever interacted with Jackson again. He deserved the world for what I did to his family, yet he was the one who was still willing to give me reassurance. Jackson is a strong guy, not just physically, but also emotionally. I couldn't imagine how I would feel in his shoes.

My mother and Mrs. West caught up briefly as we settled in. It was already evening. Mom and I were obviously tired from being in a car all day, and wanted to rest.

We had dinner with my grandparents, Jackson, and his mother. Mrs. West told us how Jackson started going to a new school and how he's become a four star recruit. That sounds amazing to me, even though I have no idea what it means. Why did he have to go to a new school? Was I the cause? I couldn't help but to ask these questions, and feel horrible for what I did. I wanted to ask him myself, but I didn't know how to open up that conversation.

After the meal, I went to my room to get ready for bed. I still had a hint of jitters. I don't know why I needlessly stressed myself over what happened, when Jackson and his mother seem unfazed by it. As I fell asleep I was being haunted by the images of Mr. West on the floor in a pool of his blood with his jaw unhinged from his skull. I needed to ask Jackson how he felt about the whole situation, because I may never have this chance again.

The next morning I woke up with the mindset of determination. Determined to ask Jackson for his point of view on everything that happened. My brave ideology was put on a halt when I went to the kitchen. I saw Jackson laughing with my grandfather. The two of them looked so happy. I didn't want to disrupt them, but I was already halfway into the room.

"Hey guys how are you?" I spoke while walking towards them to enter myself into their conversation.

"Hey Landon, we were just talking about some football." Jackson replied.

I didn't know much about football, so I was unsure of what to say. I just sat down quietly and listened to Jackson speak. The sun was glaring into my eyes from the window. So I had my full eye contact on Jackson to avoid the sun. His words were poised, and I enjoyed listening to him speak, because he was so passionate and knowledgeable about football. He was so spectacular, and he just so happened to be my best friend.

Mom and Mrs. West walked in a little later. I wondered where grandma was, because she was the only one not in the room with us. She might've been outside in her garden she loves. She came in after mom and Mrs. West, so my assumptions of her whereabouts were incorrect. Regardless we all woke up, and I was grateful to see everyone awake and happy. I was glad to see even with me ruining things, life was still manageable for Jackson and his mother.

After gathering in the kitchen for half an hour, we all dispersed into small sub-groups. Mom was with Mrs. West, my grandparents were together, and Jackson and I were with each other. Jackson and I went off into the front yard, because I offered to throw the football with him. I knew how to throw one, so I wouldn't be making a complete fool of myself. We started off in silence, just tossing the ball back and forth, but after a while we started conversing. Just simple talk about how things were, and then I popped the question.

"Are you mad at me for what happened?" I said as the ball was landing in his hands.

He took a moment to deeply sigh. I thought I might've triggered him, and instantly became scared. I knew I shouldn't have asked this. I'm just going to ruin things again.

"No, but I'm glad you asked. I was at first, but not anymore." He responded after taking a second to think.

"What changed?" I was becoming very curious, wanting to know his side entirely.

"I was mad that I wouldn't have the big house, the nice car, or my old friends. And at first I blamed you for that. You were the easiest person to blame. Then after a while I realized you helped more than anything. You lifted off a burden I could never lift myself." I was confused. I helped?

I felt as if he was only saying things to make me feel better. Even if that was the case I was still surprised by his detailed response, and how he made it into a positive. I almost missed the ball while it was being thrown to me while I was thinking.

"Jackson, you deserve the nice house, the nice car, and all of the great friends. I took that away from you. I'm sorry." The silence after my statement could be heard by all the insects making noises outside.

"You didn't take that from me. My father did. I was held captive, distracted by all of the materialistic things, and not realizing my own self worth." His responses were very thorough and I was glad that he had been thinking about this.

"So how did I help?" I was still a little confused on where I played a role.

"Nobody was willing to stand up to the bully, but you were. You knew you couldn't beat him, but you weren't willing to see someone you love get hurt so you said something. That meant the world to me, that gave me the strength to rebel against his tyranny." I was too stunned to speak.

I was all out of words, so I set the football down and walked towards him. I wrapped my arms around him and started to tear up. I've been living with these thoughts that I ruined everything, when in reality I helped him.

"This whole time I thought I ruined everything for you, and I felt horrible. I just didn't want to see you get hurt. I love you." I said while fighting my tears so Jackson wouldn't think I'm soft To my surprise Jackson was also crying. He was letting his bottled up emotions from the past two years out the only way either of us knew how to.

"I love you too, Landon." I was so glad to know that all of my overthinking wasn't warranted. I was glad to know that I didn't ruin anything for him. I was glad to know that he loved me.

Jackson and I didn't really know what to say after that. We just went to find our mothers. The day was kind of empty outside of that talk that we had. I didn't mind that conversation could be the only thing I do all week, and it would be okay. That was the talk I've been needing for the last two years. To know I hadn't ruining everything.

...

The rest of the time in Texas was pretty boring to be honest. We didn't do too much in the area. I think this was just an opportunity to reestablish our feelings for one another. I was glad to do so, but dreaded the ride that was coming the next morning.

The last night that was spent in Texas, everyone in the house gathered for a nice meal. The mood was nice, due to the nice lighting that filled the room. Everyone was happy with how the week had gone, and we were only gathering to send off my mother and I back to Colorado. We knew that Jackson and Mrs. West probably weren't going to be awake when we left so this would be the last time we see them for a while.

We had a nice roasted turkey that grandma had been preparing all day for us. It was the kind of turkey you would expect to see at a thanksgiving feast. She was always a good cook so anything she made was delicious.

As we ate mom encouraged me to talk about my plans for my senior year and college. I really didn't have a plan I just wanted for Brooke and I to be in a good stable relationship when school was finished. Despite coming here to get my mind off of everything going on in Colorado, Brooke couldn't escape my train of thought. She continued to be my top priority at all times. Even with the distance between us, I would constantly ask if she was alright, and how everything was going for her back home.

After the brief discussion of my plans, Jackson took a turn on how he wanted his senior year to go, and where he had hoped to go to college. He was really keen on going to Baylor University, seeing that it was really close to home, and a very large and well-respected school. I really enjoyed hearing how all the wishes that he had as a kid were coming true.

After we finished as much of the food as we could eat, we all became very tired. We all went to our rooms approximately the same time. I was ready to go back home to Brooke, but I didn't want to leave Jackson as I felt as if our relationship had reached a new high. I was glad that he wasn't angry with me, and it made it easier going to sleep that night.

I dreamed about the things I hoped to do with Brooke when I got back to Colorado. I thought about the things we might do when she was glad to see me after being gone for a week. I could only dream.

When I woke up the next day abruptly with mom shaking me awake, I was aware that it was time to go back. I gathered my things very quietly hoping to not wake up anybody else with the ruckus I was bound to make. As I made my way to the front door with my things, I was surprised to see that grandpa was already awake and in front of the television watching the same game that he was watching when mom and I first made it to Texas.

Mom went to grandpa and gave him a hug. I was still waking up, so I was still regaining my consciousness. I saw the look of confusion when grandpa saw me. I looked back at him with the same look of confusion, wondering why he was confused.

"Good to see you Rachel. Who's the friend you brought with you?" Was he talking about me? Surely he was just joking.

"It's Landon, dad." My mom answered him.

My eyes began to fill with tears realizing what was going on. This couldn't be happening. I must've still been asleep. I thought he would remember me.

"I'm sorry I- I don't think I've met you before." There was a genuine look of confusion on his face, as tears were becoming visible.

"We made it to the last day, and now you forget me? That's not fair." I should've been more considerate, but I was hurt.

"I'm sorry son, I just have a hard time remembering things. How should I know you?" He seemed so honest with his responses.

"I'm Landon, you're grandson. The little man you've known for the past seventeen years." I was speaking while tears streamed down my face.

I was in disbelief. He really doesn't know who I am. There was no way to get him to try to remember me, and I had to leave with that being one of my last memories with him. It wasn't fair. He was my male role model. He was the father I needed my whole life. He doesn't even remember who I am. I was hurt, but there was nothing I could do about it.

How do you accept the fact that someone you love doesn't even know you?

Why did I have to leave, knowing there was nothing I could do to make him remember me? I was just a faded figment of his memory. I thought I meant more. I didn't know what else to do, or what to say. I just stood a couple feet away from him and cried. I know he wouldn't even hug me, because I was just a stranger to him. Someone he just met.

When we got in the car mom tried telling me that grandpa still loves me, and he can't help his condition. I wasn't hearing any of it, I just wanted to go home now. There was nothing left for me in Texas. The biggest part of my family, besides my mother, is gone. I just wished there was something I could do. I wish there was some kind of cure to his illness. I wish I was worth remembering.

When we got back to Colorado, I was aware Brooke wouldn't come over like she did last time. I understood that I would have to sit alone with my thoughts. I felt defeated.

It was that same way for the rest of the summer. Even the times I would spend with Brooke I was filled with a certain emptiness. I needed something to change. I didn't know if it needed to be Brooke and I change or I change something else, but I was tired of how things were. Luckily for me there wasn't much school left.

I still had no idea what I planned to do for college. Ever since I've been with Brooke my grades have been good. Other than that spell where I was deep in my alcoholism. Other than that, I felt like it was acquirable to actually obtain a scholarship. That was my main objective this school year.

Not jeopardize my chances for college, and hopefully still be with Brooke. Once it felt like a guarantee that Brooke and I would stay together, but I doubt myself more and more everyday. My grandfather couldn't even remember who I am, so was I really even worth the bother. If my own family couldn't even find the importance in remembering me, why would Brooke?

I started to realize how much I was losing, I wanted to fall apart, but nobody would help put me back together. Brooke wouldn't, Tony couldn't, and the rest of friends wouldn't. Mom could, but she's already really stressed about how her father's doing, and I didn't want to add on to the stress. It wouldn't be fair to her. Then I thought about what would be fair to me. With as much as I've had to deal with, most kids couldn't even fathom what I've been through. I just wish someone was here for me. I just wished that I was worth remembering.

XXVI

It was about to be the start of my senior year. This was it. It was all finally coming to an end. Reminiscing about what's happened all throughout highschool was astonishing. It was strange how things seemed to be coming full circle. I even have Mr. Richards with Brooke and Paul again. I remembered him mentioning there was a chance of this happening when I was getting my schedule as a sophomore, but I didn't think it would actually happen. I wondered if he did anything to make it this way. I wondered if he knew all that happened between Brooke and I. Probably not, but it was interesting to think about how everything was developing.

The first day of school rolled around and I didn't even want to change. So I didn't, I went to school in my pajamas. The only thing I did was throw on a hoodie that I liked. You tell by the way I looked I didn't really care how school went anymore. Our dress code wasn't very strict so I knew going, looking the way I did I wouldn't get in trouble.

The grades below me were pretty annoying, so I hardly talked to any of them. Much less was I friends with them. I just knew this would be a cycle I would have to be a part of for the next nine months. After that my public education was over. At least until college.

I mindlessly listened to the teachers talk about themselves, and introduced themselves to the class. I couldn't care less about their personal lives to be honest. I knew they weren't really interested in mine, so why should I care about theirs?

The first day was going by pretty fast. Before I knew it I was already at lunch. Our table remained the same, with the exception of the gaping hole that was left from Tony's absence. It hurt less and less as time went on, but it still hurt every time I saw his empty seat. A spot that isn't filled, because of my own selfishness. There wasn't a lot of talking between any of us because Matt was also gone. It was weird now that there were only five of us, but we tried to act as if it was normal.

Eventually Paul, Brooke and I went to Mr. Richards class. It made me have a nostalgic feeling of our freshman year. Things were so simple then, only worrying about if I impressed Brooke or not. If our project would be good enough. Little things that I wish I could go back to. I couldn't imagine the amount of problems that would occur. It used to be so easy, even though I treated it like it was the end of the world. I saw Paul and Brooke the way I saw them as freshmen, and I realized how much we changed physically. Then I thought about how we changed emotionally. Mr. Richards probably still thought about us as those kids who had silly arguments, and worried about our grade on a project. He probably didn't know the pressure that was given to us by society, and each other.

I missed our freshman year. I missed how much we loved each other. I don't know if she stopped loving me, but it was evident it changed. I loved her all the same. Regardless of what would happen I would still love her. I know I can't really display my emotions well, but I tried my best to show her that I love her. I could only hope that she knew that.

As class proceeded, we sat at the same table we did as freshmen. The feeling was restored amongst the table. The three of us got the same sensation from being back here. Brooke and I smiled remembering how we got to know each other, and all of the key moments that started because of this classroom. I missed how we used to be. There's no reason for us to be distant, but we are. I feel terrible for ever complaining about anything she did in the past. I thought those complaints and everything that occurred over the years, have built on the pressure that brings us space.

I looked around the classroom to find that virtually nothing changed within the classroom. Mr. Richards grew out his facial hair a good amount, but he was still the same person I remember from all those years ago. I say "all those years" like it was forever ago, but that time feels like another lifetime at this point. We were just small kids, and soon enough we'll be in college. Time has flown, and I've been wasting a lot of it over needless problems.

The class started, but I could hardly pay attention to what was happening. I was still reminiscing about all of the things that happened. I remembered how that feeling I had while Brooke and I gave our presentation that brought us together. I thought about how that same feeling isn't much different to how I feel often nowadays. Maybe that was the reason Brooke was growing apart from me. Maybe she's dealing with her own problems, and I can only hold a selfish mindset to it. I wish she would come talk about it with me, because I can tell from just a look that she felt the same way I did upon seeing each other in our seats. I could tell that she missed the same thing I did. That had to have meant something. I wish she would come talk about it with me, because I can tell from just a look that she felt the same I did upon seeing each other in our old seats. I could tell that she missed the same thing I did. That had to mean something!

After the class Brooke and I walked out together. I was nervous to speak to her. I wanted to talk to her, but

I didn't know what to say. It felt like I was trying to win her over again. I was losing. My worst fears were taking shape before my eyes. I tried to reflect on what I've done wrong since New Year's of our sophomore year. I knew I was depressed, but was the dark void I created for myself consuming the loving feelings she had? Did it consume my own feelings, and I've been around her without feeling? I don't feel as if I have on purpose. I didn't feel purpose, because of all of the things I blame myself for. All of them were justifyingly warranted.

"Landon, can I come over after school?" Brooke was hesitant before she spoke.

"Yeah of course." I was glad she wanted to come over, because it's felt like forever since we spent time together.

I was surprised she even wanted to, but I guess being in Mr. Richards' class made her think of how things used to be. The same way I did. I was also shocked she wanted to come over, rather than meet somewhere. I felt wanted. This was the first feeling of being wanted I've had in a while. Even though Jackson was happy for what I did, it didn't seem as if he wanted me. My grandfather must've not wanted me, because he couldn't even remember me. It was starting to seem as if Brooke was next in line of people who didn't want me. A line that felt like it lasted miles.

A line I've created, because of my own problems.

The end of the day came, and I made it home waiting, patiently waiting for Brooke. I thought of things I could do to make her interested in staying for a long period of time. I would be glad to spend any time with her, but I wanted it to last. I wanted us to last, but it felt inevitable at this point that she would admit that she doesn't want me. Of course, like always, it would be my fault. It was almost always my fault, but I didn't know how to voice my concerns to her. I didn't want us to end. I didn't want to keep feeling like the problem. I didn't know how to support myself. I wish someone could magically fix the way I feel. It felt as if Brooke had the fix, but she held it to where I could only have the fix with her. She was like a drug, addictive, and I always needed to be around her to feel whole.

Brooke came over, and I felt instant warmness being around her somewhere I could consider my "safe place". She was happy to see me, it was evident by the smile that laid on her face. Maybe her feelings weren't gone. Maybe this entire time I've just been overthinking. That seems like a very probable answer, but I didn't know how to not overthink everything. How could anyone feel when the love of their life starts spending less and less time with them. Regardless of how she feels toward me, she was here.

She was smiling. I missed her.

She came up to me and gave me a hug. I reciprocated the action, and held her tightly. We were by the front door, and it made me remember this same predicament that occurred last year. It was a different feeling, but it was eerily similar to how things were when we weren't together. Her embrace made me feel needed. She was the only person that could conjure up this feeling.

"I'm sorry." I heard her whisper into my shirt.

In my mind I thought how she should be sorry. I also thought about how she shouldn't, because it was my fault. My words and actions made us distant. Even with this conflicting battle I had within myself I ended up saying, "Don't be, you did nothing wrong."

After our hug we didn't do much else, but talk. It was mostly catching up, because we just haven't been telling each other how things have been. I listened to how she applied to a college. It was Colorado State University, which she was more than capable of getting into. She then asked about me, but I couldn't indulge in how I've been feeling. I know she wouldn't want to really hear how it's actually going. Although it's been apparent of my mood change over the past year. I just feel like a completely different person. So much changed within such a small amount of time.

After we talked she saw that the snow globe she got me three Christmases ago still sat on my nightstand. She looked at it with a look of confusion. What was there to be confused about? Did she think that I would've gotten rid of it? It's stayed in the same area for the last three years.

She picked it up and shook it. The snow within it fell slowly as she watched it. I thought she was going to start crying, because I saw her tearing up. Although she never did. She looked at me and kept her mouth open showing she wanted to say something, but was speechless. I wanted to say something as well, but was scared to interrupt whatever she had planned to tell me. We sat in a long pause waiting for someone to speak. We just couldn't muster the words we wanted to tell each other. Things became stale after a while, because neither of us said any words. My brain was so loaded with things I've been wanting to say. Now that she's here I was too stunned by her beauty. I was looking at an angelic person who wanted to cause no problem, while she looked at someone consumed by their problems. I didn't try to be so problematic. It just seemed as if issues would just follow me wherever I go, and that deterred the one person I've always aimed to impress.

The night ended with us not saying much. When she ended up leaving I went back to my room to where I felt comfortable. I pictured her still being here to give me more comfort. I picked up the snowglobe and shook it the same way Brooke did. I watched the snow fall on the two figures that ice skated. What would this snowglobe look like if there was only one figure? It would feel empty. It would make the city behind the figure feel meaningless. It would make the globe feel meaningless if it was just one figure.

School was more of the same, feeling like an endless cycle. I only found joy in Mr. Richards' class. It gave me the optimistic mindset that things may be able to go back to how they were. Brooke and I have been together for over three years now. It is crazy to think that my life has revolved around another person that's only been present for a little over three years.

Brooke asked to see me after school one day after Mr. Richards class after months of minimal conversation. I still wanted to spend time with her, so I obliged to her request. I was kind of nervous about what she was wanting to tell me, but I was glad that we would be with each other nevertheless.

I was anxious after school waiting to see her in the parking lot. I waited for a little over five minutes by my car that was positioned a few spots away from hers. As I waited I thought of what she could be wanting to talk about. I was hoping it would be good, because I liked hearing about how her day has gone. The enthusiasm she carried while talking about her experiences was fun to hear.

Once she got out to the parking lot. I stood vigorously trying to look confident. I wasn't very confident, but I wanted to look like I had some authority as she walked up. I made eye contact with her, and fell back into a slouched position.

"Hey Landon." Her expression was dry.

"Hey Brooke, how are you?" I answered with enthusiasm and with a smile on my face. I was hoping that my tone would carry over to her, but me putting up a front did nothing.

"I-I don't know how to tell you this." She had a level of concern layered in her voice.

"What do you mean? Just say it." I responded almost simultaneously.

"I don't think I can do this anymore." She sounded sorrowful. It was a strange temperament she had.

"What? What- what do you mean?" I was becoming teary-eyed hearing my intrusive thoughts fulfill tuition.

"I don't think we can keep on going." I was getting more disheartened the more she spoke.

"So 'us' is over?" I said with the same dry expression that she entered the conversation with.

"Yeah, I think that's the best thing for both of us." She said as she started towards her car.

My legs started to quiver as she walked away. She only parked a few spots away, but watching her leave felt like an eternity. An eternity I didn't want to have any part of. I wanted to cry, but I couldn't grasp the reality of what just occurred. I had a grotesque feeling building in this pit of my stomach. We spoke so briefly and yet this is the end? Every experience we've gone through the last three years ceased to matter? This was the end. She left like nothing ever happened. My mind felt tormented by the thought of closing this part of my life. She became so important to me, and now she's gone. It doesn't feel real.

Although he doesn't remember me I just want to hear my grandfather. Even if it was just mom talking to him, he would know what to say. I could correlate his words with my situation in some facet. I just wanted to hear anything to make me feel any kind of emotion, besides despair. It's like she ripped every emotion out of me with such a simple conversation. After all of the conversations we've ever had, it was all over with one sentence? I was just hurt.

When I made it home I wanted to speak to mom, but I heard her either crying or laughing hysterically. The sound was unrecognizable, but I could tell she was either drastically happy or sad. I decided to enter the room and I saw a flush of tears streaming down her face. What was there to be sad about? Something important must've happened to warrant this amount of tears. Something must've been terribly wrong.

"What happened?" I asked with a comforting voice, hoping to bring her any level of comfortability.

Initially she couldn't even formulate a sentence. She just clutched onto me and kept balling her eyes out. I wanted to reassure her that things would be alright, but I didn't even know what was going on. I sat by her on the edge of her bed holding on to her the same way she would hold onto me when I was upset.

"Your grandfather, my dad…" She began to speak, but left her statement incomplete.

"What happened to him?" I felt my heart begin to

drop into the grotesque area that was already built in the pit of my stomach.

"He's…dead." Once I heard her, my heart felt broken. Shattered into a million pieces with nothing that could attempt to put it back together. It felt like I was stabbed with a knife continuously with no remorse.

Mom began to cry again. I tried to remain strong so she wouldn't feel completely hopeless, but tears started to fall from my eyes uncontrollably. This couldn't be real. I couldn't fathom the idea that I lost two of the most important people to me. I lost them both in one day. He died not remembering who I was. Why was this happening to me? What did I do to deserve this? I was already at a low place, I thought the imbalance of negativity would be fixed by any positive, but there was nothing there. I just sat there holding my mom falling apart. I tried not to make it apparent I was hurting, so mom wouldn't feel how I did.

Her face was a ghostly pasty white. What could I say? I was in no place to help anyone. I needed help, but the people who could help me were gone. Only a memory that was hard to access. A memory that would reconcile pain. I was completely broken. Only not falling weak, because I didn't want my mom to see me at my lowest point. She didn't deserve to see her only son hurt beyond belief. I knew she would take on the burden of my pain, but I couldn't let her do that. She just lost her father. I just lost my father figure. I lost my love. I lost everything.

XXVII

For the next week I just layed in my bed, surrounded by the dark void that was my room. I was still in complete shock by what had occurred. I didn't know a proper way to react or to cope with what happened. I saw no light emission besides the one on my phone. I didn't get up to eat or drink. I felt my stomach craving any kind of substance, but I didn't have the energy to move. I didn't get a text from anyone checking on me. I just went through my phone looking at old texts between Brooke and I. I looked at old photos I had with my grandfather. I didn't even have enough energy to cry at this point. I was just completely empty.

After this week my mom came into my room and turned the light on. I cowarded away under my blankets. I was a vampire to the light doing everything I could to stay away from it. Mom couldn't stand me not doing anything, so she yanked the comforter off my bed. The light was visible even with my eyes closed. I groaned in agony to see the light blaring sensations into my head. My head was pounding, because of the drastic change in my room.

"Look, you can't be like this forever. I know it's hard, but you can be great. You are so capable of doing so much. I can't let you just lay in your room and waste all of your potential. Do you think that's what my dad would've wanted?"

After hearing me not answer for a while, mom exited my room. I replayed what she said a couple times in my brain. I knew I couldn't live like this forever. What would anyone think of me if they saw me in this state? I couldn't let everything that happened be for nothing.

I rolled around in my bed getting readjusted to actually moving my body. A couple of minutes passed, and I decided to sit up. My muscles strained as I haven't had any physical activation in over a week. I looked around my room, and saw the snowglobe that Brooke got for me. I picked it up and clenched my hand as if I was going to break it. Before I could make the impulsive decision I put it back down, and looked at the two figures.

Instead of thinking of Brooke I thought of my grandfather.

We once went to Dallas and ice skated when I was very young. I was maybe seven years old. I remembered how he was trying to teach me how to ice skate, while he was struggling himself. I fell a couple times, but each time I did, he would pick me up and encourage me to keep going. So I did, I just kept going until I figured out how to skate. After I got the gist of how to skate I went faster and faster. I remembered being exhilarated by the speed I was going, and the affirmation my grandfather projected to me. I went in circles around him, as he laughed happily. He was happy to see me happy. That couldn't have been for nothing.

Recalling that memory made me remember how even if I kept falling I was willing to keep going. I knew I had to keep going. I had to for my grandpa, and more importantly, I had to keep going for myself.

The first thing I decided to do was eat food, after realizing how hungry I was. I went to the kitchen and grabbed the first thing I saw. Even though it was three p.m, I ate cereal. It was the first thing I saw, and I hadn't eaten in over a week. While I was eating the cereal I made, I decided that I was going to make a change. I was going to strive to be better, and have a better mentality. Even if I kept falling I would get up and try again.

After I finished my bowl, I told my mom that I was going out to get a job. She seemed stunned by the sudden change, but was glad to see me up. She let me leave, so I made myself look somewhat presentable, as I went out to get a job application.

I went to a few different stores in the town before

heading home after a few jobs hiring, and some saying that they weren't. Most of the jobs I was really interested in were unfortunately not hiring, but I was glad to at least have an opportunity to have any job.

The next day, which was a Saturday. I went back to the places that offered me an application, and gave them the papers back filled out with the correct information. I knew that I would have to wait now, but I don't know for how long. I was hopeful that they would offer me an interview within a week, but I was willing to wait.

My hope was fulfilled. Within the week I was given the opportunity to go to a fast food restaurant that I gave an application to, for an interview. I was excited, and happier than I have been as of recently. Having this chance makes me feel wanted. Such a simple occasion gave me self-worth.

I dressed up half-way decently. I put on khakis with a button down long sleeve shirt. I was filled with nervousness not ever experiencing anything like this before. I headed out the door with optimism that I haven't had in a while. I was glad that things were on the incline in my life. At first I admittedly didn't think I would even get a job, and that this attempt would be for nothing.

When I made it to the establishment I confidently muttered to myself, "Keep skating." As I walked in, I held a smile on my face to keep my spirits high. I try to be as proper and professional as possible. I walked up to the front where people would order food to ask for the manager. Once the man taking orders got me to the manager, the manager directed me to the back.

He took me to a small cubical room that was filled with papers and a singular computer. He didn't say anything at first, he just gathered my application and looked at the paper. He went from the header all the way to the footer.

The manager was a bald older man who had a pear-shaped figure. He wore reading glasses, and as he finished he moved his glasses above his head after he finished reading. I tried reading his facial expressions to make an assumption about how he felt about my application. Although he didn't change his facial structure once. I didn't know how to take in the encounter, because he showed no emotion.

"So, uhh Landon. Would this be your first job?" He asked me while looking back at the paper, squinting his eyes.

"Yessir." I closed my body inwards being scared to say too much. I did my best to look positive and be respectful.

"Can you tell me a little more about yourself?" The manager then asked.

"I- I'm a senior in highschool. I aspire to go to college, to further my education. I live with my mother, and am not associated with any clubs within my school, so I have a flexible schedule." I responded, hoping that would suffice as an answer.

"Well you seem like a really good kid, and I think this company would love to hire you." He said while standing up.

I matched him and stood up myself, with a smile on my face that went from ear to ear. He put his hand out for me to shake and I grabbed on to his hand out of pure excitement. I had a sudden rush of adrenaline and shook his hand profusely. The shake lasted a little longer than it was probably meant to. After I realized what I was doing, I let go of his hand.

"Can you start Monday after school?" He asked, while looking uncomfortable from my hand shake.

"Yessir I can. I get out of school at three-thirty." I answered.

"Great. I'll see you then. Your schedule will be finalized when you clock in on Monday. We'll also figure out your pay as we finish your schedule."

I nodded my head, and made my way out. I held in my cheers until I got in my car. Once I was in my car I let out a loud animated reaction. I had the music blaring as I was going home.

Once I got home I rushed into mom's room to tell her the news. She looked exhausted, but I hoped that the energy I had would translate to her, once she heard what I had to say.

"Guess who is now a working citizen!" Her eyes lit up as she heard how it went.

"Oh my goodness. That's great Landon!" She became more lively seeing how exhilarated I was.

I got closer to her to give her an embracing hug that I felt was necessary. She put her head on top of mine. She was happy seeing that I didn't continue the slump I was in. I was still going and I was really striving to improve myself.

On Monday I was anxious for the end of school to come. When it eventually did roll around, after a day that felt like an eternity. I walked with a fast pace to my car ready to go to work. I didn't know what was in store for me, but I was prepared.

Upon arrival at my job, I was filled with nerves not knowing what was about to occur. I was ready nevertheless. Getting hired was supposed to be the hard part, so now I just have to do the work. At least that's what I convinced myself while I was going in. I expected to be welcomed by my co-workers and they kindly teach me what to do. That's not what happened. I heard a lot of machines making a variety of sounds, and felt an emptiness throughout the building. It seemed as if nobody was there. I quietly went to clock in as I was instructed to by the manager, and saw my schedule. I saw that I would be working five hours a day every week day. From four to nine. After clocking in I wasn't sure what to do. I just stood around looking clueless for a couple minutes. I was just waiting for instructions.

While I was waiting I was surprised to see who

approached me. It was Alana. I haven't seen her since the New Year's party. She looked equally shocked to see me. I didn't know what to say. I was speechless.

"Hey…Landon. I'm sorry." She looked at me with remorse. It was apparent that she felt bad for what she did.

"It's okay we're not together anymore anyway." I didn't want to make things more awkward than they had to be.

She instructed me to follow her, as I was shadowing her. She showed me the basics of how to do the job. She explained what everything does, and how to use it. It didn't seem right that I had to be learning from her. I know that Brooke and I weren't together anymore, but I promised her that I wouldn't have anything to do with Alana anymore. Although I never blocked her, I just ignored her completely.

A couple hours passed, and I felt confident enough to do the job. It wasn't entirely too hard. My mind just went back to my sophomore year of why I even got myself in that position. Did that contribute to why Brooke and I aren't together anymore? I had to ask Alana why she did that.

"Why did you kiss me that night?" I asked her out of nowhere. I broke the silence with that question, that was very straight to the point.

"I…was hurt." She didn't even face me as she responded.

"What do you mean 'I was hurt'?" Do you know what

that did to me?" I started to get angry. Built up aggression that I never released from all those years ago.

"My boyfriend had just cheated on me, and I didn't know what to do. I just wanted him to hurt as bad as he hurt me." She said still not facing my direction.

"Who was your boyfriend, and what does that have to do with me?" I was becoming more curious than angry.

"Carmelo May. I saw him walk in with you. You two looked like really good friends, so the only way I thought I could get back at him was through you. I'm sorry." My eyes widened when she said she was dating Carmelo.

Carmelo didn't seem like the kind of person to do that. I guess I didn't know him all that well, but I see why Brooke didn't want me around him even more now. I wish I would've known. I should've learned more about Melo before I just trusted.

"It's okay. I'm sorry too. I didn't know that Melo had done that." My words were now softer seeing that I was venturing uncomfortable territory in her mind.

"It's not your fault I was just being a dumb kid." That was the last thing she said, before our shift ended.

As we headed out to the parking lot after our first day I thought about how I contributed to everything unknowingly. I was causing so many problems unknowingly. I blamed her for my issues, when in reality it was me the whole time. I was only wanting to be friendly to her, but I would've never guessed that she was falling apart, and I just so happened to be there to catch her. She was resorting to alcohol the same way I did after I lost Brooke. I was so oblivious to everything. She was just an innocent person reaching out, crying for help.

"Alana!" I called out right before she got into her car.

"Yeah?" It didn't seem like she didn't really want to talk, but I had to tell her what was on my mind.

"I'm sorry for what happened. I never would have imagined the pain you were going through, and I just want you to know that... I'm really here for you. I don't want to seem as if I was using you then or now."

"Thank you Landon." She closed her door, and walked my way.

She came up to me and gave me a tight hug, and began to cry. I was confused at first, and didn't really know what to say, or how to react. I thought about what I told Brooke, and I felt like I was betraying her. We weren't together anymore, and Alana is still hurt. I just want to help the problems I've caused.

Once the hug was over I smiled at her, and watched her walk away. I then got into my car, and just sat there with the key in the ignition. I wondered how I should feel. Did I help Alana's mental state? Would Brooke be mad? I shouldn't even think of her, it's been two weeks. She doesn't think of me anymore. I know she doesn't care about me. I just couldn't accept the fact that I still cared about her.

We've been together for years. We were so close to making it to the end of High School. I needed her. It felt weird not having her around. It was like a punishment for all of the mistakes I've made. I wanted to do right by her, but I couldn't.

When I got home I was too tired to even take a shower. I just went and flopped on my bed. When I was laying there I started thinking about Brooke more and more. She was tattooed in my brain. I could still see her like an afterimage. I reached out to the snowglobe that still sat on my nightstand. I refused to get rid of it. It was the best gift I've ever received. I saw the two figure skating on the ice, and felt empty. The Denver skyline still felt empty. Even when I shook it to watch the snow fall, the snow felt meaningless. It was just empty.

I have to keep skating. Even if I'm alone, I have to keep skating.

XXVIII

Months have passed and Brooke and I still aren't together. There's been minimal communication between us. We had become strangers with memories that felt like a lifetime ago. Memories when played back felt as if there was no reason that we weren't together anymore.

I still work at my same job. Alana and I have become good friends with a good rapport at work. Every now and then we would go out to eat somewhere, or go spend time outside of work together. We've established that our relationship would extend to a friendship and nothing more. Not because we had something against each other, but because we understood that it would be the best thing.

I applied to the University of Denver. The school I've always wanted to go to. Although when I was accepted I felt no instant joy. I was happy, but not overwhelmingly. A part of me wanted to go to the same college as Brooke, but I knew it just wouldn't happen. I know I should just let it go, but I can't. Graduation was in a month and I felt isolated from everyone. So it was probably for the best that I would be going to somewhere where I can have a clean start.

The money I would make from my job was helping me pay for my books and other things so I could be prepared for college. Everyday I realized that the end was nearing. There was still so much I haven't done. There was still so much I wanted to do. I missed how things were. I barely even hangout with Paul or Ryan anymore. Of course there was no sign of Brooke being in the picture. I felt truly alone.

I learned to appreciate nature more. It was spring so the trees gave beautiful colors, but the colors didn't illuminate the same without Brooke around. Nature didn't give me the same breath of fresh air. I still felt an empty darkness inside. I was doing well enough to hold myself together, but I just needed my friends and Brooke back. I was tired of looking at the same old snow globe without her around. Things just haven't felt right in a long time. Things were getting better, at least that's what I was telling myself.

Graduation was getting closer and closer. I was spending the days before graduation had come, going to old places that Brooke and I have been together. They weren't the same without her. Why was I still torn up about something that happened months ago? How could one person have this much affect on me? Why was there nothing I could do to win her back?

Mom found out what happened between Brooke and I a couple weeks after the fact. She must've thought I was in a hibernating state because of losing grandpa. Little did she know I spent the last three years losing everything.

Mom had met Alana after the third time she and I went out together. Mom suggested that I should give a relationship with her a try, but I couldn't picture me with any other woman that wasn't Brooke. Why did it affect me so much, when I know she doesn't care?

A week before graduation Mr. Richards kept me in his class a little after the bell. I thought that I might've been in trouble, but I couldn't think of anything I've done. I minded my business and was very quiet now that Brooke and I weren't together anymore.

"What's been going on Landon?" He asked with a concerned look on his face.

"Nothing." I tried to shrug it off, hoping that he wouldn't spare any pity on me.

"Well I've noticed that you and Miss Rose haven't been talking as much anymore. I know you aren't doing that for my pleasure, so tell me what's going on. I'm here for you." I loved the way he was able to lighten the mood no matter what. He's been the best teacher I could've ever asked for.

"I don't know to be honest. It's just...I-I guess I'm

not good enough for her." I said in a melancholy tone. I felt tears building up, but I held them back to continue to speak to Mr. Richards.

"You're more than good enough. You are an amazing person that anyone would be lucky to be with. Whatever happened I assure you that you weren't the problem. You, Paul, and Brooke have been my favorite students I've had the honor of teaching." His words were so touching. I felt appreciated again.

"Thank you Mr. Richards. I just want her back." The tears were becoming too difficult to hold back.

I went up to him and hugged him while letting the build up tears fall down my cheeks. He patted my back. I was glad that this was his free period so nobody would see me cry.

"Everything will work out, don't give up Landon." I nodded after he told me that and grabbed a tissue to blow my nose.

After I made myself presentable, and not like I spent the last ten minutes crying, I headed to my next class. I went through the day replaying his words, and determined to not give up. I couldn't give up. When I was sitting with Paul and Ryan at lunch my gaze was set on her, as I watched her laugh with her friends. Beyond everything I was feeling. I smiled seeing that she was happy. It still bothered me that I wasn't the one making her laugh, but I was glad she was. I had faith that the opportunity to talk to her to either get closure or rekindle our relationship would come. I didn't want to force it, I just hoped that it would occur.

Graduation day had come and it felt unreal that we had actually gotten to this point. My mom was more excited than I was. I was expressionless. I didn't want to leave my highschool life. I wanted things to be normal again before I left. I wanted Paul, Ryan, and I to be friends again. I wanted Tony to be with us again. I wanted Brooke and I to be happy again. I had my cap and gown on, and the silk feeling gave the realization that this was going to happen. There was nothing I could do to prevent it. I just had to accept that things were coming to an end.

I felt a cold shiver down my neck upon arrival to the graduation ceremony. It was held on the football field similar to how it was, for Matt. As I was directed to my seat I felt grim. I wasn't ready to move on. I could see Brooke a few rows ahead of me, and even in a cap and gown she was beautiful. She stared off into space. I kept looking at her, wondering what she would have possibly been thinking about. We haven't had a conversation in months, but she seemed to be doing well for herself. I wanted to tell her how I was doing good for myself as well, but I'm not sure if she would listen. I'm not sure if she has a new boyfriend, her college situation, or anything. It was weird to me how I went from knowing everything there was to know about her, to knowing nothing. I tried to read her body language from a distance to try and distinguish what she was thinking. I still knew her well enough to do that. She was slouched over, and I could tell she didn't want to be at the ceremony. Was she also scared to move on from highschool? I assumed that everyone here had to have some level of trepidation built up. As much as school prepared us for the real world, none of us were prepared to move on.

The graduation began when the salutatorian started speaking. I wasn't very keen on what she was saying. I still kept my eyes on Brooke. Even if it was the back of her head I was glad to see her. After the salutation was given, names began to be called. I listened to the names being called, as I danced my eyes back and forth from the student getting their diploma, and looking at Brooke. I kept looking at her as if I was scared to lose her. I already lost her, so I don't know why I kept trying.

Eventually Paul's name was called, and I broke out of my trance. I started clapping for him. I saw how happy he was getting his diploma. I wanted to share the happiness, but I didn't know how to. I felt selfish for not being able to look beyond myself, but this meant that all of our shenanigans would come to an end. Does this mean our friendship was over? He's stated how he planned on going to college outside the state. I wasn't sure if he would keep communicating with me.

I heard a little from Jackson after my grandfather

passed, but besides that our communication hasn't been good. I understood he was very busy with football and everything going on in his life, but I thought we would have better communication.

Students named continued to be called. I was nervous to approach the stage. I didn't want to hear my name be called. I couldn't help, but to think so narrow minded.

"BROOKE ROSE." I heard her name being called out of nowhere. I lost my sight on her for a moment, before I saw her approach the stage. Her smile was breath-taking. I couldn't help but admire her gorgeous features.

I heard her parents cheer from a distance. I missed them. They were always so kind to me. I had each of their numbers, but I never felt as if it was appropriate for me to contact them. Even if they were like my second family, they weren't my real family. So I had to let them go. The same way I have to watch Brooke go. She's happy though, and beyond all of my selfish needs I knew that her happiness outweighed anything I could ask for.

Although the only thing I was asking for was for her to be back with me.

My name was called around five minutes later and a shockwave was felt throughout my body. I didn't want to move from my seat that I had gotten accustomed to. My body was moving involuntarily. Before I knew it I was up on the stage. I couldn't tell if people were cheering for me, because of the stage fright that I had. As my diploma was being handed to me I didn't smile. My face remained expressionless and on display for everyone in attendance.

I hurried and went back to my seat with my diploma embarrassed as I watched the rest of the ceremony go on. The valedictorian of our class went up to give us our speech before officially moving on. I wasn't really hearing what he had to say. I didn't care, and I was in my own head overthinking what everyone would've thought about me.

"...And as times get hard we will never forget those we have met and befriended on this journey. With that being said I can assure you that Anthony Sims will never be forgotten, and will forever be loved. Thank you." There was a standing ovation for his speech. My heart felt warmed that people hadn't forgotten about Tony even after an entire year. His loss really impacted everyone. I just wish he was here to get the diploma he deserved. He deserved so much more than what a piece of paper could've given to him.

After the valedictorian's speech everyone threw their cap in the air. Everyone except me. I sat and watched all of my peers caps' fly in the sky, as I sat with a blank stare on my face. It was really over. My heart felt as if it sank. I was completely empty. My former peers were all leaving, I just sat in my seat waiting for the field to be empty. A lot of people stayed and took pictures. I knew my mom was probably waiting for me, but I just wanted to stay where I was. I didn't want to move on. My highschool career was incomplete.

"Hey Landon." My name was called by an angelic voice. To my surprise it was Brooke standing over me. Watching me with my emotionless face.

I looked up at her, as if she was someone I had been missing for years. I couldn't believe that she really approached me. It didn't seem real that she was willing to come to me. I missed her.

"Hi…Brooke." my voice trembled, as I was scared to speak. I was afraid I would ruin any chance of us having at least a friendly relationship.

"How have you been?" She asked me with the same kind, welcoming tone she did when we first met as freshmen.

I've been waiting for this opportunity to come, but now that it's here I'm starting to become shy. I tried to speak in a nonchalant tone, so she couldn't tell I had a lot on my chest to say. Hearing her speak again with the same nostalgic voice, made me realize I was the only one that changed.

"I'm good. How about you?" I wanted to have a strong conversation, but how could I in this setting?

"I'm good too. I just saw you sitting here, so I thought I should at least come say hi." She had a childish smile on her face.

If she just wanted to say "hi" why hasn't she before

this? Why would she wait till it's all over before saying anything? She acts if we are just old acquaintances that just so happen to stumble across one another. Does anything we've done together matter to her? I wanted to keep talking to her, because I missed her, but it was so strange. I had to say something while she's standing here. I leaned forward to engage in the conversation.

"Are you ready for college?" I had nothing else to start talking to her about. I already knew she probably got accepted to Colorado State University.

"I absolutely am. I got accepted to Colorado State." She sounded delighted to share her acceptance. I was just glad to see her smile again.

"Oh that's fun. I'm going to the University of Denver, so we'll be pretty close, right?" I responded hoping she would be intrigued.

There was an awkward silence between us. It was apparent that things weren't the same anymore. I just had hoped that there was some part of her that still cared, but I guess there wasn't.

"Yeah...I don't know, maybe we'll cross paths again one day." She said in an attempt to not make things as awkward.

After that there wasn't anything to be said between us, so she walked away to go see her parents. I watched them hug her as I was slouched over in the chair I was sitting in. My chin laid on my hand as I thought about all of the memories I wouldn't be able to forget with her.

I gave my mom a hug that didn't have much passion behind it. I just wanted to go home. There was nothing left for me here. I only had one place that would give me comfort. Which was also the root of where I kept my depressing thoughts. I just wanted to be in my bed, and get away from everyone.

When I got home I walked in my room and threw my cap down. I didn't even take the time to turn the lights on. I laid face down on my bed wanting to scream. I had so many built up emotions I didn't know how to portray. I turned over to look at the snowglobe that used to hold so much meaning. Now it feels like an empty city with no meaning. As I looked at it I could feel the tears stream down my eyes. I came to the realization that this chapter of my life was now over.

XXIX

The summer went by pretty fast. I was in a constant routine of working, and going home to do nothing. Sometimes I would hangout with Alana or Paul, but for the most part I did nothing.

Once the summer was finished I turned in my two weeks notice, because I had to move away for college. I had my things that I would be moving into my dorm ready to go. I told the few people I still conversed with my goodbyes as time neared. I realized that I didn't have much, and that all of the things I would be bringing to my dorm would fit in my car.

I had previously gone to the University for housing openings, to get a room. I picked a dorm that had not been chosen by anyone else to try to have a room for myself. About a week later I was notified that another person had chosen to be in my room. All I knew about him was that his name was Dawson Williams.

Today would be the first time I would meet Dawson, because it was the first day that students were allowed to move their property into dorm rooms. I wasn't too excited to meet him. I wasn't very good at meeting new people. Although I would have to get through that mental block, because I would be living with this person.

Upon arrival at the University, there were hundreds of cars. So many people were excited to move in. I was just going through the motions. I was doing things without purpose. I knew I should be very ecstatic to move out and start a life of my own, but what life did I have? I was completely starting from scratch.

Once I found a place to park, which took forever to find, I grabbed two boxes of clothes and headed towards my dorm. The door was propped open for students. Probably because they knew that we would be holding various things, and it would be hard to also open the door.

When I got inside, there was an elevator that I had to use to get to my room. I used my leg as leverage to hold the box as I struggled to click the button that called the elevator. A heard a girl behind chuckle at the sight of me struggling. My mind instantly thought it was Brooke, but when I turned around it was just a random girl. I laughed out of the awkwardness that I had made.

"Do you need help with carrying your stuff?" The girl asked me, as I started to turn away.

"No, I'm good, but thank you." I responded respectfully, while turning to face her again.

As I was about to indulge in conversation the elevator rang a small bell sound, alerting me that it was on my floor. The girl I was going to speak to slipped past me to get in, and I followed in after her. She clicked the floor she was going to, and I almost forgot to click mine. Once I realized my mistake I clicked my floor, and peered over to the girl to see if she had the same realization. Luckily she didn't and the elevator trip was silent.

The elevator stopped for her floor, and she got off. When she got off and the door closed to proceed me to my floor, I gave out a sigh. I didn't think I was going to be capable of getting through college. I miss how easy it was talking to Brooke. I don't think I'll ever be able to talk to another woman the way I was able to talk to her.

When the elevator got to my floor I readjusted my boxes to make it easier so I could mobilize more efficiently. I got the key to my dorm ready when I approached my door. As I was fumbling to put the key in the door, it was opened. A dark haired guy around my height answered the door, to the sound of me struggling to open it. I presumed it was Dawson.

"Thank you." I said, as I moved past him to put my boxes where I already planned to have my room.

"You're Landon, I'm guessing?" He questioned. His voice was deeper than I expected.

"Yeah." I answered him while exhaling, after putting down the boxes I brought up.

"I'm Dawson, it's nice to meet you." He put his hand out for me to shake.

I met his gesture with my hand, and was surprised by how aggressively he shook my hand. He was a pretty stocky guy so it made sense, but hurt my hand a little. Whenever he let go I checked my hand to see if it was alright.

I looked around the dorm to see that he had his side decked out with all of his stuff. Some of his clothes were in a box, while some were already ready to put up. He moved in pretty quick.

"Are you already done?" I asked him, surprised to see how much he had up already.

"Yeah, I practically am. Do you want some help with your stuff?" He asked kindly.

"I'm okay, you don't have to help." I responded without trying to bother him.

"No no no. I insist. You can see that I'm done with moving in, and I would love to help you." His willingness to help shocked me, but I agreed to let him help.

Once he followed me to my car he grabbed one of my heavier boxes, and a smaller box that had Brooke's snow globe in it. When I realized that he had that box I freaked out. I didn't want him to accidentally break it.

"Hey would you mind, if I grab that top box from you? It has some sentimental valued things in there." I tried to say in a friendly tone.

"Oh, my bad. Didn't mean to intrude on your things." He said while lightly cackling.

"You're fine. I just don't want anything to happen to the things in there, unless it's my fault. You know?" I remarked trying not to seem rude.

Once I acquired the box from him, we headed back to our room, and put down the box on my third of the dorm.

Our room was set up like an apartment. There was my room, Dawson's room, and a living area that had a bathroom with it. Dawson and I were able to bring up my belongings in just two trips. He was very helpful, because it took me many trips just to pack the things in my car.

Dawson and I started conversing more as we put up our things. He would ask me general questions about myself. I would answer as appropriately as possible, and question him about the same thing. We weren't in each others' line of sight, which made it easier for me. All I had to do was call out to him.

He finished unpacking his things before I did, and headed into the living area. He continued to question things about my life until I myself was finished. Once I was done I met him in the living room. It was starting to get dark out, and I was exhausted. Although I enjoyed talking to Dawson. He was a really good guy to talk to. He also talked more than I did, and I was delighted by that.

"I'm probably going to head to bed." I told Dawson, while I was yawning.

"Alright, but I have one more question for you." I was intrigued by what he had to ask.

"Shoot."

"Is there any special partner I should expect to be around here?" Referring to any kind of relationship that I might've had.

"Well...not anymore." I was saddened thinking about the distance between Brooke and I.

"Dang, what happened man. I couldn't imagine anybody not wanting to be with you, you're a stellar guy." His words seemed genuine and I appreciated them.

"Thanks, I-I guess we just grew apart." I was pretty confused by how I should answer, because I really don't know what happened. I never got full closure.

"Well don't sweat it. We're in college now, you'll have many opportunities to find someone new." He reassured me.

"I guess so...Goodnight Dawson."

"Goodnight Landon." He said in a still giddy mood, while he headed to his room.

As I got to my room I looked at the snowglobe that I put up. If only she knew the effect she had on me. If only she knew how much the gifts she got me meant. If only she was still here. I couldn't help, but to go to sleep thinking about Brooke.

I went to my first day of class, and I still could only think about Brooke. I was a business marketing major. I didn't know what I wanted to be, but I thought it sounded like something I could take up. I sat in class with my book bag ready to follow what the other students did. Everyone got out a notebook, and pen so I did the same.

The professor came in and gave a very brief overview of what to expect about the class, and immediately started lecturing. I couldn't pay attention, because everywhere I looked I saw a ghost of Brooke. I looked at my paper to start writing notes. I heard what the professor was lecturing about, but my hand started writing Brooke's name in cursive. It was like she was haunting my brain. I couldn't do anything. I heard the intense writing from everyone, and the calm demeanor of the professor as he started pouring information out. I was overwhelmed, and needed to get out of the stressful environment. I raised my hand to go to the restroom.

"Yes Mr. …?" He asked me while stopping his lecture. Everyone's gaze was on me.

"Morgan. May I use the restroom?" I asked nervously, and aware that my peers were looking at me.

"Believe it or not, you are grown now, and don't have

to ask to use the restroom." The entire class started to giggle at me.

I felt ashamed, and scurried out of class. I went to find a restroom, so I could relax. I was having a panic attack. My breath became short, and I could feel my heart racing. My breathing started to become audible, as I continued to panic.

When I found a restroom I rushed in there and sat down. I stayed on the floor until my breathing was stable. She wouldn't get out of my head. I convinced myself that I would be okay. So I headed back to class after about fifteen minutes.

I came into the classroom quietly. Most people had their heads down writing as it was, so I wouldn't bring any attention to myself as I came in. I sat down and wrote the few notes I could before the professor dismissed class.

That was my only class of the day luckily so I went back to my room so I could get away from everyone. I know it wasn't healthy that I isolated myself whenever I wasn't okay, but I didn't know what else to do. I was accustomed to doing this whenever a problem occurred.

Dawson came in sounding enthusiastic. I was curious as to what he was excited about, but I wasn't going to go out of my way to ask. I heard him put his things in his room, and make his way to mine.

"How would you like to go to a party sir?" Dawson asked me, keeping his enthusiastic tone.

"Uhh…I don't know." I still didn't like the idea of partying, because of what happened when I was with Brooke.

"Come on, you'll enjoy it. It beats doing nothing." He was persuasive, and easily got me to oblige.

"Sure, why not." I thought that they would at least have alcohol at the party that would get me to not worry as much.

I knew it would be bad to start my alcoholism problem again, but I convinced myself I would drink responsibly. It was probably the only way I could get Brooke off my mind.

I got up and got ready to go to the party. I still didn't really want to go, but I already opted in. I tried to think of the situation positively, because that's what it was meant for. I was most likely going to find a couch to sit on and a bottle of alcohol to drink. That was my positive and ideal alternative to doing nothing.

Dawson told me I could ride with him, because he didn't intend on drinking. He just wanted to have a good time. So we headed off to the party. was becoming tense while we were listening to music in the car. Dawson was jamming out to the music. I just sat fearful that much older people would judge me.

We arrived at the house, and I stayed tense. My hands were balled up in a fist. Not with aggression, just fear. I could hear the people inside the house before we even got in. I was hesitant to go in thinking about what happened last time I was partying. I was conscious of my decision about wanting to consume alcohol, but I was prepared. There shouldn't be any fear in having fun. It's not like I could disappoint Brooke anymore. I had my own image, it was just blurred without her.

I eased my way into the party, as Dawson and I split up. He went and did his own thing, similarly to how Carmelo did. I was just waiting for another Alana to come and distract me. I did find a nice place that I could relax at while I enjoyed the music. I tried to avoid any direct eye contact with anyone.

There was a bottle sitting next to a lamp. I could hear the bottle calling my name, tempting me. I could feel myself itching to find it. Why was I wanting it so bad? I hated the taste, but I hated the lingering thought of Brooke more. Alcohol can't leave the same way she did. A part of me still wanted to talk to her. I could only imagine what she was doing right now. I felt my hand grabbing the bottle, as my mind stayed on the millions of things I could think of.

I opened up the bottle and started to chug it. I hated the taste, but I didn't care. I wanted as much as I could get. Whoever it belonged to could start a problem with me, and I wouldn't mind. I got up after, and went to find Dawson.

went through the house to find Dawson, hoping that he would still be in his enthusiastic mood. While I was looking for him, I ran into the girl I saw when I was moving in. I could feel the alcohol in my blood, that was giving me confidence.

"Hey!" I called out to her.

"Hey?" She seemed confused by me calling her out. She seemed to recognize me.

"Aren't you the nice lady I met while I was moving things in?" I asked her.

"Ah! I remember you." She started to laugh recalling the awkward moment between us.

"I never caught your name." I said while beginning to dance to the music.

"Oh my name is Brooklyn, but you can call me Brooke." I started to laugh when hearing her name.

No matter what state I was in I couldn't get her away from my mind. I did well for a little bit I guess. I couldn't help but to laugh at the odds of me meeting another girl named Brooke. This Brooke couldn't compare to mine at all.

"My name's Landon. I wanted to thank you for offering to help." I tried my best to sound sober, knowing I didn't sound that way.

"It was no problem, but it's nice to meet you…" I nodded her way, and walked away from her before she could finish talking.

I looked at my phone, and thought about Brooke. The confidence in me convinced me it would be a good idea to text her. So I did. I sent her a text that simply said "hey", I didn't want her to know that I wasn't sober. She would be really upset if she found out.

eventually found Dawson. He was talking to two girls. He looked as if he was having fun, and I didn't want to ruin that. I could feel my sober mind acknowledging that my heart was racing, but I was trying to ignore it. I felt my phone vibrate, and I could feel myself being nervous. I was so nervous I could've thrown up. I saw a text from Brooke saying "hi." I didn't want to keep texting her drunk, but I had to answer her.

I decided to ask her about how college was going. I thought it was a kind enough thing to ask that could potentially start a conversation. As I hit send I knew it was a terrible idea.

"Are you ready to go?" Dawson asked me, while grabbing my shoulder. I was startled, because I was glued to my phone.

"Yeah." I answered after giving out a sigh, followed by a smile.

We went back to our dorm. I kept my phone faced-up on my lap, waiting for a response. I had the same tense feeling I did when arriving at the party, but now it was a little different. I was more anxious than nervous now. She wouldn't just ignore me, at least I hope so.

By the time we made it to our dorm, and settled into our beds, I received another text from Brooke. I read the message in her voice, to make it seem like she was here speaking to me. She said that college has been fun and is a lot different from high school. I was glad to see that she was having fun. I wasn't really sure how to respond other than saying I was happy for her. She should be here with me. I missed the conversations we would have while she was in my arms. The only thing that was in my arms now was a pillow.

Before I went to sleep that night, my phone buzzed again. It was her, but I didn't want to keep bothering her, because it was getting late. I put the phone next to the snowglobe. As I looked at the snowglobe, while I was drifting to sleep, I thought there was a sliver of life still left in the city. I dreamed about being in the city with her.

There was no reason to continue my bad habits when she's around. I did well for so long, but I needed her. My life felt empty without her around, and I hoped that at the very least she would keep answering my texts.

...

A couple of months have passed, and Brooke and I frequently texted. We've even got to the point where we will call each other again. I had hoped that there was still something that held us together. I felt as if no matter what happened I would be connected to her I also got more accustomed to the "college life." College has been pretty fun, and I know not to ask to use the restroom. Class has been pretty stressful, because I've never really been good at studying, but it's been alright overall.

I wished that I would've applied to the same college as Brooke. Even if we remained separated I would at least get to see her. Winter break was around the corner, and I planned on asking to meet up with Brooke. I didn't know if she would agree to it, but I had nothing to lose by asking. So after the last day I started a texting conversation with her.

After the conversation had started I asked the question. I thought she would say yes, but I wasn't one hundred percent sure. She said that she wanted to see me, and would be "glad to meet up." I was shocked that she actually wanted to see me. Does this mean that she still cared? I could finally ask what happened. Find out why she broke off our relationship. I would finally get to see her again.

I was full of excitement. I still loved her, and was enticed by the thought of seeing her. I asked to meet her at the same park she and I knew so well, and she agreed to see me there. We all were going home for the break anyway, so I was packing a few of my things to go home with me.

I packed a couple outfits that I could wash, and keep me looking presentable throughout the week. I took the snowglobe as well to show Brooke I still kept it. I couldn't care less what happened today, because I was going to get to see Brooke again tomorrow.

Dawson could see the joy the news brought me. He shared the same energy I was carrying. He didn't even know what was happening. He couldn't fathom how important this was to me.

"What's got you in a good mood?" Dawson asked me.

"Remember that girl that I 'grew apart' from?" I asked with a smile laying on my face.

"Yeah, you didn't seem to be happy about that situation." He looked confused.

"Well I still have feelings for her, and I get to see her tomorrow." I said keeping my smile attached to my face.

"That's awesome dude. I'm happy for you." He was so good at keeping a good mood.

I hugged him, because I needed the affirmation at that moment. I know he doesn't know the full extent of Brooke and I's story, but he cared enough to listen. He was really a stand-up guy, and I was thankful for him. Dawson did his best to make me feel welcomed, and reciprocated the hug I gave him.

I really get to see Brooke tomorrow. I don't know what she could be thinking right now, but I know her excitement couldn't match mine. I've missed her beyond belief. Now, I finally get to see her, after all this time.

XXX

Today was the day that I get to see Brooke again. The last time I've seen her in person was at our graduation. A conversation I wish I could go back to, and confess my true feelings to her. I shouldn't have been nonchalant at that moment. I should've admitted the fact that I still cared for her, but today I have the opportunity to tell her.

I headed to my car in sort of a skipping motion. I couldn't hide the fact that I was ready to see her again. At this point I don't care if she didn't look forward to this, I was just ready to see her. I put my things in my car with nice smooth movements. I was imagining my actions matching a song in my head. I probably looked like an idiot to everyone watching, but I didn't care. They had no idea how happy I was.

I started to drive and as I started to get on the interstate I was filled with a blast of energy. Making my car go as fast as it would let me. I was going around ninety miles per hour within the first mile of me getting on to the interstate. I was ready to get home, and see my mom. I was going to tell her that I was seeing Brooke, because Brooke and I agreed to see each other around six in the evening. I realized how fast I was going after the sudden rush was depleted, and eased up on my speed. I enjoyed the entire trip to my house, and was prepared for anything.

By the time I made it to my house, my mom was delighted to see me. She gave me hugs and kisses, as well as asking a million questions about my college experience. My mind was blank, and focused on the encounter I was going to have later.

I put my clothes in my old room, and took a moment to admire my room. I can't believe this was my safe space. It seems so small and insignificant now. This is where I would hibernate for days. This is where I changed. This is where Brooke and I laid. So many memories stayed in this room. Good and bad.

After putting my things up, I realized it was already four o'clock. I chatted with mom, and told her my plans to see Brooke. She sounded as excited as I was, because she understood how much I really cared for her. Mom tried giving helpful advice on what I should say, but I already had determined what I planned on saying. I did want to ask her why she split up with me, and if there was a possibility of us getting together again. I was really looking forward to hearing her answers, because my mind was set on her still caring about the relationship we built.

By the time I had to go, I started to get nervous again. I could feel the anxiety rush through my veins as I was getting into my car. This was the moment I've been waiting for. I set the snowglobe on the dash, and headed to the park that we both knew so well. It was the same park we confessed our love for each other, and would be the same park where we continued our love saga, or where it would end.

On approaching the park I didn't see her car, but I was early. I was about fifteen minutes early. I went and sat on the bench I knew she would know to come to, and I waited for time to pass. I sat with the snow globe in my hand as snow began to fall around me. The snowglobe didn't feel empty anymore. I felt the city alive when I shook the globe. I wanted to show Brooke that despite everything that happened I kept it. No matter if the city felt alive or dead. No matter if the two figures skating felt meaningless or not. I kept it, because I couldn't let go of the memories we had together.

I looked at my phone to see that thirty minutes had passed and she still wasn't here. The snow was beginning to fall harder. Did she stand me up? It was the same thoughts I had when we planned on going to that basketball game together our freshman year. She was late then so maybe she just got a little busy and was late now. I wanted to text her, but I didn't feel the need to rush her. If she wasn't here by six-thirty I was going to text her. What if she really doesn't want to see me? Am I doing all of this for nothing? I loved her, and that couldn't mean nothing, could it? There was purpose in my actions. At least that's what I believed. That everything I did would account for something, or would it transpire down into nothingness.

It was six-thirty and I sent her a simple "hey" text. Just to see if she would respond, because it was still possible she was busy, and running behind. I started going through my phone to look at old pictures Brooke and I took together, as I continued to wait on her. I knew that she wouldn't just not come, right? She had to becoming here.

I kept waiting for her, and my phone got a notification that it was close to dying. I dismissed the message and kept going through it. I let it pacify me until Brooke was here. Although it was almost seven-thirty now, and I still haven't got a text from her. Did she really not come? Do I really not matter to her?

As I was getting ready to leave, I weirdly got a call from Mrs. Rose. Was she being the middleman, in telling me that Brooke wasn't coming? I answered the phone quickly, worried about what she had to say. As I answered the phone I heard her crying on the other side.

"Mrs. Rose? What's wrong?" I asked her scared for what she had to say.

"Brooke...She was coming to see you...and-and

she got into an accident. She's in the hospital." She said, stammering through her tears.

I dropped the phone in the snow, as I continued to hear Mrs. Rose speak. She told me what hospital she was at, and I ran to my car. I threw my phone and snowglobe in the passenger seat and began to race to the hospital. I was going twenty over the speed limit, dodging cars, and weaving traffic.

A cop turned on his sirens, and began to pull me over. This couldn't be happening, not now. I have to get to the hospital. I pulled over, and got all of my things ready to give to the officer. To my surprise the officer that pulled me over, was the same officer that pulled me over when I first got my car.

"Please officer, I have to get to the hospital." I pleaded to him, hoping that he would remember me.

"What happened son?" He asked me.

"I don't know if you remember who I am, but a couple years ago you pulled me over with a girl. That same girl is in critical condition in the hospital right now." He looked shocked by what I said, and felt immediate guilt for doing his job properly.

"Follow me. I'll get you there." He rushed back into his car, and kept his sirens on so I could follow him to the hospital.

The officer and I went fifteen miles per hour over the speed limit on the way to the hospital. When we made it there I ran out of my car, grabbing only my phone. I thanked the officer swiftly as I made my way inside.

"Where is Brooke Rose at." I asked the receptionist.

"I'll be with you in a moment." She answered me in a non-caring tone.

"Please the love of my life is about to die! I don't have time to wait." I angrily said while tears began to form.

The receptionist looked appalled at first, but then got me the information I needed to go to Brooke's room. I sprinted to her room as fast as my legs would take me. I've already wasted so much time.

When I got to the room she was lying unconscious on the hospital bed. I was mortified by the sight of her despaired-filled parents. Tears blurred my vision, making the scene unrecognizable. I couldn't believe what I was seeing. She looks lifeless. She had cuts on her face from glass shards, but she was still beautiful. Even in this state she was as beautiful as the first time I met her. I felt my legs tremble. I didn't know what to feel, but none of my emotions were positive.

"Brooke!" I exclaimed to her, while clutching onto her hand. I was hoping there was some way she could hear me. I needed to hear her voice just one more time.

"Brooke…please!" Her parents and I started crying uncontrollably. She wasn't answering. I couldn't lose her. I needed to feel her grab my hand back. I can't let go of her. There is some way she can hear me. My heart clogged my ability to speak, and I couldn't formulate words to say anymore. I had to watch the woman I love suffer in silence.

Brooke's parents and I stayed for as long as possible. I was determined to stay until someone physically removed me from the room. I sat on the side of the bed in a chair continuing to hold onto her hand. I watched my tears splatter on the ground waiting for her to give me a sign that she was okay. There was no indication that she was okay. It was unbearable to look at her with her eyes closed, and her pulse barely stable. Why did this happen to the most perfect woman? Why did this happen to Brooke Rose? Why couldn't it have been me? She wouldn't even be in this predicament if it wasn't for me. I'm the reason she got into the accident. All of the cuts and bruises that were on her body were because of me. The numbness that was felt throughout my body made me nauseous. It's always my fault. I ruined the most perfect angel, because of my selfish wants. Why did I do this to her? I'm so sorry, I wish she could hear me say those words. I wisht there was something I could do to heal her. Whatever it took to make sure she was okay I would do. The guilt built in my stomach making me feel as if I needed to throw up, but my tears blocked me from being able to make any other physical reaction.

My tears kept hitting the floor as my hope began to dwindle. Hours passed and she still hasn't shown any notable sign of life. She couldn't leave, I needed her to stay. She had to stay. It's not fair that I get to stay here after being a cause of my best friend's life, and now her. I love her. I'm sorry. I wish it could've been me. She deserved to live way more than I did. If I could exchange our positions I would in a heartbeat. I love her more than I do myself. She needed to hear that, so she would know that no matter what happened, I love her.

XXXI

As I was instructed to leave the hospital, I knew this could possibly be the last time I see her. I never knew I could feel like dying without actually passing away, but I guess this is what it felt like. There was no feeling that could feel worse than this. I was a ghost that was stripped of my emotions.

A day later the news came that she passed away. Broke Rose was pronounced dead. I was broken beyond imagination. Nothing could have prepared me for this. It felt as if my breath was taken away from me. I never stopped crying when I left the hospital, and tears blinded me. Anger and anguish flooded my vocal chords, not allowing me to speak. I was deafened by the memories of her voice.

Why her? She was so perfect. I didn't get to say what she needed to hear, I never got to ask her the questions I had, and now I'll never be able to tell her. I loved her, I wish I could tell her I did just one more time, or hold her one more time. I needed her embrace. I wish I could bury myself next to her, so I could still be with her. I wish I could show her how much I loved her, just one more time.

It's like life spat in my face for giving someone my all, but this was my fault. I was the only reason she was even in the accident. Why do I mess everything up? Why was I the cause of all of this? Why did I let my selfish needs be the reason she's gone? Why did she of all people have to go?

Why do I now have to live with the fact that all of my love for her will never bring her back?

When the funeral came two days later I couldn't manage myself anymore. Not enough to be in front of the Rose family. So I stayed in my room, a deep void of darkness, the same void I was feeling in my heart. I couldn't get rid of the feeling of being shattered. There was no recovery for me. She was my everything. What was I supposed to do now? Life was meaningless without her in the picture. She was my story, she was the movie, she was the star of everything in my life. Gone like she never even mattered. Nobody could understand how hurt I am. No words or phrases can describe my pain. I thought I was dead for the next three weeks. I didn't try to take care of myself at all. I didn't care about anything else that was going on in my life. Paul, Ryan, Sara, and Matt all tried to visit me when they heard the news, but I couldn't even get myself to see them.

They could never understand that I lost everything.

Once I could finally manage getting up, and handle myself well enough out the house, I had to make one trip. Brooke's tombstone. Seeing her was going to leave me in the same state I was when she first left, but I had to tell her something. I know she wouldn't hear, but I still felt obligated to tell her what I wish she could hear. It was cold outside, but I was freezing, my hands were trembling on the car ride there. Silence filled the car, while all of the things I wish she could hear tormented my mind. It was windy, but I felt a tornado. A tornado that threw my mind out of whack, causing me to not think logically. A terrible sensation flooded me physically and mentally.

Whenever I saw her grave I saw two roses on the gravestone. I saw them and imagined us being those two roses. All the life we spent together. Seemed as if they were trapped within those two roses, that would eventually rot, and turn into nothing, but dust. Similar to the snowglobe I decided to bring her. The one thing I wish she could've seen. Proof that I loved her unconditionally. The two figures mocked me, with the joy they intended to bestow. All of the things we experienced together. I fell to my knees crying uncontrollably. I couldn't make sense of why she was taken away from me. She was perfect, and never did anything wrong to anybody or anyone. I couldn't believe that I was ever mad at her, I needed to apologize, but I couldn't. All of her right-doings equated to a terrible fate. How is that fair? Why do I get to cry down on my knees here, while she lies gone, forever.

Once I could somewhat control my crying, I pulled out the note I made for her eulogy. I opened it up and read aloud, hoping there was some way she could hear me. "Dear Brooke Rose, the woman who changed my life forever. What more can I say other than you altered my life for the better. I'm so sorry I wasn't there, like I said I always would be, I'm sorry I couldn't protect you. I failed you, when you never failed me, and I know this is all my fault. I wish I could tell you the millions of reasons why you were perfect, or the billions of things that were on my mind, or the trillions of ways you made me happy. I'm sorry, but I feel as if there's only one thing I can say to the most perfect woman: Thank you."